Promise
To Obey

Promise to Obey

STELLA WHITELAW

ROBERT HALE · LONDON

ISBN 978-0-7198-0978-1

Robert Hale Limited
Clerkenwell House
Clerkenwell Green
London EC1R 0HT

www.halebooks.com

2 4 6 8 10 9 7 5 3 1

Typeset in Palatino
Printed by MPG Printgroup, UK

To

My beautiful Rosie who dozed in the filing tray,
keeping me company while I wrote this book.

ACKNOWLEDGEMENTS

As always, overwhelming thanks to Dr David Thomas. I bombarded him with questions, every one of which was answered in detail and with patience. If there are any medical mistakes, then they are entirely mine.

The staff of the Tourist Office at Worthing and at Brighton for helpful information.

And again, the libraries at both Oxted and Worthing for endless assistance and encouragement.

And to the editorial team at Robert Hale who are always so friendly and kind. It's a pleasure to work with you all.

Won't you come into the garden?
I would like my roses to see you.

Richard Brinsley Sheridan
1751-1816

ONE

'Hello? Is there anybody there? I think someone is supposed to be meeting me.'

Jessica Harlow's voice carried along the empty platform. Dried leaves scattered like little insects. Dead geraniums drooped in flowerpots, like exhausted dancers at the end of a long ballet.

Jessica came out of Eastly Station and stood on the forecourt, still wondering if anyone was going to meet her. She was already regretting her decision to accept a three-month private nursing contract at Upton Hall. This place was out in the wilds, masses of trees, and it was beginning to rain.

She stood under the inadequate ironwork porch of the station entrance, peering through the fine drizzle at the bleak view, wondering where she was. It was all hills and woodland, hedges and fields. It was part of the South Downs but even that meant very little. She was a town girl, born and bred in North London. This green countryside was alien. She could barely recognize a rabbit. They had long ears, didn't they, and hopped about, Beatrix Potter style?

It was a forlorn view and she was getting wet and cold. Her shoes were poor protection and her toes were squelching. There was an anorak in her case but it would be foolish to open it in this weather. Everything inside would get wet.

There wasn't even anyone she could ask for the whereabouts of Upton Hall. The station was unmanned with only a machine for tickets. There was no one to help with her wheelie case and travel bag, no bus stop, no taxi. Surely they didn't expect her to walk? Which way, left or right?

'I might as well give up and take the next train back,' she said aloud. 'If there is ever a next train from this godforsaken hole.'

She huddled into her damp clothes. Her smart navy suit and high heels were glistening with raindrops. Her fine tawny hair was already clinging to her cheeks like a wet curtain. She could feel the fringe catching on her eyelashes. She was going to make a fine impression in this state.

There was a discreet cough from somewhere. 'Please don't do that,' said an amused voice, deep and resonant. 'I've come out in this damned awful weather to meet you and my mother will be furious if I don't return with you in tow.'

It was not easy to take in the meaning of the words. She was adrift, like someone on a treadmill, pumping toxic fumes. There was no way out.

Jessica turned to find a tall stranger standing a few yards away in the rain, not suitably dressed either, checked blue shirt soaked, jeans creased, dark hair plastered to his head. He was regarding her with cool courtesy but Jessica refused to be cowed. He was good-looking and probably knew it. His jaw-line was firm and dominant. He was someone who was used to getting his own way.

'You are Miss Harlow? There can't be two young female passengers alighting at Eastly Station today. We get about one a month in a good year. That's our allocation. Southern Railways don't make their profit out of us.'

'I'm Jessica Harlow,' she said. 'I'm here to nurse Lady Grace Coleman of Upton Hall after her hip replacement operation.'

'My mother.' The tall man moved closer and held out his hand. 'I'm Lucas Coleman, son of Lady Grace. Glad to meet you. And father of the two children you are also going to keep an eye on. You're going to save the day for us.'

'The children, yes. Not usually my domain,' said Jessica,

shaking his hand. 'But I can do that. Keep an eye on them if you are away.'

'I'm often away,' said Lucas Coleman, enigmatically.

I bet you are, thought Jessica. A playboy, if ever I saw one. He looked like a dissipated layabout, someone who lived off his mother, who never did a day's work. She probably kept him to run errands and meet visitors at the station. 'Can we go now?' she went on. 'I'm getting soaked. Do we have to walk?'

'Heavens no,' said Lucas Coleman, abruptly. 'We are quite civilized out here. We've moved on a bit from the horse and cart days.'

Jessica hadn't noticed the car. It was behind him, parked at some distance against a hedge, a low slung machine in glistening metallic blue. Too low to get into with any dignity. Still, it was a vehicle of sorts. She pretended to be interested, put on her enquiring face.

'Great looking car,' she said. 'What is it?'

'A Porsche Boxster, Spyder class, very fast, very reliable. Lovely vehicle. Are you interested in cars?'

'No,' said Jessica. 'They are merely a means of getting about.'

'I agree,' said Lucas smoothly. 'There's far too much importance attached to status cars these days. But I do like this one. It's fast and suits my purpose.'

He opened the door for her and Jessica lowered herself into the low-slung seat. The dashboard was like an aircraft cockpit with dials and knobs and blinking screens. She struggled to find a seatbelt further down in the depths. She heard Lucas Coleman heaving her case and bag into the boot. The rain was becoming a blanket. She couldn't see anything through the rivulets of water on the windscreen.

This was going to be a disaster. Jessica could already feel that everything was going wrong. She should not have accepted the offer but she had three months to fill before she took up a new hospital appointment in Sheffield. This represented her mortgage repayments and other commitments. She had to keep earning money and the terms on offer were good ones. Lucas

Coleman wanted someone to take care of his mother, Lady Grace, when she came out of hospital.

Lucas folded himself into the driver's seat and fastened his seatbelt. Jessica had a chance to look at him more closely. Not that she cared about men anymore, not after Fraser Burton. Fraser had shattered her fragile confidence, and he had done it unforgivably in public, but the experience had made her become a stronger woman. Not many men could do that. It was an evening she wanted to forget.

Lucas had a good-looking face but it was rigid with a lack of emotion. She wondered what had happened to cause this reserve. At this rate she would never know. There was no way she was going to dig beneath that cold exterior. She'd let him drive her to Upton Hall and then she need never see him again.

'And the children?' she began. 'How old are they? What are they like? You didn't say much about them in your letter.'

'Lily is five and Daniel is seven, going on eight. He'll have his birthday in a few weeks' time.' It was a blunt statement.

'We must have a party,' said Jessica, exhausted already at the thought of jelly and games, party hats and crowds of noisy children.

'I doubt it.'

What an odd answer. Didn't most children have parties on their birthdays? Every child deserved a birthday party.

'We could go to McDonald's. Is there a McDonald's nearby, at Brighton or Worthing? They do great parties. They lay on every-thing. Daniel would enjoy it.'

'No, thank you, Miss Harlow. We'll talk about this later.'

Jessica shrank back into the low seat. What kind of father was he? All children wanted a party on their birthday.

It was a long and winding drive, leaves brushing the top of the car, rain streaking the windscreen. Jessica had no idea where they were. He could be driving her to the end of some remote moor, a forgotten quarry or desolate headland. She was absolutely in his hands. There was no knowing if he was who he said he was, or where he was taking her.

12

She thought of the book she was reading. A crime novel with an abduction and a victim who was never found. A little unsettling.

Jessica felt a surge of panic. Panic was a recent thing. An unrealistic fear. It was all part of the aftermath of the faithless Fraser. The man had almost destroyed her but she was fighting back. She was clinging tight to the seatbelt now as if they were on the point of crashing over Beachy Head.

'There's no need to be so tense, Miss Harlow,' said Lucas Coleman. 'I can drive this beast. I know what I'm doing. We are not going to land upside-down in a ditch. You're safe in my hands.'

'Sorry,' said Jessica, trying to relax. Her skirt was damp, clinging to her legs like a wet sandwich. 'It's been a difficult day, such a long train journey. So many changes. I'm feeling really tired.'

'Shall I play you some music? To soothe your shattered nerves? How about Rod Stewart in his most nostalgic mode? The Great American Songbook. *It Had to be You*. It's one of my favourites.'

He slid in the CD and pressed the starter button. The soft opening notes and rasping voice of the maestro were a perfect contrast. Jessica felt her breathing slow down in time to the music. Maybe she could survive these three months after all. It was not forever. The time would fly by if she kept busy. A hip replacement patient could not be that difficult and she could easily manage two small children.

'Cheer up, Miss Harlow. We'll soon be there,' he said. 'Upton Hall is only a few more miles, to the right, behind the trees. This damned rain.'

'I'll believe it when I see it.'

'My mother may be a dragon but she doesn't bite.'

'I do bite.'

'Then you may have met your match with my mother, Lady Grace. She's a fighter. She gives as good as she gets, just like you.'

Was there a glimmer of laughter in his voice or had she imagined it?

Jessica was beginning to wish she had stayed at home or turned back after one bleak look at Eastly Station. This fancy sports car was no consolation, nor was its cool looking owner. It was starting to rain in earnest, the windscreen wipers hardly coping. The hills were swathed in fog like a creepy Johnny Depp film.

She felt Lucas shiver in his wet clothes. He switched on a heater.

'Why are you soaked?' she asked. 'Didn't you know it was raining?'

'I was late meeting you, so I didn't stop to get a raincoat. Then I found the petrol was low so I had to make a detour to fill her up. I didn't want to run out of petrol with a special passenger on board. You wouldn't have believed such a tall story, would you? Running out of petrol in a leafy lane?'

'I doubt it,' said Jessica. 'I've heard it all before.'

'I was very late in last night, early hours, so I hadn't checked.'

Late in? Party? Out clubbing? Girlfriend or girlfriends? Jessica sighed. She guessed that any one of those might be true, probably all three. He looked the kind of man with a string of doting women friends and he'd said nothing about a wife. She wouldn't be joining the queue. She had learned her lesson. No more men for her after Fraser. From now on it was going to be work and more work.

She watched his hands on the steering wheel. They were strong and capable hands with long tapering fingers, nails cut short. The smooth hands of an artist. He'd never done a day's work in his life, that was obvious. She wouldn't waste any sympathy on him, even if he was trying to be pleasant.

'Thank you for meeting me,' she said, in an effort to bridge the gap, but not using his name. Her wet clothes were clammy and uncomfortable. She needed to be dry and warm. 'I appreciate your kindness.'

'Don't worry,' he said, his silvery grey eyes still cold and blank. 'You won't see much of me, day or night. I'm a creature of uncertain habits.'

He was putting her straight, right from the start. Lucas Coleman was out of bounds. She needn't harbour any romantic thoughts about the heir to Upton Hall. She was, after all, the hired help. The temporary hired help.

'Don't worry,' said Jessica, deliberately repeating his phrase. 'I won't get in your way. I shall be far too busy with your family. It looks as if I shall have my hands full with two children and a convalescent.'

She turned away, staring out of the window at the passing countryside. It was a blur of trees and branches, swaying in the wind. What on earth had she let herself in for? It was going to be a battle of staying power.

'Miss Harlow,' said Lucas Coleman, eyes fixed on the road ahead. 'Let's get this sorted. You are only employed to work here, to help the family though a difficult period. There is no ulterior motive.'

'I don't understand what you mean.'

'I don't have any designs on you. Even though you are quite pretty. If a drowned rat can look pretty.'

TWO

Lucas Coleman drove the last two miles from the station with occasional small talk that passed for conversation. Jessica was cold and wet and not listening. She appreciated that the man was trying to put her at her ease, but she could only wonder what on earth had possessed her to come out here to the wilds of the country. There was nothing but fields and hills in the pallid light. Civilization was receding fast.

'Do you drive?' he was asking.

'Yes, of course. Doesn't everyone?'

'While you are with us, you can have use of my mother's car. It's a vintage Vanden Plas Austin Princess, and she's very proud of it. In fact, I think she loves it more than she loves her family. It's got little picnic trays in the back that let down, with a place to stand your drink. Very posh.'

'Useful for picnics,' said Jessica drily.

'Automatic gears.'

'I can change gears.'

'I'm sure you can. Automatic takes a little getting used to. I've stalled it a couple of times. A bit tricky to start.'

'It's surprising that your mother lets you drive it then.'

'She didn't know,' he said.

Jessica was beginning to think she had brought all the wrong clothes. It looked like Wellingtons, jerseys and anorak weather. The windscreen wipers were working overtime. Upton Hall would probably be unheated and her bedroom like ice. She should have brought winceyette pyjamas, bed socks and a hot water bottle.

'Does it rain every day down here?'

'This is the wet season,' he said, as if they lived in Asia.

'I hope you are not expecting me to wear uniform all the time,' she said.

'No, of course, not. The kids would think they were in hospital. Just wear your own clothes. Be comfortable and warm. Lots of layers.'

The sounded ominous as if he was warning her that Upton Hall could be a chilly house. Well, she would soon change that. This fit and healthy looking man could flex his muscles chopping wood for a fire. She'd soon find him a couple of trees. There were plenty around.

'What about my hours of work,' Jessica went on, relentlessly. 'Your letter didn't say anything about my time off.'

'Didn't it? How very remiss. I should prefer it if you were with the children every weekend, both Saturday and Sunday, but you can certainly take time off during the week. They are both at school and the school bus picks them up at the end of the road. But there is always Lady Grace to look after. I don't want her left alone for any length of time, not so soon after her operation.'

'Patients usually recover quickly from a hip replacement. They need to keep moving. It's not like the old days with endless bed rest.' It didn't sound as if she would have any time off. Jessica wished she had asked earlier.

'As you think fit and proper,' said Lucas, a renewed coolness entering his voice. 'But I would remind you that you are employed to look after my mother and whole days off to go gallivanting to the shops are out of the question.'

'I wasn't planning to go gallivanting.'

'Then we can work something out.'

'Surely you could be around too, occasionally?' said Jessica, with a note of sharpness. 'There are times when you could look after the children and your mother and I could have an afternoon off. A few hours perhaps?'

'No, I'm not,' he said curtly, closing the subject. 'We're nearly there. Look out for tall chimneys through the trees. This is Upton Hall.'

All Jessica could see were trees. They were driving through an avenue of close trees, the canopy of dripping leaves overhead like a cathedral roof. Her spirits fell. She didn't even know what kind of trees they were. This was going to be disastrous. She could feel the despair growing. She was already homesick for her little London flat and wanted more than anything to turn round and go back to its safety. Then she remembered that she had let it to a friend of a friend for the whole three months, banking the rent. There was no going back.

'Upton Hall,' he said, with a degree of pride and utter masculinity. 'The home of the Colemans for over a hundred years.'

Upton Hall was impressive, standing within the lea of a low pastured hill, sheltered on two sides from the worst of the wind. It was a two-storeyed stone building with leaded windows, with a tall tower at one end with wide curved bay windows, crenulated like a mock castle. The front door was of heavy oak, flanked by two columns and a porch of slate. Virginia creeper was turning to russet on the walls, warming the austere lines of the house.

'It's . . . it's very grand,' said Jessica, eventually, unable to find the right words. She had a hundred sudden impressions, crowding in. 'How old is it?'

'It's a Victorian folly, built onto a medieval farmhouse and stables, we think. The farmhouse is at the back, part of it now the new kitchen, a utility room and garages. It's rambling inside. You'll get lost.'

'I'm lost already,' said Jessica .

Upton Hall was awesome, so much larger than anything she had ever seen before. But its grandeur had a certain gentleness, a timeless warmth.

The unhappiness in her voice was not lost on Lucas. He bent forward, his fiery, silver grey eyes for once tinged with concern.

'Cheer up, Miss Harlow. You'll love it once you get used to it. Upton Hall will grow on you.'

Jessica did not believe him. Nothing was going to sway her or make the next three months any easier. She would have to grit her teeth and get on with it. The handsome Lucas Coleman could be as pleasant and welcoming as he could manage, it would not make any difference. She hated the countryside, she hated trees and especially she hated wet trees, dripping everywhere.

'Does it ever stop raining?'

'Occasionally. We put out the flags and eat in the garden.'

'Even in winter?'

'Especially in the winter.'

Now he was laughing at her and that made the arrival even worse. The sooner she escaped to whatever damp bedroom was to be hers, the better. She would lock the door, become distant and withdrawn and go into a Jane Austen decline.

Lucas stopped the car in the curved drive and climbed out. He went round and opened the car door. Jessica was struggling to undo the safety belt.

'Let me do that for you,' he said, bending over her. For a second his unruly dark hair brushed her face and the shock was electric. The freshness of soap and water with his own manly scent was overwhelming, scant inches away. For a second Jessica could not breathe. It was an endless moment.

'There. It's an awkward one, too far back. Damned designers.'

He straightened up and held out his arm to assist her. The passenger seat of the Porsche was so low down, again Jessica was struggling. She had to use his arm as a lever, to get herself out of the seat. She was angry for being made to look such a fool when she was normally so calm and efficient. It washed over her in a turbulent wave. She brushed back wet hair from her face.

'Thank you,' she said, trying to regain her composure. 'Damned stupid seat,' she went on. 'Built for a midget.'

'And you are about five foot seven. I do agree. I have the same problem.'

Now that Lucas was standing beside her, she realized that he was over six feet. He would have to fold himself up to get inside the car. He was already getting her case out of the boot and carrying it towards the front door.

He turned round, seeing her hesitation. It was a long, challenging look.

'Are you coming, or have you changed your mind already?'

Jessica did not know what to say. He was giving her a chance to back out. Say yes, and in twenty minutes she could be sitting on a wet platform, waiting for a train back to London, if there were any trains back to London at this time.

'I'm coming.'

It didn't sound like her at all. Some other person was speaking. Some strange woman that she didn't know. The real Jessica Harlow had gone into hibernation.

The hall floor was tiled with black and white squares. A curving staircase led to the upper regions. Busts of Greek philosophers stood on marble pillars and portraits of ancestors in oil glared down from the walls.

Someone had put bursts of wild flowers on side tables and their scent was overwhelming. The huge vases looked antique and valuable.

'Mrs Harris, the housekeeper,' said Lucas, putting down her case and bag. 'She has a mania for picking flowers but no sense on how to arrange them. It requires a special skill. Perhaps you can do flowers. Let me show you round.'

He opened a door to the left. It was a long, gracious room in ivory and pale blue with a grand piano, armchairs and more portraits. 'The sitting room,' he announced. 'My mother uses it when she has bridge parties.'

Jessica could not imagine anyone sitting there and feeling comfortable. It was stiff and unused. A room that was kept for best and best never happened.

Lucas turned right off the hall. 'The library. No overdue fines.'

The room was wall to wall leather-bound books, ninety-nine per cent unread. But Jessica spotted a small clutch of modern novels on a side table. It also had a computer at a desk overlooking the drive. The several armchairs were deep and inviting, well used. There was a small wine cooler in a corner.

'Can you use a computer?' he asked.

'I'm not from outer space,' she answered, biting off each word.

'You may use this one. Remind me to give you the password.'

Lucas nodded, then opened sliding doors in a wall between the bookcases. 'This leads into the dining room. So if we hold a party, we can use both rooms. Unfortunately, we rarely hold parties. Such a pity. This house was made for parties.'

The dining room was beautiful with eau de nil walls, toning carpet and curtains. More portraits on the walls. A long polished walnut table that could seat at least twelve people. Jessica hoped she would not have to eat here.

'How do you talk to each other?' she asked. 'With walkie-talkies?'

'No,' he said. 'We don't sit marooned at either end. We sit together, here at the top. It's really pleasant. Nearer the kitchen, so the food is always hot.'

He took her up a few steps into a strangely bleak area, whitewashed walls and low ceiling. There was nothing in it, apart from a stone inglenook fireplace. The floor was made up of huge slabs of uneven slate. Their size was amazing.

'We think this is the oldest part of the house, perhaps even before the farmhouse. Maybe it's all that is left of some medieval hall. This middle post has been dated back to 1412. All the rest has gone.'

The post was thick and blackened, gnarled and sturdy enough to hold up a roof. Lucas stood with his arms laced easily round the post in an embrace, something he had done since a child. He was looking at the post fondly.

'How do they know how old it is?' Jessica asked.

'They took a core sample,' he said. 'It's the tiniest plug of wood. They can tell the date by the year rings. It's very clever and very accurate.'

'No graffiti?'

'Not on our rings.'

'I'm relieved.'

They went back into the hall and began climbing. The stairs divided halfway and Lucas took her first to the left. 'The kid's bedrooms are in this wing. They have a bedroom each, a family bathroom, and their nanny's room is next door.'

'Do I have the nanny's room, then?' Jessica felt this was to be her place in their life. She was the nanny, single bed, no radiator, no fire, cramped and soulless..

'No way, Miss Harlow. Follow me.' He led her across the wide landing. Jessica reckoned they must be nearing the tower. 'My mother has the front bedroom in the tower. It's a beautiful room with big windows that look out onto the garden, the best in the house. You are in the guest room, next to hers. It's called the Primrose Room. I think you'll like it.' He threw open the door.

It was as big as her entire flat in London with pale yellow walls and cream paintwork; buttermilk damask curtains with matching cover on the double bed. A sofa covered in saffron velvet toned with the carpet; a desk by the window, and an upright chair with upholstered seat in the same velvet. The room was warm and radiated light. 'En suite through there,' Lucas added, pointing to a far door.

Jessica went over to the window. The view was of rolling hills and dappled fields, the hedges and crops of trees like a painting. Nothing moved. It was so still, emptiness and clarity stole the scene. It had even stopped raining. So unlike the rooftop view from her North London flat of ugly buildings, refuse bins and scaffolding, parked lorries and neon street lights.

'Thank you,' she said with genuine warmth. 'I love the room.'

Lucas did a mock sigh of relief. 'Glad to have got something right at last.'

'So where's your room?'

Jessica had not meant to ask but it came without thinking. She did not want to bump into him in the night. Coming home late from a party.

'I have a makeshift sort of room, somewhere to bunk down, over the garage stables. I'm not here much. You won't bump into me in the night,' he added, reading her thoughts. 'You may want to tidy up before meeting my mother. She's very particular. I'll bring up your case.'

The buttercup tiled bathroom was as pretty as the bedroom. Jessica had another sigh of relief. She was going to be so comfortable here. Some of her misgivings faded, her spirit recovering. But she still tested the lock on the door.

She was dishevelled by the wind and rain and all her subtle make-up had disappeared. She set to and repaired the damage so that Lady Grace would get a good impression. Her high-heeled shoes were muddied and she changed into a pair of flat black suede slip-ons. Her wet jacket was hung behind the bathroom door to dry.

She tucked her white shirt into the plain navy skirt, added a red patterned silk scarf to her throat and she was ready to face the dragon.

'So you are the nurse who is supposed to look after me and make sure I do all the right things,' said Lady Grace with a decided lack of grace. 'You're a bit too young and skinny for my idea of a nurse. Are you properly trained? Supposing I fell?'

'I'm stronger than you think,' said Jessica.

'You don't look strong enough to lift a bedpan.'

'I should hope you are bathroom trained.'

'I'm convalescing after a serious operation, I'll have you know. I need a great deal of care and attention.'

'Hip and knee replacements are routine these days and highly successful,' said Jessica. 'You'll be as right as rain in no time, and free of pain.'

Lady Grace snorted. 'I'm certainly not free of pain yet. I need regular medication.'

'I can do regular medication,' said Jessica calmly.

'Any idiot can pop a couple of capsules and fill a glass with water. I don't need your help.'

'I'm glad to hear it. I shall be free then to make sure you eat the right foods and take the right amount of exercise. Exercise is the key. It will all help to make your recovery quick and painless.'

'I can do all of that by myself, thank you, Nurse, Matron, whatever you are,' said Lady Grace. 'Well, if you have got to stay, I suppose I'll have to get used to it. What am I supposed to call you?'

'Jessica will do fine,' said Jessica.

'I don't like fancy names. I shall call you Jess.'

Jessica fumed. She hated her name being shortened. It made her sound as if she was a dog. A shaggy dog at that.

Lady Grace was indeed tetchy and short tempered. She was sitting in an armchair by the big bay window in her bedroom, dressed in a fawn skirt and blue twin set, a double string of pearls at her neck. Her fine grey hair was drawn back into a French pleat and pinned with combs. She had a certain pallor after her operation and the lines on her face were not all bad temper and impatience.

'Shakespeare didn't think Jessica was a fancy name,' said Jessica. 'He used it in one of his plays, *The Merchant of Venice*. Jessica was the daughter of Shylock, in love with Lorenzo.'

'Makes no difference. I'll still call you Jess, Shakespeare or not. Never could stand all that rubbish. Shakespeare indeed.'

Jessica let it pass. There were more important things to discuss. She had a feeling that Lady Grace was not moving about much or doing any exercises.

'How are you getting on with the exercises they gave you at the hospital?' she asked. 'Have you got the printed sheet?'

'They are too painful so I'm not doing them,' said Lady Grace. 'Getting from my bed to this chair is all I can do at present.' She nodded towards the window. 'I like the view. It's perfect, don't you agree?'

Jessica moved towards the bay window. She could appreciate the glorious countryside now, hill upon hill of the South Downs, once deeply forested, now for grazing sheep and growing corn. The view from this window was of the gardens which she had not noticed, arriving in the rain in Lucas's low-slung car. The rain had flattened some of the flowers, the heavy heads hanging with abandon to the elements. But the droplets were glistening in the late sun and the garden looked magical.

'It is indeed a beautiful garden, a beautiful view,' said Jessica. 'You'll be able to walk round it very soon. Once we get you downstairs.'

'I can't go downstairs!' Lady Grace was aghast. 'I can't do stairs. Far too painful. I can barely reach this chair.'

'The more exercise you do, the less painful it will be,' said Jessica patiently. 'The long term success of this operation depends on the patient strengthening the leg muscles that hold up the hip. So, regular exercise.'

'I'm not just the patient,' said Lady Grace indignantly. 'I'm Lady Grace Coleman, not a nobody. I know what I can do and what I can't do.'

Jessica held back a sharp retort. She paced the bedroom, judging its size. It was a big room, decorated in a style of thirty years ago, heavy walnut furniture with dark rose flowered curtains and toning carpet. Silver-backed brushes lay on the dressing table with an old-fashioned glass powder bowl and puff. A single tube of Max Factor dark red lipstick and bottle of clear nail varnish stood beside a large bottle of Elizabeth Arden eau de cologne.

'You have a beautiful room, too,' said Jessica. 'But it will become your prison if you don't get some exercise. I suggest you walk from one side of the room to the other once every hour, holding onto something. Then tomorrow you can walk to the landing and back and perhaps try one or two steps of the stairs.'

'The stairs? Are you trying to kill me, young woman? I can't do the stairs. My son, Lucas, will have to have one of those new-fangled stair lifts put in.'

'On the contrary, I'm going to get you downstairs and into the garden. You won't need a stair lift, I promise you. It would spoil that lovely staircase. You need lots of encouragement and a positive attitude.'

Lady Grace swung round in her chair and the sudden movement was painful. She gasped, her fury overriding the pain.

'I won't be spoken to like this. You can leave my house immediately. Lucas can get another nanny for the children.' She sat back, her face reddening, her hands clutched together.

Jessica searched the bedside table for prescription painkillers. She couldn't find them. But Lady Grace's leather handbag was on the floor by the bed. She opened it and a packet of painkillers, with her name from the hospital dispensary, was inside. She fetched a glass of water from the adjacent bathroom and took two tablets to Lady Grace.

'Here you are. These will help. You shouldn't lean forward in a chair or in bed for the first couple of weeks. The hospital told you that, didn't they? And you need a high-rise toilet seat. I'll get one for you.'

'You've been in my bathroom,' Lady Grace spluttered.

'That's right,' said Jessica. 'I'm a nurse. I go in bathrooms.'

'Not in mine, you don't.'

The air was strained and Lady Grace abruptly fell silent.

'I'll go and make some tea. I think we could both do with a cup of tea,' said Jessica. She had to get away from this exasperating woman.

'Is that hair colour natural?' was her parting shot.

'It's certainly not a wig,' said Jessica.

Jessica escaped to the peace of the landing, her heart pounding. She had never, in all her days of nursing, had such an impossible twenty minutes with a patient. She could easily grab her coat and her case and walk back to the station. It might take an hour, two hours. But Jessica knew she couldn't walk out on a difficult patient: Lady Grace needed her or that operation would have been wasted.

Jessica took several deep breaths to steady herself.

This prickly old woman needed help. The hip replacement would not be a success if she refused to exercise and she would be back to square one. Back to constant pain and unable to get about at all.

It was a challenge. Jessica could not resist a challenge.

Mrs Harris, the housekeeper, was busy in the kitchen supervising the children's tea. The scene was pleasant and homely. Jessica noted the big Aga range pumping out heat and moved towards it. This was somewhere to get warm.

'Hello, Mrs Harris. I'm Jessica Harlow, nurse of sorts for the next three months, looking after Lady Grace. I think she would appreciate a tray of tea, if you have time. Something to calm her nerves. She is a little frayed by my arrival.'

'Of course, Miss Harlow. I'll take a tray up to her ladyship immediately. Perhaps you'd like some tea yourself. You could join the children.'

'That's exactly what I shall do,' said Jessica gratefully. 'And no need to call me Miss Harlow, Jessica will do.'

She sat down at the kitchen table, aware that the two children had been listening to the conversation. They looked at her expectantly. Now she was going to meet them and make friends. She hoped that they were not as prickly as their dragon grandmother.

'Hello,' she said, turning her attention to the little girl. 'And who are you?'

The little girl was squirming in her seat, her eyes bright with excitement. She was about five years old, a little on the plump side, but as pretty as a picture with a riot of dark curls and bewitching lashes that were outrageously long.

'I'm Lily,' she said, wriggling. 'I'm five. I go to school now.'

'Nice to meet you, Lily.' She shook a sticky hand with a solemn dignity. 'You must show me some of your school work. I'd like to see it.'

'Do we call you Jessica Willdo?'

Jessica laughed. The first genuine laugh of the day. It lit up her face and she was transformed. Her true face was often hidden behind professional calmness. But when she laughed, her periwinkle blue eyes sparkled like gems and her mouth curved into an irresistible shape of happiness.

'Jessica Willdo, will do.'

'I like you already,' said Lily, still chewing on her jam sandwich. 'I like you better than our last nanny. All she did was smoke all the time and watch television.'

'First of all, Lily, I will put you straight. I am not your nanny. I am a nurse who is here to look after your grandmother after her operation. But at the same time, I'll be around for you both, keep an eye on you. You can come to me any time, ask me anything, and we'll do things together.'

'What sort of things?'

'For a start, I thought we might go to Worthing and see what's there, walk on the beach if the tide is out. You'll need your Wellington boots.'

Lily jumped up and down in her chair, wheezing. 'Can we go now, Willdo?'

Jessica laughed again, so much that she nearly spilt her tea. 'It's far too late, poppet. We'll see about tomorrow or the next day.'

She turned her attention to the boy who had not said a word. He was concentrating on his tea. She noticed that he had lined up the jam, the butter dish, and a jar of Marmite in front of his plate, like sentries. His cup of tea was exactly in line with his plate and he had put the spoon rigidly straight by the saucer.

'Hello,' she said gently. 'I'm Jessica. Who are you?'

'Who are you?' he said.

'I've just explained. I'm Jessica, a nurse who has come to look after your grandmother after her operation. Nice to meet you.'

'Nice to meet you.'

Lily piped up, her mouth lined with jam, 'Daniel doesn't say much. He likes being alone. He doesn't like people.'

Jessica noticed the lack of eye contact. Daniel would not look at her. There was no communication between them. She tried again. It might be initial shyness.

'I'd like us all to be friends while I'm here. It could be such fun. I have lots of plans.' This was not true, but she had time to make some instant plans. 'We'll do all sorts of things together. And I know that someone soon has a birthday.' There was no response. 'You don't want to be stuck in the house all the time, do you?'

'All the time,' said Daniel.

Alarm bells were ringing in Jessica's head. The repetition of her words. His whole posture had not moved. He lived in another world, no contact with this one. He was cutting his sandwich into exact squares and lining them into rows. He then ate them in order. At least, he was eating, methodically.

'Never mind, Daniel. We'll talk another time.'

'Another time,' he said.

Jessica finished her tea. She was not hungry. The emotion of the last few hours had drained her appetite. Perhaps later, she would poke around and make herself a cheese sandwich.

'Willdo?' asked Lily, still wheezing as she started on a big slice of home-made sponge cake, 'are you going to put us to bed? Are you going to read us a story?'

'I guess I can do all that. What story would you like me to read?'

'The one about the baby mole who couldn't find his way home in the fading light.' Lily was perfectly sure about her favourite story.

'That's a new one on me,' said Jessica. 'And what's your favourite story, Daniel?'

This threw the boy off balance. He was seven, coming on eight, and looked a lot like his father. He was going to be lean and tall, incredibly handsome, break a few hearts one day. He had no answer to that question. He drew swirls on his plate with smears of Marmite. He did not look at her.

'Perhaps you'll tell me later,' said Jessica, throwing him a lifeline.

'Later,' he said.

29

Jessica stood outside the house in the falling dusk and wondered where she would find Lucas. He said he had a room over
the stables. She had no intention of going to his room but she
might find his car parked in the stables.

She wasn't angry but she was annoyed that Lucas had not
been straight with her. He had got her down here to Upton Hall
on false pretences about the children and there was no way he
was going to escape her tongue.

She had an anorak over her shoulders because the trees were
still spilling their raindrops. The garden scent was heady and
the landscape was mesmerizing her. She wondered if she could
cut some flowers and put them in her room. A few wouldn't be
missed. She loved fresh flowers. She always bought herself a
bunch in a market.

The peace of the garden was soothing, the mist spinning
round her like a cocoon. Perhaps she would be beamed up to
some alien ship and transported to an Elysian community. It
would be peaceful there.

'Have you survived?' Lucas was coming out of the mist, clad
now in Wellington boots and worn anorak, his hair still plastered wet to his head. He looked breathtakingly handsome. 'You
don't look too shattered. How did you get on with the dragon,
Lady Grace?'

'I think I won,' said Jessica.

'First round to you, then.'

'Do you have the walker frame? Surely the hospital issued
one for your mother to use? She needs it.'

'It's downstairs, in a cupboard. My mother won't use it.
Says it makes her look a cripple. It does look a bit like sheltered
housing gear.'

'She will be a cripple if she doesn't get some exercise. Can
you resurrect it and take it upstairs? I shall get her to use it.'

'Your word is my command.' Lucas bowed his head in
mock deference, looking grave, almost grim. 'I obey the dragon-
slayer.'

'Daniel and Lily,' said Jessica, changing the subject.

'My two delightful children.'

'You didn't tell me.'

'Tell you what?' He looked defensive, a hard set on his face, but still someone in charge. He looked over her head, out into the garden.

'You didn't tell me that Lily was overweight and asthmatic and that Daniel is autistic. They both need trained help.'

'And aren't you exactly the right person to do that?' said Lucas, coming so close that she could barely stand straight. 'I looked into your qualifications. You've done a lot of work with difficult children. I don't want them regimented and put into specialist centres where children are numbers and shuffled about like pieces on a chessboard. I want them looked after at home. I want you to change their lives.'

'In three months?' Jessica was astounded at his impudence.

'However long it takes.'

Jessica took a deep breath and moved away from his closeness. Rain was dripping off his nose. His tongue came out and licked away a drip. A sharp, guilty thrill ran through her and he caught the change of expression.

'You'll stay?' he asked with a sudden sweetness, mentally on his knees but not physically on his knees. There was an unexpected warmth in his eyes.

'I suppose I'll stay,' she said reluctantly.

'Thank you, Jessica.' Lucas brought his hands out from behind his back. He was holding a bunch of freshly cut yellow pom-pom dahlias and white daisies. 'I thought you might like these for your room. I think you like flowers.'

'Thank you,' said Jessica, taking the flowers. 'But there is one more thing I must ask you. What about your wife? Will she be here too, telling me what to do, ordering me about?'

His face froze. 'No,' he said. 'Forget my wife. She's not likely to interfere in any way.'

'How can I be sure?'

'You can take my word.'

He snapped out the words and walked away. His back said don't ask me again. It was a wall of ice. Jessica was suddenly afraid.

She walked slowly back into the house, wondering what she had taken on.

THREE

It was a long time before Jessica got her breath back. Lucas had tricked her into this job and that made her really mad with a complex mixture of emotions. She had been gullible, not asking the right questions, taking all he had said at face value.

But she could also see his point of view as a father. He cared about his children and he knew they both needed help. No nanny was qualified to take on the complex task. And would she have come if he had told her the truth? Probably not. She would have said that she didn't know enough about autism and that Lily needed a dietician, not a nurse.

She was here now and she would have to make the best of it. She might be able to make the smallest difference, but at least she would get Lady Grace up and downstairs. Even if she had to fight that lady for every step of the way.

It was going to be a fight. Two strong wills in opposition. Jessica might end up feeling a fool, but she knew she could genuinely make a difference.

Bathtime with Lily was hilarious. The family bathroom had been converted from a small side bedroom. It was plain cream tiled, but there was plenty of space and a comfortable lloyd loom basket chair to sit on, and there were more ducks than the Royals could shoot in a day. Lily blew enough bubbles to launch herself into space. Jessica was glad of a plastic apron. It was ages since she had towel dried a little girl, and the small cuddly, sweet smelling bundle was delightful. So different from washing a sickly child in the antiseptic confines of a hospital ward.

'You are going to read me a story, aren't you, Willdo?'

'Of course,' said Jessica. 'I always keep my word, if I can.'

'And you are not going off down to the pub after we've gone to bed?'

'No, I'll be here. Wherever did you get that idea from?'

'The nanny before the last one was always down the pub.' Lily giggled. 'We called her Ginger Beer because of her hair and the pub. She was always down at the pub drinking ginger beer. And she had ginger hair.'

'That wasn't very kind. She might have been drinking champagne.'

'She wasn't very kind. She wouldn't read to us at all.'

'Perhaps she couldn't read very well.'

'I can read. Only small words, of course. Daniel can't read properly yet.'

Daniel bathed by himself in awkward silence. He didn't want a story but Jessica noticed that his door was left open so that he could listen to the baby mole story. Lily managed her nightly inhaler dose with a careless regard to the correct procedure. It was more gasp and puff and blow. Jessica made a mental note to show Lily tomorrow. She wondered if anyone had ever checked.

'Goodnight, Lily, sweet dreams,' said Jessica, tucking her in. 'Sleep tight.'

'Night, night, Willdo. I like having you here. You will stay, won't you?'

Again that anxious note as if Lily was used to being let down. Perhaps nannies came and went. It seemed they did.

'Don't you worry, Lily. I'll be here tomorrow.'

Jessica switched on the dim battery light on the wall and half closed the door. Mrs Harris had told her that Lily had nightmares if she was left in the dark. Jessica wondered what the nightmares were about.

Jessica looked into Daniel's room. He was already in bed,

huddled under the clothes, only the top of his head showing. He also had a dim light on the wall.

'Goodnight, Daniel, sweet dreams,' she said. 'You can stay up a little later tomorrow if you like. You don't have to go to bed at exactly the same time as Lily.'

There was no answer. But she hadn't expected any.

She tidied up the bathroom, leaving nothing on the floor that they could slip on, in case one of the children got up to use the bathroom in the night. She gave her hair a quick smooth, tucking away the damp ends, and went across the landing to Lady Grace's bedroom. After a polite knock on the door, and a moment's pause, she went in.

Lady Grace was sitting on the edge of the bed, looking distraught and dishevelled. Her hair had escaped from its neat French pleat.

'Where were you when I wanted you?' she cried out, her voice low and full of pain. 'I've been calling and calling.'

Jessica knew this was not true. She would have heard. The children's bedrooms were only across the landing. And the baby mole story had been read in a hushed silence.

'I'm here now, Lady Grace. What do you need?'

'I need to get to the bathroom, idiot. I can't make it without help.' She was struggling to stand up but making a poor job of it. 'You know that.'

'My name is Jessica by the way, not idiot. Take my arm and I'll help you to the bathroom. Lucas is going to bring up your walking frame which you will find a great help. You can lean on it as two extra legs.'

'I'm not using that damned contraption.'

'Oh yes, you are. You'll be surprised at how much support it gives. No need to tell anyone. Use it in secret if you like. Hide it in the bathroom. Give it a name. Call it Fred. Fred is a nice name. Unless you actually know someone called Fred.'

Jessica saw a fractional quirk to the woman's lips. It was the nearest Lady Grace ever got to smiling. She would never show that anything amused her. A bit like Queen Victoria. It was slow progress to the bathroom, and once safely there, Jessica left Lady Grace on her own. She knew further help would be an insult to her dignity. She heard water running and thought it safe to leave her.

Jessica took the tea tray down to the kitchen. Mrs Harris was busy preparing supper. She was a comely woman in her late fifties, with greying hair still tied back in the ponytail of her youth. Jessica could imagine her in the carefree flower power days, dancing to the Beatles barefoot in a long flowing dress with flowers strung in her hair and round her neck. Very rural and poetic. Mr Harris had been lucky.

'I'm doing you and the master a cold buffet on the sideboard in the dining room, with a tureen of hot leek and potato soup. Will that be all right, Miss Jessica?'

'Perfect. Is Mr Lucas still around then?'

'He's fiddling with the Austin, I expect. Making sure it's all right for you to drive. He'll probably give me a lift home if it's still raining, though I've got my bicycle. I live in the village, you see. Dove Cottage, down by the green.'

'I didn't know there was a village.'

'It's called West Eastly which is the daftest name, proper Sussex, that is. We've got a lot of daft names. Some people collect them. It's only a few houses and cottages, a church and a pub. The mobile library calls once a week. There's a small grocers shop. My brother, Ted, runs the shop. You can get most things. Here at Upton Hall, we have a weekly delivery from that Avocado firm, ordered on the Internet. Newfangled shopping. How can you tell what you want from a photo?'

Jessica moved over to the Aga and lifted her hands towards the warmth. It was raining in earnest again, large drops pelting onto the path, spurting brown earth.

'Always ask me if you want a lift home, Mrs Harris.'

'That's real kind of you, miss. Thank you.'

'And Lady Grace's supper?'

'I'm doing a tray of the same for her ladyship. It's her favourite soup.'

'I'll help you carry it up.'

'Thanks. I always hate carrying soup upstairs in case I spill any.'

'Why not take it in a lidded jug and pour it out when you get there?' Jessica suggested, seeing a bowl of hot soup sliding everywhere on a disaster course.

'Now that's an idea. Why didn't I think of that?'

'It's an old hospital trick,' Jessica grinned. 'Hot soup is dangerous.'

It was quite a procession taking supper up to her ladyship. Jessica privately adjusted the title to her battleship. Lady Grace was sitting in her chair, looking regal and triumphant. She had tidied her hair.

'I shan't be needing Fred,' she said with a straight face.

'He's handy to have around,' said Jessica, equally straight faced.

Mrs Harris looked bemused but immediately began laying a small table which she lifted across to the armchair. A white lace cloth and silver cutlery appeared.

'Your favourite soup,' she said.

'I don't have a favourite soup,' said Lady Grace, reverting to normal.

'Leek and potato. You said it was your favourite.'

'Pour, not talk, Mrs Harris. It's getting cold. And please draw the curtains. It looks dark and miserable outside. I don't want to look at it.'

Mrs Harris did as she was told. Jessica wondered how long she had put up with her employer. Maybe work was hard to get in West Eastly. Or perhaps there was another reason she stayed. Some dark secret that she knew nothing about. Jessica thought about the possibility of a secret, but quickly gave up.

It was none of her business.

Lady Grace dismissed both women. 'But I'll need you later,' she added, nodding towards Jessica.

Jessica checked on the children who were both fast asleep. She noticed that Daniel's toys were all lined up in rows. And his shoes were in rows. A sad young boy, living in a world of his own.

She changed into a cornflower blue tracksuit for supper, as her skirt and shirt were still damp from bathtime. There was no need to dress up for Lucas Coleman and it was going to be a snack supper. She would be warm and comfortable. She wandered into the dining room, not knowing if it was the right time.

Lucas was already there, struggling with opening a bottle of wine. He'd screwed the corkscrew in diagonally so the cork would not come out. He looked annoyed then amused. He peered at the bottle.

'I'm hopeless. Can't do anything properly,' he drawled calmly. 'Are you any good at this?'

'I'll have a go,' said Jessica, jerking her gaze away. She withdrew the corkscrew and started again, making sure it went in straight. Then she folded down the levers and the cork came out, ruined in shape but out. She noticed that it was a very good New Zealand Merlot from a vineyard in Onion Bay, wherever that was.

'Efficient at everything. I hope you've put opening wine bottles on your CV,' said Lucas, pouring out two generous glasses. 'None of this precocious sniffing and tasting business, please. I know what corking means. It's going to be good.'

The glasses were elegant old crystal, their fine cut catching the light and flashing sparks through the red wine. She couldn't put a price on their worth, but it would be a lot. She would not be able to afford them.

'I wouldn't care if it was the cheapest supermarket plonk in these glasses,' said Jessica, relaxing a few degrees. 'They are beautiful.'

'I'll remember that,' said Lucas. 'In case I'm ever hard up.'

The soup tureen was already on the sideboard, standing on a hot plate. There was an array of salads and cold meats and a cheese board. Suddenly Jessica was hungry. She had not eaten since breakfast and that had been a hurried affair, using up bits and pieces from the refrigerator before leaving her London flat.

'Let me serve you,' said Lucas. 'You look worn out. Sit down.'

He had changed too. He was in black jeans with a black polo necked shirt, very casual but still smart. His hair hadn't seen a comb and was all over the place, drying itself from his shower. Instinct was telling Jessica not to look at him. It was too dangerous and too much of an effort.

Jessica did not argue. She let him bring her a bowl of soup. The china was beautiful too, almost too old to use. It was cream with a turquoise and gold border. The side plate matched, a brown roll on it, ready to crumble. A slab of butter was on a silver serving dish. None of those horrid little packets that were hopeless to open. Jessica sighed. It was all so civilized. She craved civilization after years of NHS hospital routine and crowded canteens. It was a seductive delight.

'Are you regretting it?' Lucas asked, sitting opposite her at the top end of the long table. 'Do you still want to go home?'

The soup was good, hot and creamy with a delicate taste. Mrs Harris knew how to make soup. Jessica did not answer straight away. She was too hungry.

'I don't know,' she said eventually, with a surge of confidence. 'You did trick me and I'm annoyed about that. But I can understand why. No one in their right mind would have come if they had known all the problems.'

'No one but you. You are different.'

'That's not the point. I still have to deal with these problems. And deal with them every day. It won't be easy.'

'Does that mean you are going to stay?' He was staring at her as if trying to hypnotize her answer, sweep away her defences. She could sense his anxiety overflowing like a flood. But he still had an air of coolness. A Coleman would never plead or beg. He had inherited that trait from his mother.

'It goes against all my good judgement, but yes, I will stay. I can see that your mother, Lady Grace, needs a firm hand. She is the most awkward patient I have ever had and she will dislocate that new hip if she is not careful. Daniel is difficult. He lives in a world of his own, sees the world through a different lens. I'm not sure how I can help him. Little Lily is a delightful child but she is going to put on weight in a big way if she doesn't change her eating habits. An obese child will have health problems later. And she doesn't know how to use her inhaler.'

'I didn't know that she didn't know. I thought someone had shown her.'

'Did you ever think of checking? And you should have seen the cake and jam she put away at teatime. She should have been eating fruit. An apple or a banana. There's not even a fruit bowl in the kitchen.'

'Not a fruit bowl?'

Jessica laughed. 'Ah, now I know. So that's where Daniel gets it from.'

'Gets what from?'

'Repeating the last phrase of whatever is said to him. It saves him thinking or having to say anything. There's a word for it: parroting.'

'It's better than not speaking at all,' said Lucas, helping himself to a second bowl of soup. He offered some to Jessica but she shook her head. She stood up and served herself some salad and cheese. She rarely ate meat but made no fuss if meat was offered. She had refined a neat way of pushing it around the plate as if she was eating it. She could not bear to eat something which had once lived.

'Would you allow me to do the weekly shopping order from Avocado? That's not the proper name, is it? Mrs Harris couldn't remember what it was.' Jessica hoped this was not too pushy but Lucas nodded in agreement.

'Please order what you think fit. It's a Brighton firm. You'll see the link on the computer under Favourites. My card is registered with them. It will pay for anything. Order crates of apples, grapes and oranges. Whatever you like.'

The good wine was making her feel warm and mellow. She tried not to look at Lucas in case her thought processes stopped working. She was looking forward to sleeping in that pretty primrose bedroom, her body now aching with tiredness. But first she would have to see Lady Grace to bed, and that would be another battle.

Jessica wanted to know where the children's mother was in all this, but it was obvious that Lucas had no wish to give her that information. He said nothing about their mother. They talked about the garden and cars and other mundane matters, never touching on anything personal.

'My mother has made a complaint,' Lucas said eventually, helping himself from the cheeseboard while stabbing at an olive. 'Complaint number one.'

'So what's new?' Jessica sighed. 'I'm sure she complains about everything.'

'You went into her handbag without permission.'

'Oh, my God. She was crunched up with pain and then complains when I try to find her prescription painkillers. I don't believe it.' Jessica was astounded.

'Apparently she considers that an invasion of her privacy.'

'Like she might have a packet of condoms in there or a stash of ecstasy?'

'Hold on, easy, easy there. I know she is difficult, but I would be grateful if you could try to remember that she is an old fashioned lady in many ways. Her handbag is a fortress of privacy. No one is allowed to look in it.'

Jessica took a deep breath, worried she might tremble with indignation. 'I will try to remember in future. Her tablets will be where I put them.'

'Thank you.'

Lucas made fresh coffee for them and brought it through from the kitchen. He was not the usual helpless male. He could make good coffee. Perhaps he had been on his own for a long time, somewhere else.

'I've brought in the walking frame and given it an antiseptic wipe down. No hospital germs. I know how important it is that my mother doesn't pick up any infection. The early days are tricky ones,' he said.

'I wish your mother would understand that. You could speak to her. She doesn't seem to want to know that exercise is vital. The stronger she gets, the less pain she will be in. It can't be that she enjoys being in pain.'

'I think in a strange way she enjoys the attention,' said Lucas, stirring a black coffee. 'She hasn't got much else left in life to enjoy, poor soul.'

'That's nonsense,' said Jessica briskly. 'She has lots to enjoy. The Sussex coast, theatres, having friends in, walking, swimming. You said she liked playing cards. Swimming is excellent for hip replacements because the water is a support.'

Lucas looked appalled. 'You'd never get my mother to go swimming. It would be equal to a total eclipse of the moon.'

'You'd be surprised what I can get people to do. And it would be good for Daniel and Lily too. Daniel would find a kind of freedom in the water, freedom to be himself, not having to talk to the water. And the exercise would help our tubby little girl immensely, especially if I buy her a very pretty swimsuit.'

Lucas sat back, laughing, those silvery eyes twinkling for once. 'Well, I wish you luck. How about a wager? I'll take you out to dinner at the Grand Hotel in Brighton if you get my mother into a pool. Champagne if you get her to swim more than three strokes. A length would be an impossibility.'

'Done,' said Jessica. 'Tell them to put the champagne on ice.'

A small sharp ringing sound broke into the moment of equality. Lucas took his mobile out of his pocket and answered the call.

'Yes? OK, I'll come right away. You could take all the necessary pre-op scans and X-rays for me to look at. Sedate him lightly in preparation. I'll be there in about twenty minutes.'

Lucas switched off and got up abruptly, leaving his half drunk coffee. He lifted his hand in a half gesture of farewell.

'Sorry,' he said. 'Work calls. Motorbike RTA. Nasty one. I'll leave everyone here in your good hands. Enjoy your evening.'

Jessica sat back in total shock. The professional jargon was not put on. Lucas had already forgotten she was even there. She heard the front door close and then the low throb of his powerful Porsche Boxster pulling away out of the drive.

She did not understand what was going on. He'd said nothing about himself or any commitment anywhere. Was she supposed to make guesses?

She got up and took the coffee cups out into the kitchen. Mrs Harris was ready to leave with her coat and hat on, prepared to cycle home. She took the tray from Jessica.

'Don't worry, miss. I'll clear up in the morning.'

'I can put these in the dishwasher and food in the refrigerator. Mr Coleman has had to hurry off somewhere.'

'He's not just Mr Coleman,' said Mrs Harris, shaking her head. 'It's Dr Coleman. Didn't you know that? He works at that famous hospital in East Grinstead, the Queen Victoria, where the burnt pilots were taken in the war. He's a plastic surgeon: then he's called Mr Coleman. He puts faces back together again.'

Jessica listened in silence, hating herself.

'A plastic surgeon? I didn't know that,' said Jessica weakly. She remembered how she had thought he was a playboy, being kept by his mother, running errands for her. No wonder he had little time for his children.

Suddenly another name came into her head. She had heard it somewhere before. Sir Bernard Coleman was a famous surgeon. He must have been the husband of Grace and father of Lucas. It made her cringe, the way she had been making waves and saying she wanted this and wanted that, proper time off. Lucas had not said a word, quietly keeping his peace, letting her rant on.

About twenty minutes, he'd said. She hoped there weren't any speed cameras on the roads. It would surely take longer than that.

'Don't you worry, miss. He may not come back tonight so I'll leave you to lock up. I'll give you the code for the alarm. He has a room at the hospital where he can doss down for a sleep. See you in the morning.'

'Thank you, Mrs Harris. It was a lovely supper.'

Jessica was all alone in the big house except for a grumpy patient upstairs and two sleeping children. Jessica cleared the dining room and stacked the dishwasher. Then she made some hot milk to take up to Lady Grace. She braced herself for the battle ahead. Whatever happened she was going to make sure she won.

It was late before Jessica had Lady Grace safely in bed, clean and comfortable. Lady Grace had objected to the pillow between her knees but Jessica explained that it was to prevent her crossing over a leg in bed and rotating the new hip.

'Didn't they strap a foam pillow to your knees when you were in hospital? They call them knee immobilizers, to stop you bending the hip. A pillow is for the same purpose. It's not forever. Only till your new hip is stable.'

'I don't need a pillow. I won't cross my legs,' said Lady Grace, exasperated.

'You don't know what you might do in your sleep,' said Jessica.

'I shan't sleep a wink,' she decided.

'I'll leave the bedside light on, in case you want to read. And here are your spectacles.' Jessica put them where Lady Grace could reach them.

'I don't know where my book is. I can't find it.'

'I expect it's the one on the floor beside your chair. This one.'

'I don't like that one. It's very stupid and badly written.'

'When the mobile library calls at West Eastly, I'll get some new books for you. Tell me what you like to read and your favourite authors. Tomorrow you are going to start walking for real. And exercising. Straight leg raising is a good one.'

Lady Grace didn't answer. She closed her eyes with a pained expression. Jessica decided she was being dismissed and left the stuffy bedroom with relief. Tomorrow she would open some windows. Another battle ahead.

Jessica locked the house, discovering so many unexpected doors, it took ages. The alarm was simple to set. If Lucas returned, he could get to his room over the stables without coming into the main house. Then she checked on the children again. All was well.

Her primrose bedroom was a refuge of peace and privacy. She was exhausted physically and emotionally. She slumped onto the sofa and stretched out her aching legs. She flexed her muscles to ease the cramp. She could fall asleep right now, but she knew she would wake in the early hours, stiff and uncomfortable.

Instead she wallowed in a bath of really warm water, letting the heat take out the ache. Geranium bath oil filled the air with its fragrance. Again she fought off waves of sleep. She didn't want to wake up in a cold bath, all wrinkled like a dried prune. Time to pull the plug and hope the noise didn't disturb Lady Grace.

Jessica dried off and wafting talc around, wrapped herself in a big towel. She had only brought her usual pretty silk night garments, not warm enough for the wilds of the country. But the bed was comfortable and in no time, her own body heat had warmed it. She fell asleep almost immediately, lulled by the quietness. Where was the traffic, the buses, the sirens, the nightly concert of London street noise?

Had she been washed onto some desert island and was the only person living there in a bamboo hut, the wavelets of sea a watery lullaby? Her dreams had no answer. Her dream was a sunburst of happiness. She smiled in her sleep.

She was awoken by a sudden heavy lump landing on her stomach. She was awake instantly, visualizing some disaster, ceiling falling down, plane crash, satellite plunging from the sky.

'Willdo! Willdo! Wake up, it's morning. You said you would still be here.'

It was Lily, jumping up and down on the bed with wild abandon, her pyjamas half undone. Her face was bright with excitement.

'So I am still here,' said Jessica sleepily. 'I said I would be.'

'But you are not up. You are in bed. We want you up.'

'I might be able to get up if I didn't have an elephant sitting on my stomach.'

Lily fell about giggling on the bed and Jessica struggled to sit up. Her peach silk nightie was half off her shoulders. She ran a hand through her flattened hair.

'What's the time?' she asked.

'I don't know,' said Lily. 'I can't tell the time.'

Jessica felt about on the bedside table in the dim light for her watch. She could not believe her eyes. At first she thought that the hands had got stuck on their circuit. The hands were luminous and bright.

'It's only six o'clock in the morning, you imp,' she said. 'I'm not getting up this early. Dawn is for the birds.'

'But, Willdo, we want you to get up.'

'Well, Willdo won't.' This was a little too complicated for Lily to understand and she continued to pound the bed with her feet and her hands, singing to herself. Jessica lifted the side of the duvet so the little girl could climb in. 'You can stay for a while if you promise to go back to sleep for one hour.'

'I promise.'

Lily climbed in and snuggled up. 'Tell me another story about that poor lost baby mole.'

'No,' said Jessica, closing her eyes. 'I said, go back to sleep.'

The door to the yellow bedroom was still open. Jessica was aware that someone had come in. She could barely force her eyes open even if it was an intruder. She sort of recognized the tall dark figure in wet clothes.

'I do apologize,' said Lucas, hesitantly. 'I was checking on the children and heard this rumpus. It sounded like a herd of elephants.'

'It was one elephant.'

His eyes roved over her bare shoulder and the peachy silk barely covering her softly rising breasts. Jessica crossed her free arm over the bare skin, wishing he had not seen her so exposed. She couldn't handle the yearning emotion.

'Lily can't tell the time,' she explained.

'I wish I had the same excuse,' he said, his eyes sweeping over the empty space the other side of her. He looked very tired. He had not been to bed at all.

'How is the motorbike rider?'

'He doesn't look like a young Brad Pitt any more. But he will live.'

'You must be tired.'

'I am. I've been up all night, working on the boy. You must know what it's like. I'll say goodnight or is it good morning? I've no idea.'

Jessica wanted to be near to him, touch him, tuck him up into bed. But of course, she couldn't. There was a limit to her nursing duties. Nothing in her contract said that she had to put him to bed. 'Do you know the way?'

'North, I think.'

Lucas closed the door behind him. He stood for a moment outside on the landing, uncertain of what he should do. He knew what he longed to do, but it was too early, too soon. He would have to wait.

Jessica listened to his footsteps fading away. They sounded like a man so tired he had almost forgotten how to walk. There was nothing she could do. But she could make life at Upton Hall easier for him. That would not be too hard. As long as she kept her thoughts to herself.

Lily slept soundly beside her, breathing shallow. Where was the child's mother? Why was she never mentioned? It was like a shadow in the room, a shadow with no shape.

FOUR

Mrs Harris was cooking a full English breakfast, bacon, eggs, mushrooms, tomatoes and lashings of fried bread. Jessica cringed at the pans of food sizzling on the stove top. Lily and Daniel were already demolishing bowls of crunchy cereal.

'Come and sit with me, Willdo,' cried Lily, waving happily. She was proudly wearing her new navy and cream school uniform.

'I'll take your grandmother's breakfast up first,' said Jessica. 'What does she usually like?'

'A lightly boiled egg, bread and butter, coffee,' said Mrs Harris. 'The tray is all ready.'

The egg will be more than lightly boiled by the time I get upstairs, thought Jessica. It'll be half cold and starting to congeal.

Jessica was wearing slim indigo jeans this morning with a crisp white open-necked shirt. If she was going to be walking her ladyship, running around with Lily and hunting for Daniel, she needed to be in activity clothes. She took the tray quickly upstairs. She had already helped Lady Grace to wash and dress and now she was sitting regally in her armchair by the window.

'You haven't changed,' she said. 'I told you I don't like jeans on my staff.'

'I'm not on your staff,' said Jessica. 'I'm employed by your son, Dr Coleman. He has no objection to what I wear. I shall be running about all day.'

Lady Grace sniffed. 'Bring the table over here and put the tray down. I don't like my breakfast cold. Mrs Harris knows how I like my egg.'

'You could have your breakfast downstairs in the dining room.'

'Nonsense, I can't do the stairs.'

'Today you are going to walk along the landing and down the stairs to halfway where the stairs divide. There will be a chair for you to sit on and rest. Then you will come up the other stairs, along the landing again and back to your room. How does that sound? It's not very far.'

'It sounds ridiculous. This egg is cold.'

'I'm not surprised. It was lightly boiled. You should know that a lightly boiled egg cools very quickly. Would you like something different? There's a full English breakfast cooking on the stove. Would you like some scrambled egg?'

'Leave me alone, you idiot girl. I can manage my breakfast by myself.'

Jessica returned to the kitchen in time to catch Mrs Harris piling up plates of fried food for Lily and Daniel. She took the plates aside.

'That's far too much food for a five year old and a seven year old,' she said.

'Lily always eats hers and Daniel leaves what he doesn't want.'

'Let's see what they would really like,' Jessica suggested. She went back to the children who were wondering what was happening. She sat down beside them.

'There must be things you like and things that you don't like,' she began. 'You don't have to eat everything that is put in front of you. Tell me what you don't like, Lily. Think about it carefully. I'd really like to know.'

Lily wrinkled up her nose. 'I don't like yucky mushrooms and hard meat.'

'You mean the bacon?'

Lily nodded. 'Ba-con.'

'Well, I never,' said Mrs Harris. 'I never knew.'

'And what about you, Daniel?' said Jessica, turning to the boy. He was thrown. Jessica hadn't given him anything he could repeat as an answer. She helped him out. 'Do you like bacon? Mushrooms?'

He shook his head.

'But you like eggs and fried bread?'

'Fried bread,' he breathed. The morning was new and young. He was not into speaking at all yet. He wanted peace and quiet. He wanted to be left alone.

'There you are, Mrs Harris. They've told you what they like.'

'Well, I never,' said Mrs Harris again. 'What about you, miss?'

'I'll have the same.'

'And I'll have everything that's left over,' said Lucas, striding into the kitchen, his eyes raking over her gently. 'I'm famished. There's nothing wrong with my appetite. Shall I join you?'

A few hours' sleep and Lucas had recovered. This was the normal doctor/surgeon self-imposed sleep deprivation routine. He looked casual in ancient brown cords and a sweater that needed mending at the elbows. He still hadn't put a comb through his hair. And it needed cutting.

Jessica had a wild, unreasoning elation that he had joined them in the kitchen for a family breakfast. He chatted away to the children, to Mrs Harris, to herself as if everything was normal. Jessica nearly forgot the time, mesmerized by his voice.

'The school bus,' she cried. 'You've only got five minutes to get ready.'

'But I haven't had my toast and honey,' Lily protested.

She hustled them into their coats, checked their school bags, and then ran with them out onto the drive. Daniel was away like the wind but Lily was panting and wheezing. Jessica slowed down.

'Have you got your inhaler?'

Lily looked vague as if she had never heard the word before. 'I dunno.'

Jessica searched the schoolbag and found the inhaler at the

bottom. It felt light and empty. She checked the expiry date. She took Lily's hand and started walking. 'Now breathe with me slowly,' she said. 'In . . . and out. Again, in time with me, Lily, in . . . and out. Big slow breathes. That's the way.'

By the time they reached the waiting bus, Lily's breathing had settled. Jessica smiled at the driver. 'Thank you for waiting,' she said. 'We had a little problem.'

'Anything for you, miss,' he grinned back.

'Will you be here when we come home?' Lily asked as she climbed the bus steps, looking back anxiously. 'Willdo, please, will you be here?'

'I'll be here,' said Jessica. 'We're going to play some games in the garden, remember? I've some new ones to show you.'

Lily smiled happily. 'Games in the garden, Willdo? And you promise?'

Jessica waved the bus out of sight, unaware that Lucas was standing behind her, hands in his pockets, rocking on his heels.

'Ah, the Jessica magic,' he said lightly. 'New games in the garden.'

Jessica started. She had not expected an audience. 'Not really,' she said. 'It's keeping a promise.'

'And do you always keep your promises?'

'It depends on what they are,' she said, as they began walking back to the house. He adjusted his step to match hers. 'If it's a promise that's been forced out of me, then I should not hesitate to break it.'

'And have you made a promise to Lady Grace?'

He was sharp. He knew that there was no way Lady Grace would do anything without a very large carrot. And Jessica had discovered a carrot.

'I've promised to play cards with her this afternoon if she will walk a short distance with me this morning.'

'Ah, cards. She's an addict. Whist, bridge, poker. She'll beat you.'

'Winning isn't important; it's the playing that matters.'

Lucas's arm went round her slim waist. It was casual, unexpected. 'And what are you going to promise me, Willdo, if I am very good and walk with you and do everything that you say?'

Jessica was lost for words, reluctant to break the spell. She wished he had not begun this teasing. She could hear the electricity humming in the wires overhead, the wind rustling the trees, the faint engine of the school bus. But her heart was pounding even louder. She twisted herself out of his grasp.

'Now that would be telling,' she said, deliberately evasive.

He drew away, putting space between them. He began to pull at a loose thread in his sweater, seemingly unaware that it needed mending.

'So what do you plan to do this morning?'

She was glad that the conversation had reverted to mundane things. 'I have to unpack my things. Everything will be horribly creased. Then I want to check the children's clothes and see if they have swimsuits. I could do this anytime. I'm really putting off the moment when I have to confront Lady Grace and get her walking.'

'Do you need any help?' He sounded genuinely concerned. 'How about a whip or a gun? I think we've got an old airgun in an attic somewhere.'

She was immediately drawn to his easy banter. She could cope with this. It gave her time to look at the structure of his face and the imprint of Daniel echoed in the fine bones. She thought of the motorbike boy and shuddered. Accidents were always dreadful, but facial injuries could be devastating. She wondered what it would be like to look in the mirror and see a different face staring back.

'Any medieval torture implements in the cellars?' she asked.

'I daresay I can find a few screws. My mother probably put them there.'

Jessica laughed and Lucas was fascinated by the change in her features when she laughed. Her smile was dimpled and delightful, her rosy lips enchanting, her teeth perfect. But it was the deep-blue eyes that drew him more than anything. They sparkled like sapphires, like gems; priceless. How appalling if anything happened to these beautiful eyes. He could not replace them.

'You will be careful when you drive, won't you?' he said without expression.

'Of course, I'm always careful. It's the other drivers who are careless and impatient. Especially those without any tax or insurance.'

'Will you have time this morning for quick trial drive in the Austin, just to get used to it? I could come with you. Twenty minutes at the most. But I do have to go back to the hospital to check on my patient.'

Jessica did quick mental calculations, some part of her alarmed at being so close to him in the front of the small car. 'Thanks. I think it's mobile library day at the village. I could get Lady Grace some new books. And some for the children. Did you know that Daniel can't read properly yet?'

'He's having special help at school. His writing is poor as well. It's all over the place.'

'I could do a little work with him, every evening, five minutes say. Nothing too arduous. Little and often, one to one, often works the best.'

'Thank you. That might help. It's an epidemic, you know. There never used to be so many autistic children. Daniel seemed to develop normally for the first eighteen to twenty-four months then he somehow lost his skill. It's a regression in ability. Some autistic children never speak, but Daniel can if he wants to. He has a limited vocabulary.'

'He repeats back what you've just said,' said Jessica.

'It's called echolalia or parrot back. He either repeats back immediately or maybe hours or days later, completely out of context, in an unrelated situation. Sometimes he picks up a phrase from the television or an advert and says it over and over again. It's very strange.'

Lucas's strong features were fractured with anguish. This was his son, his first born, and he shuddered at the thought of the boy's future.

'We know autism is on the rise. There's no explanation. He hates noise, bright light, crowds. It makes him worse.'

'Autistic children often have some talent in a totally different and unexpected direction. We've simply got to find what it is that Daniel can do,' said Jessica, aware that Lucas's pain was as raw as her own. 'He will have some talent. We've got to find it. Perhaps his guardian angel will guide us.'

Only her pain was the emotion of being discarded ruthlessly, and in public, by the man she thought she had loved. The humiliation of it was still vivid in her mind. It would take years for the memory to heal. How innocent she had been that evening. Led to the slaughter. In an expensive red silk dress. A dress that she had later bundled up and thrown away.

Lucas's strong fingers suddenly laced hers in a firm grip. 'Thank you, Jessica. I think I've found Daniel's angel.'

Jessica laughed again but this time most of her sparkle had gone.

'Lily won't think so when she finds that I have cut out cakes and jam at teatime. It's apples and pears from now on. She's consuming well over eighteen hundred calories a day at the moment. She's becoming a plump little girl.'

'She'll grow out of it. I like Mrs Harris's home-made cake.'

'You can eat as much as you like. There's not a superfluous ounce on you.'

Lucas grinned. 'And how would you know, Miss Willdo? When have you seen any of my superfluous ounces?'

Jessica coloured. The words had come out without thinking. She turned away and hurried indoors. 'Walkies time,' she said, trying to cover her embarrassment.

'Shall I bring a lead?' Lucas asked from the foot of the stairs.

'I need determination more than a lead.'

'Call for help if my mother stabs you with a hatpin.'

It took over an hour to talk Lady Grace into taking the few steps out of her room and onto the landing. She complained all the time of the pain, her stiffness, her back, her leg. Jessica gathered her patience and persuasive skill. It was exhausting.

Eventually with the aid of the walker, Lady Grace did manage to walk the length of the landing, peering into Lily's bedroom. It was a bit untidy.

'That child's bedroom is a disgrace,' she said. 'Chaos.'

'That's why you need to be up and about,' said Jessica. 'To take charge of things again. The more exercise you take, the less pain there is.'

Lady Grace snorted. 'You're merely saying that. You've no proof.'

'I'll get you some proof.'

There would be a self-help book in the mobile library, Jessica felt sure. She would get one today.

The journey back was marginally faster as Lady Grace had seen her mid-morning coffee arrive. She sank back into her arm-chair by the window, pushing the walker away. Jessica sorted out the blood-thinning medication.

'Don't forget we're playing cards this afternoon,' said Lady Grace. 'The cards are in the sitting room. I'll tell you where they are kept.'

'After you have done your straight leg exercises,' Jessica said. 'They are very boring but necessary. You could listen to music or watch television at the same time if you like. We could find some decent music on the radio.'

'I don't allow television in bedrooms. Not character building.'

It was going to be a busy day.

Jessica hurried down to the kitchen, hoping to catch Lucas before he went back to the Queen Victoria Hospital. But he had gone. His patient came first as was to be expected. She poured herself some coffee from the percolator and sipped the reviving caffeine gratefully.

'I needed that,' she said. 'Thank you.'

'I could hear you having a time of it upstairs,' said Mrs Harris. 'I didn't interfere. I hadn't done Lily's bedroom, more's the pity. I'd better do it now before her ladyship starts into me.'

'You put up with a lot,' said Jessica.

Mrs Harris nodded. 'Sometimes we have to. That's life.'

'Where's the nearest swimming pool, Mrs Harris? I really want to get Lady Grace into the water. Walking in the shallow end of a swimming pool is one of the best exercises after a hip operation. Because the water is buoyant and holds you up, there's very little stress on the hip. She would enjoy it.'

Mrs Harris said nothing. She knew about Lady Grace's aversion to water.

'A pool would be a good idea,' Jessica went on.

'She'd say the water was too warm, too cold, too wet,' said Mrs Harris, going upstairs. She paused halfway, lowered her voice. 'Yet she used to be a champion swimmer. Used to swim in the sea, off Brighton beach, any weather, I'm told.'

Jessica found a copy of Yellow Pages and roamed through, looking for leisure centres. Brighton and Worthing were both unsuitable having large pools. Lady Grace would certainly refuse to go anywhere that members of the public might be using at the same time.

Lucas was a puzzle, one minute kind and charming, and the next cold and aloof. Perhaps one day he would tell her what had made him so unfathomable. There was no antagonism between them but she never knew where she was with the man. He was unpredictable. And yet so attractive. But he was the last thing she wanted. There was no place for another man, however good-looking, in her life.

She had to keep him at a distance.

He could be dangerous. One move from him and she might find herself unable to forget him. He had spirit and texture and soul. Not many of those about.

There was a range of keys hanging from hooks near the kitchen door. Jessica glanced at the labels. There were more keys than doors. One of them was the key to the vintage car waiting for her in the garage and this was a good time to try it. She knew how to drive and it was not far to the village. If Mrs Harris could cycle the distance, she could drive it.

It was a small, low-roofed car with sleek lines, not what she had expected at all. She thought all Austin cars were saloon, family cars. This was a neat shape, park it anywhere, with a walnut dashboard, leather seats and the famous picnic trays at the back. She slipped into the driver's seat and switched on the ignition, took off the hand brake. The car shot into life, almost taking the garage doors with it.

Jessica stamped hard on the foot brake, was flung against the wheel, no seat belt fastened. She gasped. She had not realized that automatic gears need very gentle handling to ease the car away.

She sat back, regaining her breath, slowly fastening the seat belt, hoping she had not bruised her ribs. Lucas had been right. Automatics take some getting used to. Good thing that there was no one around watching. She tried again, easing the car away with only a couple of little jerks. Once moving, the car was a dream. She loved it. She drove slowly out of the drive and onto the road.

Left or right? She could not remember which way they had come yesterday. Well, she only had two choices and the village couldn't be far. So she went right.

It was a quiet, leafy lane, twisting and turning so she drove carefully, hoping to see the village of West Eastly come into sight, cottages, pub and church. A male pheasant hopped across the road, its long tail feathers gleaming. If she was going the wrong way, then the station would appear. If she saw anyone, she would ask for help.

There was no one around, not a soul. Only a few grazing sheep and they weren't much help. She doubted if they had any sense of direction. This was not the time to panic. Surely she could not get lost in such a small place?

She drove on. More leafy lanes, no signposts, nothing to say where she was. The hills looked all the same. There were no houses. At this rate she was going to end up in Brighton or Worthing or maybe back on the M27.

She was lost. She had no idea where she was. Surely Mrs

Harris didn't cycle all this way from Dove Cottage to Upton Hall? Jessica glanced down at the milometer but the figures were no help. It was more than ten minutes ago that she left Upton Hall, turned right at the end of the drive and now she could be anywhere.

She slowed down, worried about petrol. She had not checked. Always check on your petrol before setting off, the driving instructor had said, many years ago.

She drew into the next lay-by and turned off the engine, taking stock, hoping that someone would drive by. If she heard a car coming, she would flag them down and ask for directions.

There was a throb of a car in the distance, coming closer, maybe too fast to stop for her. Jessica stood clearly on the side of the road, her hand up in the air, hoping for a Good Samaritan. She prayed that it would be someone helpful, articulate and English.

It was. Someone very articulate. The car braked.

'What the hell are you doing out here, Jessica? I told you to wait for me. I said I would come with you, the first time you went out in the Austin. I suppose it was you who nearly took the garage door off? And now you are lost. Well, it serves you right.' Lucas glared at her.

Jessica stood shocked by the onslaught. She didn't deserve this. Her intentions had been the best. She had intended to get some books for Lady Grace and find out how to renew Lily's inhaler prescription. Not exactly in line with robbing a bank or stealing the church silver.

'Yes, sir, I am lost,' she said, briskly. 'All these lanes look the same. I'm hardly to blame if your council doesn't spend any money on signposts. It must be because of some literacy deficit among the locals.'

Lucas was still glaring at her. 'Did you turn right coming out of Upton Hall?'

'Yes, I turned right. I'm not stupid.'

'Then right again at the fork?'

'What fork?'

Jessica could not remember any fork. The lane had been twisting and turning. She had been concentrating on driving round the bends, keeping to the left.

'There's a fork after the third bend. It takes you directly to West Eastly. A child could follow it.'

'There was no signpost.'

'It's in the hedge.'

'Overgrown no doubt.'

Jessica was tired of the argument. At least Lucas could not refuse to see that she got back to Upton Hall. 'I think I should return,' she said. 'Lady Grace may be needing me. We've got a lot to do.'

'She may well indeed. A pity you didn't think of that when you took off in the Austin, not telling anyone where you were going.' Lucas was still fuming.

'Shall I follow you?' she asked, recovering some dignity.

'Yes. I'll lead.'

'Please drive at my speed, not like a bat out of hell.'

He was about to make a retort but thought better of it. He sat there, engine turning, while Jessica got back into the Austin. She was very careful, trying not to do a jerk start. She handled it smoothly, pleased with herself, and lined the Austin up behind the Porsche Boxster. Piece of cake.

It was a slow and careful procession back to Upton Hall. Lucas was deliberately going at a snail's pace to irritate her. Any locals would have thought it was a funeral. Any slower and the Austin would stall.

Jessica smiled to herself. She would let Lucas have his little joke and say nothing. But she was relieved when she saw the tall chimneys of Upton Hall coming into sight. Somehow she had done a tortuous circle.

She parked the car in the stables, next to the Porsche. The garage door was not exactly coming off. He had been exaggerating as usual. Lucas was nowhere to be seen. He had not waited to see if she was all right.

She went into the kitchen, hoping Mrs Harris would not

mind if she made a cup of tea. Her throat was dry and a cup of tea would be welcome.

The kitchen was empty, everywhere tidy, no coat or hat on the door. Mrs Harris had gone. Jessica immediately thought something awful must have happened to Lady Grace in her absence and she had been taken to hospital in an ambulance.

She raced up the stairs and rushed into the tower bedroom. Lady Grace and Lucas were sitting by the window. There was a glass decanter of sherry on the table and Lucas was pouring a small amount into a delicate sherry glass.

'Don't barge in like that, young lady,' said Lady Grace. 'Please knock.'

'I thought you had had . . . an accident . . . fallen or something,' said Jessica, getting her breath back.

'I'm talking to my son. Kindly leave us alone. We have something to discuss. Something important.'

'Of course,' said Jessica, turning to leave. 'I'm making some tea. Would you like a cup?'

'No, thank you. I'm having my afternoon sherry,' said Lady Grace.

'But I'd love a cup,' said Lucas, leaning back and laying on the charm. 'I've just had a maddeningly slow journey. The traffic these days and learner drivers.'

'Better slow and safe,' said Jessica, 'than fast and flashy.'

Lady Grace glared at Jessica and she retreated, smiling to herself as she closed the door. At least she had had the last word.

Mrs Harris had an urgent dental appointment and Jessica made the children's tea when they got home from school. She found some Bramley apples in the orchard and stewed them with honey and raisins. She made cheese, tomato and lettuce sandwiches with celery sticks to crunch on. No doubt there would be complaints from little Miss Sugary Sweet-tooth. No jam and no cake for her today.

Lily surprised everyone by saying she liked this tea. 'I like this sandwich,' she said, holding the celery stick between two fingers as if it was a cigarette. 'Have you got a light, miss?'

'Got a light?' repeated Daniel.

'I'm not the nanny before last, the one who smoked,' said Jessica. 'Hurry up, then we can play in the garden before it gets dark.'

'I want to play in the dark,' said Lily, jumping up and down. 'I like the dark. It's all spooky.'

Daniel said nothing. He was lining up raisins on the rim of his plate before eating them. It was a slow and deliberate procedure.

Lucas came in the kitchen with his cup and saucer. Lily was pretending to smoke the celery stick, giggling and coughing. 'Have you got a light, mister?'

'Bad habits already, young lady?' he said, gravely. 'We shall have to watch you. I'll get you a nicotine patch.'

Lily blew out pretend smoke and started coughing again. Jessica fetched a glass of water from the tap. She drank it and the coughing eased.

'Is there another inhaler for Lily?' Jessica asked. 'I think her current puffer is nearly empty. We're going to have a lesson this evening on the best way to use it.'

'I keep Lily's inhalers in a safe place. I'll get one for you before I go back to the hospital,' said Lucas, closing the dishwasher door.

'Another RTA?'

'No, I had a list this morning. I'm going back now to check on them. They should be in recovery or transferred to their rooms by now.' He spoke in a vague manner, miles away, mentally going over what he had to do. 'I'll catch a quick bite at the canteen. Don't wait supper for me.'

Jessica discovered that Mrs Harris had left a cold supper tray for Lady Grace and all she had to do was heat some soup and take it up. She would have soup and another sandwich.

They played in the garden till the light began to fail. Jessica could only remember how to play *He* and *What's the Time, Mr*

Wolf? Lily threw herself into both games with a complete dis-regard for the rules. Daniel didn't understand what they were doing but enjoyed shouting *What's the Time, Mr Wolf?* Jessica noticed that his motor skills were not co-ordinated and he ran awkwardly, sometimes almost falling.

They danced and sang *Ring-a-Ring a-Roses,* which seemed to help his co-ordination, because they were inter-acting together. He didn't know the words. Lily sang loud enough for two.

When she took Lily upstairs for her bath, Jessica told Daniel that he could stay up for another half an hour as he was older. He didn't react.

'What's the time, Mr Wolf?' he said.

'Bedtime,' Lily shrieked.

At this rate they would have Lady Grace banging on the floor with Fred.

It was quite late before Jessica took her supper on a tray into the library and settled herself into a comfortable armchair. Lady Grace had had her supper and was settled with a book.

One of the bookcases had a false door which opened and revealed a medium size television set. It was an older model but the picture was clear with a good signal and Jessica was happy to watch any programme.

She was lulled into deep relaxation with the undemanding programme, a pleasant supper by herself, a strenuous day and the fresh air activity. She was dozing off, halfway to a rambling dream about trains, when she jolted awake by a tiny noise.

Lucas was switching off the television.

'Late night film,' he said. 'Were you watching it?'

Jessica shook her head. 'No, I wasn't. I fell asleep. What's the time?' She nearly added, *Mr Wolf.*

'It's after midnight. Cops and robbers film, very violent. Not at all suitable for a young lady to watch.'

She struggled to sit up. 'Heavens. I'd better clear up the supper things.'

'Leave it for Mrs Harris in the morning,' said Lucas. He was looking at her with an expression that was impossible to fathom, his eyes full of warmth. 'You don't look nearly so fierce when you are asleep,' he added.

Her heart began to beat faster as he came over to the armchair and held out his hand. He smelt fresh and manly. It was a heady scent. 'Would you like me to tell you a bedtime story?' he asked.

'What story would it be?' she said, her throat going dry. He helped her to her feet. She was quite unsteady.

'I thought Beauty and the Beast would be appropriate.' He paused. 'Since I am so handsome and you are quite beastly at times.'

Jessica began laughing quietly and that broke the spell. They brushed against each other as they went out of the room. There was no madness in the moment, only a brief recognition of the contact, then moving apart.

'Goodnight, Willdo,' said Lucas, pausing again in the hallway, on his way to the stables. 'Do I get a goodnight kiss?'

'Sorry,' said Jessica. 'That's something Willdo, won't do.'

FIVE

Jessica drove down to Worthing sea front with Daniel and Lily strapped into the back seat. She prayed that she would not get lost or lose the children. It was a straightforward drive, nothing complicated, lots of visible signposts. She immediately found somewhere to park along the front and put money into the meter.

The size and expanse of the sea front was like tearing apart sky curtains and seeing a vast blue seascape moving in every direction. There were four miles of promenade to walk on (or cycle if you weren't caught), acres of sand and shingle when the tide was far out, the pier to perambulate on if it was high tide and the waves were lashing the high shoreline. The smell of ozone was a reminder of seaside holidays. The screeching sea-gulls set up a raucous welcome

'It's the sea. I love it, I love it,' said Lily, jumping up and down with excitement, her hair bobbing about. 'I want to paddle. Willdo, can we paddle?'

'Of course,' said Jessica. 'Let me lock up the car, get our towels and the backpack, and we'll be away down the beach. We'll find somewhere out of the wind. Would you like that, Daniel, to go on the beach?'

'Go on the beach,' he said solemnly.

They wore canvas trainers going down the slippery slope of the shingle but once free of the pebbles, they shed their shoes and ran over the wet sand, splashing through puddles, fording rivulets, skirting rocks, making for the tiny waves that lapped in the far distance. Jessica had a job keeping up with the children.

Daniel ran ahead, sensing freedom, sensing the elements that demanded nothing of him. Water made him free from a world he did not understand. No one wanted to talk to him. The lapping of the wavelets was a gentle sound. He had an unusual burst of energy, legs awkward, arms waving erratically.

They were all wearing shorts and vest tops, even Jessica. Her shorts were cut off jeans with a frayed edge. Lady Grace had been outraged.

'My grandchildren don't wear such skimpy clothes. I demand that you put them into something decent. Hasn't Lily got a frock?'

'They are going on the beach and they are going to get wet. I'm taking along dry clothes and fleeces in case it gets chilly. Would you like to come with us? It's not far in the car.'

'Good heavens, no. I don't want to walk along the front with Fred. Most improper. I might meet someone I know.'

Jessica and Mrs Harris had come to a new and amicable arrangement. Mrs Harris was to have every other afternoon and evening off. In return she would look after Lady Grace on the afternoons when Jessica wanted to take the children out. It was more time off than Mrs Harris had ever had before. Anyone could see she was pleased the way she fussed round the kitchen, cleaning surfaces that were already clean and sparkling. It was like an unexpected lifeline.

'It'll make a real difference,' she said warmly. 'Having a bit of regular time off to myself. It's always been difficult to get away and those other nannies were useless to leave in charge. No good at all, drinking and smoking. I'd like to go to the village hall afternoon Bingo. I might win a fortune one day.'

Jessica had made real progress with Lady Grace but it had not been easy. The first time she had made it down the stairs and into the sitting room, Jessica called for celebration drinks and Lucas had opened a bottle of champagne. Lady Grace had been flushed with pride, but alarmed by the thought of the climb back upstairs. A few minutes in her beloved walled garden gave her renewed courage to make the climb. She picked a few roses for her room.

'You can do it,' said Jessica encouragingly. 'Well done. You've proved that.'

'You're such a bully,' said Lady Grace. 'And yet you are so slim. I don't know how I put up with you.'

'Because you know I'm right. Exercise is the answer. You might not admit it but the pain is not so bad these days, is it?'

'I still need my painkillers.'

'I know that but not so many,' said Jessica, preparing the blood thinning medication. 'I'm the guardian of your pain-killers. Custodian, keeper, steward.'

'You do talk a lot of highfalutin nonsense. Get me a cup of tea, please, Jess. And those roses need dead-heading. Look at the poor things.'

'I'm not here to do gardening.'

'I shall have to bribe you.'

'Difficult, but you could try.'

Lily got the wettest. She had no fear of the water and was soon paddling and jumping over incoming waves, splashing through puddles. The tide was on the turn and they were surprised how the expanse of wet sand began to disappear under the incoming sea. They had the sense to obey Jessica and return back to shore.

Daniel was more interested in what the tide was bringing in with it. So many shells and bits of seaweed, dead fish and drift-wood. He was scavenging in the pools, collecting all sorts of bits and pieces in his bucket. The shells were so interesting and so intricate. He was completely immersed in his treasure hunt.

Jessica had brought a magazine to read on the beach but she didn't get past page three. A book would have been better but she dare not take her eyes off either child for more than a moment. She might get lost in a good book.

Irrational fears crowded her mind: drowning, abduction, fish hooks.

The day before yesterday she had taken the children to the mobile library on its weekly visit to West Eastly. They had never been before and were amazed at the choice of books. Jessica had found some new books for Lady Grace which were accepted with reluctant gratitude. Daniel settled on a book with colour photographs of animals which he liked a lot. Lily chose more books than she could carry and insisted on carrying them across the green to the car.

'Let me take some of them,' Jessica offered.

'I want to carry all my books from the library myself,' Lily insisted.

Now they were enjoying themselves on the beach as children should, running about here and there, digging wet sand, collecting shells. Lily was filling her lungs with clean coastal air, not coughing or wheezing at all. Pure sea ozone.

As the waves edged them nearer and nearer to the shore of shingle, it was not quite so much fun. Bare feet on sharp stones is *ouch* time. They were slipping and sliding on a shelf of wet pebbles. But Jessica had brought plastic flip-flops for them to wear and the discomfort was soon forgotten. They had a picnic tea higher up on the beach – plenty of cheese sandwiches, apples and pears, yogurts, cartons of juice. They ate every crumb, then shook it all down skimming pebbles into the waves, watching the greedy seagulls diving into the deeper water for their fish suppers. Daniel was quite good at skimming. He watched the bouncing pebbles.

'Wow! Daniel's pebble bounced four times. One more go, everyone.'

It was two very tired children whom Jessica drove home to Upton Hall, drowsy and wet and sandy. Lily went to sleep on the back seat. Daniel sat close, examining his treasures. His romp on the beach had brought a colour to his cheeks. His hair was stiff with sea water.

'Did you enjoy the beach, Daniel?' Jessica asked. 'It was fun, wasn't it?'

'Fun,' he said, from the depths of his bucket.

'You've both brought half of the beach home with you,' said Jessica later, as Lily's bath water filled with a swirl of sand. 'I shall have to wash your hair.'

'Please don't tug my hair.'

'I'll try not to, poppet. Hold this little towel over your eyes.'

Lucas appeared in the doorway, tousled and leaning on the doorway, as if he didn't have the strength to hold himself up. Jessica wanted to soothe away the fatigue, wipe away the pain, let him fall sleep in her arms. She shook away the devastating thoughts, wishing her emotions would calm down. They were burning her up. He was not her responsibility.

'So you've had an afternoon on Worthing beach? Some people are lucky,' he said laconically. 'Some people have to work, day and night.'

'I was working,' said Jessica.

'We had a picnic tea on the beach and we didn't even have plates!' said Lily, who thought this was the best part. 'We ate out of a box!'

'How civilized,' said Lucas, raising his dark eyebrows. 'It could catch on, eating out of boxes. No washing up.'

'As long as you bring them home,' said Jessica.

Lucas agreed. 'Did you bring your litter home, Lily?'

'We did.'

But Lily's attention had already wandered elsewhere. 'Are you going to have your supper with Willdo, Daddy? She will look after you, when she has put on some clothes. She will make herself look very nice, in a frock.'

Jessica was still in her cut-off denim shorts and vest top. They were indeed skimpy and clung damply to her soft curves. Lucas could see the shape of her breasts and he could not wrench his gaze away. They were too enticing, so deliciously feminine, made to be touched and explored.

And those long tanned legs were asking to be stroked. Lucas moved away with barely concealed impatience, the tension between them rising. 'Supper sharp at eight, Jessica, is that all right?' he said curtly. 'And Lily is right. Put some clothes on.

You look positively indecent.'

Jessica gave him an ironic, distant stare. 'Most medics are used to half-clad women. It goes with the job.'

'I do faces, not bodies,' he said.

Jessica went to an extreme. She made sure every inch was covered. She put on a baggy cotton jersey and black trousers and a waistcoat and scarf. Her slip-on black shoes completed the camouflage. She combed her fringe well over her eyes and brushed her hair onto her shoulders.

'The only part of me showing is my nose,' she said as she went into the dining room. Supper was waiting on the hot trays.

'Quite a nice nose,' he said, without looking at her. 'I could do a bob or a tuck but you don't need it. Mrs Harris has left us a beef casserole with lots of vegetables. It's very hot and smells delicious. Would you like some wine? I've managed to open the bottle this time.'

'It's the practice you need.'

'I'll remember that and keep practising.'

Jessica took a small helping of the casserole, avoiding the tasty chunks of dark meat. But she had plenty of vegetables, broccoli, French beans, carrots, mashed potatoes. There was home-made blackcurrant cheesecake afterwards.

'I see that you are avoiding the beef,' said Lucas. 'Is there a reason?'

'I don't much like eating animals. Not exactly a vegetarian, but near. I occasionally eat fish, but mainly because I think fish have a chance to get away.'

'Not in fish farms.'

'I know,' said Jessica, realizing this was merely polite conversation. He was not really interested in what she said. He was so self-contained, a passionate introvert. 'It's getting all too complicated these days. I won't know what to eat.'

Lucas was almost too tired to eat. He pushed away his plate. 'Do you mind if I tell you about today? I had a little girl in this morning, her name's Maggie. She was attacked by three Rottweilers. They tore at her face and broke her jaw in three places. She's a mess, but alive.'

Jessica caught her breath at the horror of it. 'Poor little thing. How dreadful. Is she going to be all right? What did you do?'

'For the moment I've done what I can. She'll need some skin grafts when the injuries have healed. Her mouth is damaged. It's going to be a long haul.'

Jessica was always shaken by injuries to innocent children. 'Can we do anything for her? Does Maggie need anything?'

Lucas thought for a moment. 'If Lily has any spare books or toys, they might help Maggie. She's going to feel really bad these early days and needs distraction. She only has a disabled grandmother who lives quite a long journey away.'

'Would it be of any help if I came and read stories to her?' Jessica heard herself saying. The offer came out without any thought of how it could be organized or when she might have time. She would have to drive to East Grinstead and back. Perhaps there was a train. She realized her offer was near impossible. There was Lady Grace to think of, as well as the two children. They were her responsibilities.

'That's very kind of you, Jessica, but I don't see how it can be worked out. Let me think about it. Some of Lily's toys might be acceptable.'

He pushed away his slice of cheesecake, unable to finish it. He looked at Jessica over his glass of wine. He wondered how she would take his news. He was knotted with tension, rigid, yet restless.

'I have something to tell you,' he said, his face changing oddly.

'So, tell me.'

Jessica wondered why he was suddenly so serious. His eyes clouded and he pushed his unruly hair back. It was easy to see that he didn't know how to begin.

'I have been thinking about it for some time,' he said. 'It's been a long time since my wife, Liz, died. They used to call us the three L's, Lucas, Liz and Lily. We were a lively threesome.' He didn't include Daniel, she noticed. How sad.

Jessica froze. No one had ever said anything about Mrs Coleman as if she never existed. Jessica dare not say anything for fear of breaking the spell. Lucas was finding it difficult, that was clear. She let him go on.

'It was a car accident, late at night. Head on crash with an articulated lorry on the M25. Instantaneous death. Horrific. They were both killed outright.'

His voice was without emotion. He could have been reading a weather forecast to an unseen audience of millions. There was nothing in his expression either. Yet he was talking about his wife, mother of his children. He was staring into his glass of wine, as if seeing the carnage again in the pool of red.

'Both of them?' Jessica said, after a moment's hesitation. It seemed like prying, opening a painful wound. The room was still. Nothing moved. The oil portraits looked down on them in stony silence. Maybe they had heard it all before, centuries ago. It was the same old story.

'Did I say both?' He stared at her.

'Yes, you did.'

'You misheard me. I said nothing of the kind. And anyway, it's none of your business. Now I've lost my train of thought. Don't interrupt.'

Lucas ran his fingers through his hair, making it even more untidy. Jessica was afraid to say anything that would disturb him.

'But what about your two children, Daniel and Lily?' she asked, at last. The silence had a positive quality. Jessica knew this was about years of anguish.

'Lily was only a baby, barely six months old. Liz didn't like having babies, losing her figure and all the pain. She didn't like children at all and had no patience with Daniel. Daniel hadn't been diagnosed as autistic but we knew something was not right. She was quite happy to leave them both with me. At least she left me the children. That was something. More than something. It was a blessing.'

'I'm so sorry,' said Jessica. 'I know words are inadequate but I am sorry. You must have been really hurt. And it was a difficult time.'

'Well, not any more,' he said, injecting some false cheerfulness into his voice though his face was set in gloom. 'Things are going to change. You see, I have decided to get married again. I'm going to take the plunge. Yes, very soon, Jessica. I have made up my mind. It's a good idea, isn't it? Don't you agree?'

Jessica couldn't think of anything to say. It was a good idea but she was thrown by the thought of having to adapt to another woman living in the house. Lucas deserved someone to help him, to look after him. He worked so hard, such long hours. He needed someone loving to come home to.

'Yes, it is a good idea,' said Jessica, taking a firm hold of her doubts. His words were stealing away the happiness of the day, the colours fading. 'You need someone to look after you and it would be good for Lily and Daniel. They need stability. I hope this woman is kind and caring. They need a lot of love.'

He poured out some more wine and gulped it down.

'Yes, she is kind and caring, very good with children. A bit bossy at times, used to getting her own way, but I daresay I can cope with that. I think Lily and Daniel will be pleased. As you say, they need lots of love and mothering. And I'm sure she's the kind of woman who will give them that.'

'So do we drink to the happy day?' said Jessica, raising her glass. Her hand was trembling. She was frightened by the depth and power of her own feelings. She could no longer smell the fruit of the grapes. 'Have you fixed a date?'

A flicker of a smile crossed his lined face. 'Unfortunately, no date in view. You see, I haven't even asked her yet. I still have that bridge to cross. And I'm out of practice in the proposal stakes.'

'Well, you'd better hurry up, get things moving,' said Jessica, engineering some sort of enthusiasm. 'Such a paragon might be snapped up by someone else. She sounds too good to be true. Make your move.'

'I do agree with you. She may well have some ardent suitor

waiting in the wings. I don't really know. I know very little about her, actually.'

Jessica was lost. She did not understand what Lucas was saying. He was going to marry someone that he knew little or nothing about? It was absurd. She rallied her good sense. He may not want her advice but she was going to give it.

'Forgive me, if I'm speaking out of turn, but this sounds crazy. You can't marry someone who you know very little about. This isn't one of those dating agency on the Internet, is it? It could lead to all sorts of disasters. She might be completely fraudulent, years older than you, foreign, merely wanting to marry someone to get hold of a British passport. Don't do it, I beg of you.'

The tension broke and Lucas grinned. 'Internet dating? I hadn't thought of that. I might try it next if this falls through. Well, I'd better get it over quick then. Jessica Harlow, fantastic nurse, glamorous nanny, funny Willdo from the wilderness, will you marry me? Will you become my lawful-wedded wife?'

Jessica said no, of course, straight away. What else could she say? It was all too sudden. They didn't know each other. It was a ridiculous idea.

'No way, sir, Lucas, Mr Coleman. Is this some sort of joke? Are you making fun of me? Well, I'm not laughing. It's not even funny.'

'Please think it over,' said Lucas, pouring coffee. 'Get used to the idea. It might grow on you. We get on pretty well together.'

'Don't you reckon on it,' Jessica said. 'Why me?'

'Because you are eminently suitable. A very good nurse. Excellent with children. Not bad-looking at times. Quite the arm candy, I could say, if I ever need a glamorous escort. I do have various medical dinners and functions that I am supposed to attend. You'd look pretty good, wearing the right clothes.'

'Thank you,' said Jessica, icily. 'You certainly know how to make a woman feel good. Did you take a correspondence course on courtship? I should ask them for your money back.'

'Then you'll consider my proposal?' Lucas was looking at her keenly, his silvery grey eyes suddenly fierce and glittering. 'I mean it. I want you to marry me.'

'I didn't say that,' Jessica said.

'You nearly did.'

'Please listen, Lucas,' she said, dredging the words from somewhere. 'Marriage isn't just a convenient arrangement. It has to mean so much more. It's between people who love each other, who can't bear to be apart, who want to live the rest of their lives together.'

'I know,' he said smoothly. 'But we are different. We have both been hurt, badly, in the past. I don't know what happened to you, but it's there in your eyes, the hurt and humiliation. So this could be second best for both of us. I'm offering you security, a pleasant home, status in society, two children who need you. I'm not asking anything for myself. No midnight romps in bed or early morning quickies. Nothing more than an obligatory kiss on the cheek in public. I ask for nothing more. Could you manage that? It might not be too hard a duty to perform.'

Jessica was breathing hard. Lucas was offering her a lifeline, a way out of the swamp she had been wallowing in, throwing a life-belt to a shipwrecked woman. But where was the love she had always dreamed about? Where was the gallant knight in shining armour, riding to rescue her? He must be somewhere on the horizon.

'It's your choice,' he went on, finishing his coffee. 'Please listen to your heart. I'll leave you to think about it.'

He got up from the dining table and came round to her side. He pulled Jessica to her feet. He steadied her hip against his body and his mouth touched her lips. There was nothing inexpert about his kiss. It was warm and gentle, incredibly familiar. She was trapped in his arms.

'Goodnight Jessica,' he said in a deep, slow and husky voice. 'Don't make me wait too long.'

Jessica did not sleep well, tossed and turned. When she awoke the next morning, she wondered if she had imagined the whole strange proposal? Lucas had been overtired, drinking wine on an empty stomach. He might regret it this morning, if he remembered it at all. Maybe he had also had a few whiskies before the wine.

The light streamed through the window, turning the primrose to gold.

But Lucas had already left for the hospital. She heard the Porsche Boxster leaving at some inhuman hour. She had wanted to talk to him about Daniel's coming birthday. There had been no response from Daniel himself. The concept of birthdays did not register. Time and age meant little to him.

When she put her head round his bedroom door, Daniel was already up. He was sitting on the floor in his pyjamas, all his treasures from the beach lined up in front of him. He had one of his school books on his knee and he was busy drawing on a blank page. It was the drawing of a shell, in great detail, very small and intricate. Unlike his handwriting, which was all over the place, this drawing was perfect.

'Time to get washed and dressed, Daniel,' she said.

He didn't answer but kept drawing.

Lily on the other hand, had dressed herself in shorts and T-shirt, ready to go to the beach. She had decided it was going to be the beach again. The T-shirt was on inside-out but what did that matter, and she had odd socks on.

'Have you practiced your inhaler this morning, Lily?'

She shook her head, dark hair bouncing around. 'I have to breathe slowly,' she said. 'Do it properly.'

'That's right. Let's do it now. Sit down and check inside and outside the mouthpiece to make sure it's clean and clear.'

'All clean.'

'Shake the inhaler. How many times?'

'Four or five times. To mix all the stuff up inside.'

Lily held up the inhaler and breathed out slowly which she did not find easy. She always wanted to breath in again quickly, scared of not having any air in her lungs, of starting to gasp.

'Don't panic. Hold your breath. Put the mouthpiece in your mouth and press down on top of the canister to release a puff.

Then you can breathe that in. Breathe it in slowly. Well done, steady now. Don't rush.'

'Not rushing.'

'Now do it again, Lily. Excellent. You've got the hang of it now. Put the cover on firmly. Next time we'll clean it with a dry cloth or tissue.'

'I'm getting better at it,' said Lily happily. 'Now can we go to the beach?'

'Not today, Lily. We're going to do something quite different today. I'll get you a peak flow meter so we can check how you are doing.'

'Is that like a parking meter?'

'In a way, yes. It tells us if your airways are relaxed. If they are, then you get a high score.'

Jessica had a new idea. She was fast running out of new ideas. 'Over breakfast, I'm going to tell you about a little girl called Maggie who is in hospital.'

'Is it a sad story?'

'It's a true story and quite sad.'

Mrs Harris had breakfast ready in the kitchen. She had adapted to the healthier eating without any problem. It was poached eggs this morning, and fruit. Jessica did the ordering now after discussing the family's needs with Mrs Harris first. There was far less cooking involved, lots more fruit and salads.

Lady Grace resisted all change. She ordered her own menus every day and Jessica had no wish to be involved. It was the children that she cared about and Lucas. She knew what hospital food was like, even in the staff canteen.

It was exercises first this morning. Lady Grace always tried to get out of them. She thought up new arguments every day. It was like a game show.

'I don't need to do them every day,' she protested. 'I shall get ugly, bulging arm muscles like an athlete. As long as I walk a bit, I'm doing fine. You must admit I have made excellent progress, Miss Know-all.'

'Indeed, Lady Grace. Your progress is good. It's remarkable

when you have argued every step of the way. You must admit now, that regular exercise is the answer. So let's start. Let's put some music on. Straight leg first.'

'Do we have to? I don't like that music.'

'Yes, we do. Think of that lovely glass of your favourite dry sherry when you get downstairs. Then your walk round the garden. The roses are magnificent. I've even done some dead-heading. I'd like to know some of the names.'

'I know all the names.' There was no thank you for the dead-heading.

'I'm sure you do. Your memory is amazing.'

Sundays were not easy. No school. Lily and Daniel were at home all day with Lady Grace demanding constant attention. But today Jessica told the children about Maggie, the little girl who had been bitten. She didn't go into too much detail but said that they had been three fierce dogs and she was in hospital.

'She's very lonely and she hasn't any toys or any books. And I thought we could make Get Well cards to send her, lovely pictures with glitter and ribbons.'

'Yes, yes, we'll make lots of cards,' said Lily, immediately brimming with enthusiasm. 'And she can have some of my toys.' She raced upstairs to her bedroom, turning floor and cupboard chaos out into more chaos. Jessica sat back and laughed. Lily was a bundle of energy, despite her weight.

'Lily is such a funny, little girl,' she said to Daniel. She was hoping he might reply.

He didn't look up. He was already drawing on some cardboard which Jessica had found. It was an old chocolate box lid on its way to the refuse collection. He was absorbed in what he was doing.

When Lucas returned from the hospital that evening, there was a box of goodies for Maggie, toys, a teddy, books and cards. Lily had been busy all day making cards for everyone. She had gone into serious card production. She had made a large pink one for Maggie with silver angels and stars, lots of glitter and ribbons. She had also made a hospital one for Lucas with rows of beds, on which she had written 'I love you, Daddy.' Jessica had helped with the writing.

Lady Grace got a card on which Lily had drawn a picture of her doing a cartwheel down the stairs. Not exactly tactful, Jessica thought, nor appreciated. Lady Grace had sniffed and said, 'very nice, dear.'

'At least you got a card,' said Jessica,

Lily's card for Daniel was a secret. 'For his birthday,' she whispered to Jessica. Mrs Harris was presented with a card covered in photographs of food cut out from a magazine. It said: To the Bestest Cook.

'I'm amazed at that,' said Mrs Harris.

Even Jessica got a card. It was more glittery angels and stars and inside Lily had written 'I love you', copying the writing on her father's card.

'Thank you, Lily,' said Jessica. 'I shall treasure your card. I'll put it on the mantelpiece in my bedroom.'

'So you can see it when you wake up.'

'Every morning when I wake up. It's the first thing I shall see.'

Lucas was the first to spot the near identical message. He was not slow in spotting the implication, though he had said nothing about the previous evening.

'These cards should stand together, don't you think, Jessica?' For once, his silvery eyes were twinkling. 'They were made for each other The same message.'

It wasn't easy to find the right reply. It made her realize how strong he was. The dark stubble on his chin was her undoing. He looked so vulnerable.

'You didn't have time to shave this morning,' she said. 'Was it a busy night?'

'Saturday night drinking always brings a wave of emergencies,' he said, passing a hand over his chin. 'Bike accidents, car accidents, falling down stairs, falling off balconies. No one has any sense of balance on a Saturday. It's a wonder anyone is still standing upright.'

Daniel got up off the floor and brought over his card for Maggie. He had been working on it all day, not letting anyone see what he was doing. He had folded the chocolate box lid so that it became card shape. The front said Terry's All Gold Milk Chocolates on a swirling gold and blue pattern.

Daniel said nothing but indicated that the card should be opened. Jessica opened the card and drew in her breath sharply.

The inside was covered with intricate drawings of shells, all in rows, every kind of shell in every position. Some were the ones he had collected from Worthing beach, others were dreamed up shells. The pencil lines were fine and delicate. They reminded Jessica of ancient Japanese art. She handed Lucas the card.

'I don't think you need worry about Daniel's future,' she said. 'This is his future. He is a born artist. He will be able to make a living from his work.'

Lucas took the card and studied the drawings. 'They are perfect,' he said, nodding. He smiled at Daniel. 'All the more reason to give my son the stability of a loving family. Don't you agree, Jessica?'

Jessica could not look at him. Lucas could not dictate her future in that cavalier fashion. When she married, it would be for love. Not convenience.

SIX

The revelation that Daniel could draw tiny objects with exquisite detail amazed and raised everyone's spirits, except Daniel's. He was unperturbed by the fuss.

'I can't draw like this,' said Lucas.

'Very few people can. Each shell is quite perfect.'

'My grandmother used to paint, delicate watercolours and pastels. She did mostly wild flowers. There's a little book of hers up in the attic somewhere,' said Lady Grace, modestly accepting her place on the talent tree. 'He's obviously inherited the gift from my side.'

Daniel made no response. Jessica longed for some kind of communication with the boy. Every evening she spent some time with him, helping with his writing practice but still his words and letters had no coherence. His b's looked like p's and m and n were interchangeable. S was always curved the other way round. In a funny way, it was readable, like an ancient Persian or Egyptian script. She could read it. His alphabet was re-invented, drawn backwards, upside-down, sometimes he added a completely new letter shape. ^ and > were two of them. They meant something.

'You probably had another grandparent who lived on the Easter Isles,' said Jessica. 'But I suppose it won't really matter in the future if you can't write a letter. All letters will be via the Internet. And when you become really famous, you can employ a secretary. I think you should learn to use the Internet.'

Daniel looked marginally interested as Jessica moved over to the computer in the library, switched on, logged into Yahoo, the free server, and began signing Daniel in as a new user.

He went and stood behind her, watching what she was doing, not saying a word. There was no way of judging if he understood the process.

'This is for sending letters. Now what do you want to be called?' said Jessica. 'Daniel Coleman is your real name but it is a bit too long for an email address. And it might be already in use. What do you think about DanCole?'

Daniel shook his head slowly. 'DanCo,' he said. 'DanCo.'

'I like that,' said Jessica. 'DanCo. Very neat. Let's see if it has already been used. Let's hope it's available. It is! Good, now that's your email address, Daniel. I'll write it down for you. And you will need a password, something secret that only you will know, that you have to type in this space, every time you switch on.'

Jessica thought this might be a real headache but Daniel understood and typed something in without hesitation. She couldn't see what he put. Whether he would remember it was a different matter.

'Now you can send emails to your friends.'

'No friends,' he said.

'You could send one to me, now and again,' said Jessica. 'I'm your friend. This is my email address. JessHar@yahoo.co.uk. I'll type it in for you and add it to your contacts. Watch me. Any time you want to say something to me, you can send me an email letter. I'll show you how to do it. Does that sound good?'

'Good.'

'And here is my email address at the hospital,' said Lucas. 'You should have that in your contacts.'

Before she went to bed that night, she checked on her emails. She had eight emails from DanCo. She tried not to laugh but it was a success of sorts. At least he had got the hang of how to send emails. It took ages deciphering their content. They were mostly incoherent ramblings, weird spellings and incorrect typing, but there were snatches which made a lot of sense.

'Paper 2 poot markz on.' 'I have no Mummy.' 'Skool iz bad.' 'U help me.' And so it went on . . . reams of Daniel's thoughts.

It was heart-breaking. Jessica showed the emails to Lucas when he came in from the hospital. Lucas was dropping with sleep. It had been another long day. Jessica knew that he still had some reserve energy or she would not have waited.

Lucas became both elated and dejected. 'Daniel's got the hang of email already? That's terrific. It's the way to the twenty-first century. OK, they are practically unreadable but he will get better in time. My spelling is just as bad.'

'But look what he is writing,' she said. 'This is what Daniel really thinks of his life. How can we help him? We must help him.'

Lucas gave her a penetrating look and took hold of her hand. It was a magical touch. His fingers were firm and warm, his thumb circling her palm. 'You know what you can do. Say yes, right away, Jessica. That would solve one of his problems. He would have a mummy. That's what he wants. You would be so right.'

'It's not that easy,' said Jessica, marvelling at the touch. How would this touch feel all over her body? She went weak at the thought, skin shrivelling, sliding away. 'You're talking about me making a commitment for the rest of my life. How do I know what I want to do with the rest of my life? I can't make that sort of commitment to someone I don't even know.'

'We could make it a marriage contract,' said Lucas, slowly. 'If you would prefer something that is less of an emotional commitment. I realize that a life-long marriage would be unfair to such a young and beautiful woman as you. You deserve something better. Would a ten-year marriage contract be more acceptable? I promise that I would set you free at the end of it. That would cover Daniel reaching eighteen and Lily over fifteen. It sounds feasible to me.'

Jessica was shocked to the core. She snatched her hand away. 'I can't believe that you could be so callous. A marriage contract with a time limit? As if anyone could just turn off care and affection for your children at the end of so many years and walk away. You simply have no idea.'

'I thought it would make it easier for you to decide. For you to know that it was not forever.' Lucas was trying to control his anger.

'Well, I have decided and the answer is no. No, no, no. There is no way that I am going to marry you. So you can forget it.'

'I don't believe you for one moment, Jessica,' said Lucas, his eyes darkening. 'Your head says one thing but your eyes say something quite different. And that kiss last night – there was something special about it and you know that. You are not totally immune to me. You have some feeling for me and my children.'

'For both your children, yes. I care about them. For your awkward mother, I have a lot of sympathy. But having feelings for you, definitely not. I don't have a scrap of feeling for you, Lucas Coleman. I feel nothing for you at all. I rarely see you and I hardly know you. When you come in, you are usually half-asleep, wet and exhausted. We exchange a few polite words and that's that.'

'That's true,' said Lucas, with a touch of mockery. 'We don't know each other. A few suppers and family breakfasts hardly count. I suppose I should give you the chance to know me better. I don't remember when I last had a day off. We could go somewhere together, get to know each other.'

'It won't make any difference,' said Jessica vehemently. 'You can't turn on feelings with a few hours of making small talk over a candlelit dinner.'

'I wouldn't talk at all,' he said, hiding his laughter. 'I'd simply let you find out what a really nice person I am.'

'In a day?' Jessica scoffed. 'It would surely take months.'

'I'll wait months.'

'And only on clear days, no rain, no fog, no sea mist.'

'I can't guarantee the weather but I can guarantee my undivided attention.'

'Oh, such sweet words. Clever words, too. They don't sway me.' Jessica marched away, trying to still the hammering of her heart.

Lucas was as good as his word. He reorganized his work schedule and arranged to take a whole afternoon off. Mrs Harris was happy to give the children their tea when they came in from school, and keep a friendly eye on Lady Grace.

'I thought you might like to go into Brighton to buy Daniel's birthday present. I need to find something suitable. You could help me,' Lucas said. 'Is that a good idea, Jessica? Would you like to come?'

Jessica was not sure what tempted her most. She'd like to wander round Brighton. She'd also like a drive in his Porsche Boxster with the roof down. But she'd really like the chance to buy Daniel something nice for his birthday. She did not admit to herself that she might want to enjoy some time with Lucas.

He was ready for her on the dot of two o'clock. He had changed into black jeans and an open necked black shirt. His hair still needed a cut but he looked devilishly handsome. The car was at the front door waiting. A fresh breeze combed the gardens, sending waves of scent from Lady Grace's roses.

Jessica had tried not to make an effort, to show that she didn't care a jot about going out with Lucas, but she looked wonderful in slim white linen trousers and a belted flame-red shirt, her hair tied back with a red scarf. She threw a navy fleece into the back of the car.

'You'll need a coat for coming back,' she said. 'Summer is on its way out. It'll be chilly.'

Lucas nodded, hurried back into the house and returned with the same well worn sweater that needed mending. 'Sorry, that's all I could find,' he said, seeing her dismayed expression. 'Donkey's years old.'

'I'll mend it one day.'

'No wife of mine is going to mend clothes,' he said.

'I'm not your wife.'

'Not yet.'

It was an exciting drive. Jessica loved the speed of the car on the main M27 dual carriage road to Brighton that allowed some speed. They sped through the over-lit tunnel that cut under the South Downs. Lucas was an excellent driver and she felt perfectly safe in his hands. It was such a different day to her arrival in the rain. A September sun was flinging burnt golden rays of sun down onto the earth, a sort of last gesture before autumn set in and decay began the tombstone slide. Jessica put on her sunglasses to cut the glaring light.

They drove in through the genteel residences of Hove. There were so many beautiful elegant Regency terraces, Brunswick Terrace and Adelaide Crescent, white and curving houses with big windows and ironwork balustrades. They had the long ago stamp of past elegant living, long dresses, bonnets, carriages.

'They are mostly flats now,' said Lucas. 'Very sought after and expensive, I expect. A lot of show business people live down here, television and theatre stars, because of the decent train service to London. Keep your eyes open. This is spot the celebrities time. They are everywhere. Some have a small dog.'

Parking was apparently a nightmare in Brighton but Lucas had an arrangement with the Royal Sussex Hospital. He had a visitor's pass.

'I never normally use it for a private visit,' he said. 'Mostly when I'm called to see a patient or assist in some surgery. But today is special.'

Jessica had not been to Brighton for years, since childhood, and it had changed beyond recognition. It was all shops and boutiques, crowds of visitors and tourists, overflowing with pubs and wine bars. Lucas had to take her arm or they would have been separated by the milling throng of tourists. Lucas was steering her through the narrow passages and cobbled streets of The Lanes.

'The Lanes used to be the paths between an area of allotments or gardens,' he said. 'Can you imagine what it was like when Brighton was just a small fishing port? It was really tiny. It used to pay its taxes to the crown in fish.'

The shops were a mixture of fancy boutiques, ancient antique shops, expensive jewellery shops, music collectors' havens. The oldest shops, with faded paintwork, were held together with dust and cobwebs. Their old books and records dying in untidy piles. The past struggling to survive in the modernization.

Jessica could have lingered for ages in The Lanes but time was already flying and Lucas had promised her tea somewhere special and Jessica wanted to be touristy and go on the Palace pier.

Jessica spotted it first. It was a specialist shop that sold artists' materials. This was exactly what she wanted. Lucas guessed what she was thinking.

'Daniel's present? This is it. Right first time,' he said.

They spent some time in the shop, exploring all its wonders, remembering that Daniel was at a very early stage in his exploration of drawing and it would not help to push him too hard with expensive equipment or give him bewildering choices. Everything had to be slowly, slowly.

Jessica found some good quality sketching paper, 140 gm. She bought pads in two sizes, large A3 and a small A5 sketch pad for him to carry around. She also bought a packet of heavy coloured paper, blue, pink, green and pale yellow, which Daniel might find interesting to use.

Lucas browsed through a collection of instruction books which helped very young artists with their initial efforts. Not that Daniel seemed to need any help. He was an instinctive artist. Lucas bought a paperback on How to Draw Everything and a hardback called Sixteen Drawing Lessons which seemed overly complicated for Daniel. But the pictures were beautifully produced.

'That's quite enough books to begin with, isn't it?' he said. 'We don't want to swamp him with loads of different ideas or a different media.'

'Quite enough,' agreed Jessica. She was enjoying his casual friendliness. 'I think he might like some decent soft pencils too.'

They found a packet of eight sketching pencils from 6B to H2. They added a soft putty eraser. Lucas was tempted to buy an artist's satchel.

'No, Lucas, not yet,' said Jessica, hastening to damp the thought. 'It makes his drawing all too organized. Let Daniel find his own bag. He'll have his own ideas. He'll find something strange that is all his own.'

The girl assistant was obviously smitten by Lucas and his easy manner and wanted to know everything about Daniel. Perhaps this was work experience and she would make notes. It took them ten minutes to get out of the shop. The girl stood in the doorway, watching them walk away. She gave a brief wave, cursing her bad luck not to have met Lucas first.

Tea was a calorific cream tea in a crazy, picturesque tea room called Mrs Kipling's where everything was home-made. By this time they were both ravenous as neither had had time for lunch. They went upstairs where the tables had lace clothes and they served pretty china which was a change from thick white mugs that most places seemed to go for these days.

'This is so lovely,' said Jessica. 'A choice of tea, a choice of milk, even a choice of jam. I'd like strawberry jam, please.'

'Pot of tea for two, Earl Grey, semi-skimmed milk and strawberry jam with our scones, please,' Lucas ordered. 'And a plate of your delicious cakes.' It even came with a pot of hot water for their second cups.

Jessica sat back into her chair, enjoying the atmosphere of the tea rooms. It had been a wonderful afternoon, doing normal things with Lucas.

'Civilization is rare these days,' said Lucas. 'I often used to come here when I was a student. I had to save up.'

'Was Brighton one of your favourite clubbing places?'

He grinned. 'You obviously know about students. We were all broke so we used to take food and beer down onto the beach and stay there to watch the dawn come up. What did you do when you were a student nurse?'

'Nothing so exciting. We were mostly too tired. Sometimes

we'd go to a disco or a party. People drank too much, as they do. It wasn't always fun.'

Jessica tried not to think how much she was enjoying herself in Lucas's company. He was sitting close by. They were together. They agreed about most things. He was being amusing and informal, pleasant to get along with. There was no pressure. Jessica relaxed into the warm feeling of togetherness.

'Have we got time to go on the West Pier?' Jessica asked.

'Unfortunately I fear we're a few years too late,' said Lucas. 'The West Pier has collapsed into the sea after two fires, a violent storm, neglect and more neglect. It was once a very elegant Edwardian pier with a concert hall and ballroom. There's only a gaunt wreck now, standing out to sea. People take photographs and paint pictures of it. But we could go on the Palace Pier, if you like noisy entertainments.'

'That's where I meant, the Palace Pier. Yes, I'd like to be very touristy but I draw the line at wearing a funny hat.'

'Absolutely no funny hats,' said Lucas, paying the bill for their tea. 'And I refuse all scary rides. I've no head for heights. I might be an embarrassment.'

Palace Pier was non-stop entertainments, both sides crowded with side-shows and kiosks selling candy floss and seaside rock, fortune tellers and bars. Everywhere smelt saccharine sweet. The domed amusement arcade rang with loud music, clinking coins and money squandered on machines in search of instant riches. Jessica won a white rabbit with long ears for Lily after three goes on a crane machine.

'I suppose we ought to go on something,' said Lucas reluctantly, as they walked round the thrill rides and the roller coaster. 'But I can't see anything that my delicate constitution would cope with.'

'Especially after that big cream tea.'

'Exactly. Now I wouldn't mind a go at that rifle shooting range. What about you, Jessica?'

Jessica shook her head. 'No eye for it.'

Lucas did have an eye and a nonchalant way of shouldering

a rifle. He won a cowboy hat for Daniel. So each child had a present.

It was turning chilly, the sun already sinking. There was no feeling of being at sea on the Palace Pier yet they were a third of a mile out over the water. They watched the seagulls wheeling and diving in formation. The birds were tracking a fishing boat returning, waiting for the gutted bits to be thrown overboard. Jessica pulled on her fleece. Lucas had left his threadbare jersey in the car. He tucked his arm into hers, smiling down.

'I'm afraid you'll have to keep me warm,' he said. 'A brisk walk to the car and then home to Upton Hall? Is that all right with you?'

Jessica nodded. 'We don't want to be too late because of Mrs Harris.'

It struck her that she sounded like a much married wife, showing concern about a baby-sitter. She didn't want Lucas to think she was getting ideas. One pleasant afternoon did not a marriage make.

'I hope I haven't been clamped or towed away,' said Lucas as they climbed the steep road to the hospital car park. 'I shouldn't have parked there today.'

'Why shouldn't you? You haven't done anything really wrong.'

'It's not a question of right or wrong: I have the wrong make of car. One look at this beauty and officials go berserk. I'm a target for every fine invented. If I haven't broken some by-law, they'll invent one.'

'That's not fair.'

'I'm sure, as you will have discovered, a lot of things in life are not fair. I should be driving a clapped-out Volvo. The Porsche is my one indulgence and I've earned it. I like the speed. As you've probably gathered, I've no time for shopping for clothes or CDs or DVDs or any other trappings.'

The cool scent of a crisp autumn heralded the end of the last day of the summer. Evenings would be cooler from now on. It had been a pleasant afternoon, wandering about, but that didn't mean Jessica wanted to marry him.

'I'm going into the hospital a bit later tomorrow morning,' he said, as they drove through the tortuous back streets of Brighton, searching for the main road out of the town. The tall white Regency houses of Hove sea front were melting into shadows. A sea mist was folding the beach into a shroud. 'You might like to come with me. I'm sure young Maggie would enjoy your company for half an hour. You could read to her some of your famous bed-time stories.'

'I'd like that but how would I get home?'

'You could leave my mother's car at Eastly station in the morning, and get a train back to there. A bit complicated, but worth the effort. I think you'd have to change trains. Maggie's grandmother can't get down to visit her. It's such a shame.'

'What about Lady Grace?'

'I'm sure she could do her exercises on her own for once.'

Jessica was happy to go and read to Maggie but the return journey would be a long one. She remembered that first train journey down to Eastly and shuddered at the thought of enduring part of it again. At least there would be a car waiting for her at the station, her current little car. That would be a big improvement.

Was this what it would be like as Lucas's wife, having to do wifely things like visiting patients or going to see ailing ex-patients? She knew Lucas was a conscientious doctor and surgeon and his wife might find herself acting as a second string. Jessica did not object to this. As a nurse, she knew the importance of visits and family contact. Young Maggie would be feeling strange and lonely by herself, face stitched up, in pain, feeding tube attached.

'It's going to rain,' said Jessica. A mantle of purple light was bruising the sky as rain clouds gathered. 'Thank goodness you put the roof up.'

'The holiday brochures call this part of the coast *Sunny Sussex*. But they always forget to mention the rain. And the wind. It can be ferocious. We get gales of up to seventy miles per hour. Almost impossible to walk in or cross a road. The twittens become wind tunnels. It can take your breath away.'

'Thank you for the lovely tea,' said Jessica, getting the gratitude bit over in case she forgot. 'Wonderful home-made cakes. Very calorific.'

'The first of many,' said Lucas politely.

Soon the windscreen was weeping with rain. How could Lucas see to drive? He must have laser eyes to do that intricate surgery, and he used the same laser eyes to pierce the curtains of rain.

It slowed down their return journey, although several madmen overtook them on the M27, despite the fact that they could barely see ahead.

'The Monopoly game with death,' said Lucas. 'Move to Intensive Care,' he added as another impatient driver swept passed them, his wheels spraying up dirt and water. Lucas switched on the spray washers to clean the windscreen.

Jessica was tense, the bass of her spine aching. His driving was perfect. It was the jolting of the road surface that did not help.

It was a relief when they turned off the busy dual carriageway and found the quieter side roads and twisting lanes that would take them to Eastly. It almost felt like coming home when Upton Hall loomed into sight among the dripping trees.

Lily and Daniel came rushing out into the rain carrying big umbrellas. Lily's face was alight with excitement. Daniel was having trouble keeping his umbrella open. It was threatening to turn itself inside out.

'You're back! You're back,' she shouted, as if they had gone on an expedition to the Himalayas. 'Have you brought us presents from Brighton?'

'What a greedy little girl you are,' said Lucas, bending himself in half to get under the umbrella she was holding up. 'Why should we bring you presents?'

'Because you love us!'

'Do we? Who said so?'

Jessica dodged under Daniel's umbrella, helping him to get the mechanism to stay up. 'This is an awkward one,' she said. 'It never works properly.'

He nodded, not meeting her eyes. But she did feel some sort of awareness from him. It was different to his normal indifference.

They stood in the hall, both wet, trying to remember what it was like to be warm, the children clamouring around them, wondering if there were any presents.

Lily loved her floppy-eared rabbit. 'A wabbit! A wabbit,' she shrieked. It was going to be a noisy evening.

Daniel was also taken by his cowboy hat. He put it on immediately and went to bed wearing it.

Lucas disappeared to his study. Paperwork, he said. It was never ending.

It was late when Jessica came downstairs after putting the children to bed and checking on Lady Grace.

'No cards this afternoon, then,' said Lady Grace, sitting up in bed, reading. 'Better things to do?'

'We'll play cards tomorrow afternoon,' said Jessica, forgetting about her visit to read to Maggie. It was going to be difficult to fit everything in. But she had promised.

Lucas was wandering about downstairs, talking on his mobile phone. He looked apprehensive and Jessica felt an urge to put her arm round him. She watched the changing expression on his face with a sudden chill.

'OK, I'll come right away. You were right to call me.' He switched off his phone. 'I'm afraid you'll have supper on your own. It's young Maggie. She's running a high temperature. Not good news. I don't like it. I'll have to go back.'

'You'll need an anorak. It's still raining,' said Jessica. 'I'll make you a sandwich to take with you. It won't take a minute.'

'I haven't time for a sandwich.'

'I'm the fastest sandwich maker in the West,' said Jessica, speeding into the kitchen. Minutes later she was in the porch, standing back from the rain, with a packet of cheese and tomato sandwiches. She tucked them into his pocket as Lucas shrugged himself into his anorak.

'You're going to make somebody a wonderful wife,' he said, brooding.

Suddenly he moulded her slender body to him. Jessica ached with the warmth of his closeness, his rampant attractiveness. His eyes lingered on hers for a second too long. Neither of them could stop the tidal wave of feeling.

Lucas had no idea what he was doing, being swept along. He could drown in her sweetness. Jessica was so lusciously willowy and slender. It was an agony as his lips touched her mouth briefly. His fierce kiss was burning with undisguised longing and desire.

'Oh, Jessica, if only you knew,' he murmured.

'Drive carefully,' she said against his cheek.

Then just as suddenly he was gone. Jessica had not had time to respond to his kiss. She stood in the porch, shattered and trembling, and it was not because of the rain. This was the moment that Jessica realized that she loved him.

She had not admitted it before, but now she knew.

It was dark and she was glad that no one could see her face. This was a secret that she had to keep to herself. Even if she loved him, she could not marry a man who did not love her, who wanted only a token wife to care for his mother and his children. It was not a bargain she could accept.

He'd said he wanted nothing else. He would go elsewhere for the pleasures of the body. And that kiss had been telling her that he would go elsewhere. Perhaps to a nurse or a grateful patient.

She shuddered at the thought. As before, he was asking too much. She was a human being with real feelings.

Jessica went back into the kitchen, still trembling. At least she had put the best Stilton in his sandwich. No meanness in her heart.

SEVEN

Jessica took a sandwich and a mug of tea into the library and switched on the television. She did not really want to watch any programme. She wanted to relive every step of the afternoon but knew it would be a dangerous occupation. Lucas was someone she should blot from her mind, and fast.

Poor Maggie. Instead, she should think of that little girl, still not out of the woods from her frightening experience. But Lucas would do all that he could with his skilful hands. The whole team would be there at her side. Jessica had lived through trauma many times in different wards. It was always an alarming situation, especially with sick and vulnerable children.

She didn't take in a word of the programme. It was mindless sound track running through her head and disjointed figures moving across the television screen like puppets. Wallpaper television.

It was pointless staying up any longer. Lucas was not coming home. He would spend the night at the hospital, near Maggie, fighting for her.

Jessica went round locking up the big house, making sure all the windows were closed. She activated the alarm. It was a bit scary and still raining. The gardens were trapped in darkness, rain slicing through the night with relentless obstinacy.

She checked on the children. Lily was asleep with Floppy Ears, as he was now called, cuddled in her arms. Daniel had placed the cowboy hat on his pillow and Jessica gently removed it, putting it beside his bed, where he would see it first thing when he awoke in the morning.

If only she could get through to him. It would be such an achievement.

'Goodnight, young man,' Jessica whispered.

'I suppose you're going to bed,' said Lady Grace, still sitting up in bed, propped up with pillows, reading a new library book. 'All that gallivanting about. Tired you out, has it? Young people have no stamina these days.'

'Brighton is so bustling and crowded. Masses of people. It's hard work finding room to walk on the pavements.'

'It's all those gays and lesbians,' said Lady Grace. 'They flock there, filling the place up, taking all the accommodation.'

'They have a right to live somewhere,' said Jessica, drawing the heavy curtains. 'Would you like some hot milk?'

'Yes, please, Jess. And two digestive biscuits. And make sure the milk is hot. I can't stand lukewarm milk. It's disgusting. That skin forming on the top.'

Sleep did not come easily. Jessica tossed and turned as if her bed was a ship at sea, making a nest of all her worries and fears. Dawn was filtering eerily through the sky before she fell into a deep sleep. Those few hours were not enough and Jessica awoke at her normal time, groggy and thick enough to spread on toast.

Lily was hopping about on the landing with Floppy Ears. 'I'm taking him for a walk,' she told the world. The world wasn't listening.

'Take him for a very long walk,' groaned Jessica, turning her face into the pillow. There was no way of getting out of it. The household was waking up. She could hear Lady Grace's strident bell. This was a new idea so that her ladyship could command attention at all times.

Jessica stumbled into the big front bedroom, still pulling on her bathrobe.

'Hello,' she said, blinking sleep from her eyes. 'This is a bit early.'

'I've lost Fred.'

'You don't need Fred to get out of bed. Fred is for long journeys. Do it slowly as I've showed you. Swing your legs over the side of the bed and feel the floor firmly first before putting your weight on your legs. Stand still for a few moments before starting to walk.'

'I prefer using Fred,' she insisted.

Fred was left overnight in the bathroom. Jessica hauled out the walker and took it round to Lady Grace. But she stood it some feet away from the bed.

'Here's poor Fred, banished as usual. Now, get out of bed as I showed you and then you can have Fred,' she promised.

Lady Grace pulled her bed jacket round her. 'You are a tyrant and a bully, Nurse Jess. I don't know why I put up with you. You're supposed to look after me, do what I say. I'm your employer.'

'I'm supposed to be getting you through your hip replacement. Because you know, even if you won't admit it, that this is doing you a lot of good,' said Jessica, her good humour returning with wakefulness. 'Look who can get downstairs now? Look who has been out into the garden to admire her roses?'

'I'd have done that anyway, with or without you, young minx.'

'Of course,' grinned Jessica. 'By installing an expensive stair lift. I'm sure you'd rather spend the money on a dozen crates of the best extra dry sherry.'

Lady Grace simply grunted and swung herself out of bed. She could do it quite well. She grabbed hold of Fred as if he was the staff of life. Maybe it was confidence she needed first thing in the morning. Or attention.

'And stop those noisy children stamping about out there on the landing. You know I can't stand noise in my delicate state. I shall get a headache. Take them out to play or whatever you're paid to do.'

'Sure, they'd love to go out and play, half dressed, at seven o'clock in the morning. Grass damp with dew, trying to rain, before a crumb of breakfast. Anyway, rabbits don't stamp. They hop.'

But Jessica did take Lily off to the bathroom where it was difficult to stop Lily brushing Floppy Ears' teeth. 'He doesn't need his teeth cleaning,' said Jessica, rescuing the creature from a watery grave in the washbasin.

'But look, he's got big pointed teeth.'

'He doesn't eat anything.'

Down in the kitchen Mrs Harris had arrived and was taking off her hat and coat. Jessica escaped into the warmth, still in her bathrobe, to beg for a cup of tea. The kettle was singing on the Aga as she knew it would be. The kitchen was a haven.

'This is going to be some day,' Jessica said. 'I have that gut feeling.'

'I hope you are wrong,' said Mrs Harris, wrapping herself in the flowered overall she insisted on wearing. 'I don't want one of those days. Lady Grace nearly drove me round the bend yesterday. She was in the worst of moods. Jealous because you had gone out with Lucas, I reckon. I can always tell.'

'I'm so sorry,' said Jessica, contrite. 'We went shopping for Daniel's birthday presents.' She didn't mention the cream tea or the walk on Palace Pier, or the drive home, or the kiss. Definitely not the kiss.

'And you both deserved some time off, some time together.'

Jessica wondered about that last comment. Some time together? Surely Mrs Harris was not part of the marriage conspiracy? No, it couldn't be. She was far too open and honest.

'I don't know how you have put up with Lady Grace all these years,' said Jessica, curling up on a kitchen chair with a cup of hot tea cradled in her hand. 'You could have got a job anywhere. Maybe housekeeper in one of the big hotels or another big house. You are such a good organizer, so efficient. Great cook.'

'It's a long story, miss. I won't bore you with it. All lost and gone in the past now. Nothing left.' Her voice was emotionless, it also said: *don't ask me.*

Mrs Harris sat down, her drink of tea in her own special cup. She always used the same cup, a 1981 Diana and Charles bone-china wedding cup, their faces and royal logo entwined. No one knew why she had the cup. It was the finest bone china, almost too good to use. Yet she used it every day. She always washed and dried it carefully by hand. It never went in the dishwasher.

She saw Jessica looking at the cup and smiled.

'Yes, I know. It's lovely, isn't it? I should keep it as an heirloom, stand it on a mantelpiece, but I prefer to use it everyday. It reminds me, you see, of someone I used to know very well, someone who gave it to me. So it's a very special cup.'

Jessica held her breath. Was Mrs Harris going to tell her one of the secrets of Upton Hall? The house was full of secrets. It echoed with secrets, corridors filled with ghosts. She thought of Lily's mother, Liz, and her strange disappearance. The wife that Lucas lost. The wife who died needlessly on the M25. Lucas had not told her everything. He had been hiding something.

'It's beautiful,' said Jessica, sipping the reviving tea. 'And how much better to use your cup everyday, rather than leave it on a shelf to be dusted once a week. Theirs was a very sad love story. A sad fairy-tale.'

'That's what he said,' Mrs Harris said. 'This is going to be a sad love story, he said to me, when the engagement was first splashed all over the newspapers. He was a man of great emotional depth. He knew exactly how people felt. It was an instinct. No one knew how much he suffered, mostly for other people.'

Jessica knew what she had to say. It was obvious. She could not stop herself.

'Is that why you loved him?'

Mrs Harris nodded. 'Yes, of course, miss. That's why I loved him. We had loved each other for years, on and off. Since our schooldays really. He always carried my satchel home from school. Sometimes I had no lunch and he shared his with me. We went dancing together on Saturday nights, then to open air pop concerts, lived in tents, deep in the mud. He looked after me, then he went away to study medicine. He had the brains, a skill, a talent that he had to use. He had to go.'

'Then what happened?'

'I got married. Bloody fool. I was out of my stupid mind. Some foolish romance that meant nothing. Somebody I met at the flicks. I knew as I was walking down the aisle in my white satin wedding dress and veil, all done up to the nines, that it was horrible mistake. I thought: this is the wrong man. But it was too late. I had to go through with it. My mum had paid for everything, you see, the church, the cars, the reception. She would have been livid if I had backed out at the last moment.'

Jessica did not know what to say. This was a story she had heard so many times, patients confiding to her in the still of the night, finding relief, often their last night in this world. People make mistakes. The kitchen was quiet, splinters of light like diamonds. Even the children were quiet, somewhere in their rooms.

'It didn't last. He drank, he was useless, clumsy. I left him. It was the only sensible thing I did. Then I got this job at Upton Hall. I was broke and needed the money. It was like heaven opening to me again. He was here, but with a classy aristo-cratic and demanding wife. I didn't mind too much. I was near him. I could look after him because she didn't look after him. Especially after Lucas was born. She didn't want any more preg-nancies, couldn't go through that pain again.'

Mrs Harris was sitting with her hands round her precious cup, staring into the past. Jessica did not move. She knew who Mrs Harris was talking about.

'Sir Bernard?'

'Yes, he was knighted for his work and deserved it. He was a great surgeon and he was a wonderful man. I did everything I could for him. He needed a woman to love him and look after him. I always loved him. He remembered those schooldays and gave me this cup and saucer. They are all I have of him.'

'But you have other memories?'

'Oh yes, miss. I have many good memories. He made me promise to look after Lady Grace if anything happened to him. It was not an easy promise to make, but I agreed, thinking it would never happen. No one knew that he had worked himself to the bone, that he would collapse and die at the hospital. They brought him home to Upton Hall and I was the one who washed and dressed him and held his cold body in my arms. She wouldn't even look at him.'

Jessica was shattered, her mouth turned to sawdust. She could imagine the suffering. She could not bear the thought of Lucas working himself to the bone, of him collapsing and dying at the hospital as his father had done.

What could she say? There was no way she could comfort this woman, after years of putting up with Lady Grace, all because of a promise she made to a man she loved. Mrs Harris had devoted her life to that promise.

'Mrs Harris, you have carried out your promise,' said Jessica earnestly. 'Sir Bernard wouldn't have wanted you to devote your entire life, chained to Lady Grace's every whim. It's not fair. There's still time to find yourself a new life, new friends, even a new happiness.'

Mrs Harris got up and started to rinse her precious cup and saucer.

'Well, I really appreciate the regular time off that you are giving me now. That's enough for the moment. It feels like a proper bit of freedom.'

'You ask for all the freedom you want,' said Jessica. 'I think you have fulfilled your promise to Sir Bernard, many times over. He sounds a special man and would understand.'

'That's nice of you to say so,' said Mrs Harris, starting to lay the table for breakfast. Jessica yawned, ready to drop off. 'Remember, school today, miss.'

Jessica raced upstairs with a second cup of tea. She had a quick shower to wake herself up. As she was dressing in jeans and a warm jersey, her phone rang.

'Hello?'

'Jessica?' It was Lucas. He sounded a long way away, as if he was holding the phone at a distance. 'I'm afraid your visit here is off for the time being. Maggie is in intensive care.'

'Oh, that's bad news. How is she doing?'

'Not good,' he said. He sounded as if he had been up all night. 'I don't know when I'll be home. Maybe tonight, maybe tomorrow.'

'Take care, Lucas,' said Jessica. She didn't know what else to say. She knew Maggie was in good hands. She knew he was doing his best. Any comment would be trite and hackneyed. 'I'll look after everyone here.'

He rang off without another word. He would be home when he could. All she could do was wait, trapped at Upton Hall beneath ashen skies. It was going to be a wet day. The clouds were already spilling token droplets.

They had to run through the rain for the school bus. Jessica managed to persuade Daniel that a cowboy hat was not part of the school uniform, and Lily also had to be persuaded that Floppy Ears did not need to learn to read.

'We can teach him at home,' she promised. 'You and me, together.'

Lady Grace was determined to have a difficult day. Jessica was so afraid she would dislocate her new hip. It was one of the major complications following a hip replacement. She kept attempting to bend her hip past a right angle, pointing towards the other leg.

'I've told you before,' said Jessica, containing her exasperation. 'You simply mustn't do that. A dislocation is a painful event. During the three months healing period, thick layer tissue is forming round the new hip, and this tissue is helping to keep the hip in place.'

'I thought it was screwed in,' said Lady Grace with a grimace.

'They use a plate and screw if there's a major fracture. There's lots of different methods. I believe your stem was cemented in. A press-fit stem is hammered in and tends to be used for younger patients as their bone is less likely to fracture in the procedure. A cemented stem doesn't last quite as long, but long enough for you.'

'Good heavens. Cement? I wasn't told it would be cement.'

'It's orthopaedic cement. Not the road works stuff.'

'Indeed I should hope not. But I'm not sure if they got it right. One leg seems to be shorter than the other.' She peered down at her feet. She was wearing sensible flat shoes with cushioned soles, and hated them intensely. Her wardrobe was full of smart court shoes in every colour and style which she wanted to continue to wear.

Jessica tried not to sigh. Nearly all hip patients had this worry. At some time they seemed to think their legs were not a matching length.

'Now that is something the surgeon is very careful about, but it's not as simple as you might think. Your real leg length might be different to the apparent leg length,' said Jessica, seeing that this was an explanation that could take hours. Leg length was obviously going to be Lady Grace's newest complaint. It made a change from everything else she complained about.

'They don't feel equal,' said Lady Grace. 'And they certainly don't look equal.' She wriggled her feet slightly, trying to judge a comparison.

'It all depends on whether the pelvis is level or tilted. That can make a difference as to how your legs feel and look. It's very confusing. Be assured, the surgeon made precise measurements and did his best to get it right.'

'His best might not be enough. I'm not at all happy. The operated leg feels shorter.'

'Then you must mention it to your surgeon at your next appointment. Most patients can tolerate a tiny difference, perhaps a centimetre, that's a fraction more than a quarter of an inch. It's a small price for getting rid of the pain.'

'I certainly shan't tolerate it,' said Lady Grace emphatically. 'I can tell you that. Please phone my consultant this morning and ask for an immediate appointment. I insist on seeing him.'

'If you say so, Lady Grace. But it really isn't something to worry about.'

'I'll worry about what I want to worry about, young lady. It's my leg. Make that phone call now.'

Jessica escaped from the bedroom, leaning against the door outside, getting her breath back. No wonder employees at Upton Hall rarely stayed long with the Coleman family, whatever status, nurse or nanny. Lucas was lucky to keep Mrs Harris. The good woman had her own reasons, and loving someone for years was always the best reason in the world.

This was a slight dilemma. An imagined difference in leg length was not exactly an emergency. Jessica would not hesitate to phone the surgeon's office if it was something like a dislocation or a clot. That would be an emergency. She couldn't phone Lucas. He would not appreciate a call about leg length.

Caffeine might provide an alternative answer. She went into the kitchen and made herself a black coffee. She had the room to herself and stood by the Aga, warming her hands. So many hospital staff rooms had been icy, the chilliest room in a big building. She remembered pacing with her hands tucked under her armpits, trying to bring her fingers back to life after a long night shift. She remembered Fraser finding her there and warming her hands for her.

She thought he had been sent from heaven. An angel in green theatre gear.

Fraser had been her life for two years. She had been young and inexperienced, new to everything. It had been so easy to fall in love with Fraser. He was ruggedly handsome, tall and fair, Sir Lancelot material without the horse. He made her heart thud, her senses reel. His lips were lingering and passionate. She drank in the scent of his masculinity, expecting this happiness to last the rest of her life.

But it didn't happen. She shut her mind to the evening when he humiliated her in front of all her friends and colleagues. For a moment she hung onto the back of a kitchen chair to steady herself. The memory was so vivid. She swam to the surface.

'Swimming,' said Jessica to herself. It was not the perfect answer but it would help. Swimming was the best exercise for a hip replacement and Lady Grace might feel more equal leg-wise after a few swims.

But Lady Grace wouldn't go to a public pool that was for sure. Both Brighton and Littlehampton had excellent swimming facilities. Mrs Harris had said Lady Grace once swam in the sea off Brighton, so she must have enjoyed swimming once.

Jessica wanted to take both children swimming too. She had a gut feeling that Daniel would love the water. It might give him another sense of freedom, a world of his own without talking. And roly-poly Lily would benefit from more active exercise. As long as she did not insist that Floppy Ears had to learn to swim.

Mrs Harris had left the local newspaper open on the kitchen table. It was a good balance of local news stories and advertisements. But it was the advertisements that drew Jessica. Her agile mind was already juggling with words. She thought of the film, *Desperately Seeking Susan*. Would an item headed Desperately Seeking Water do the trick? She pulled a pen and pad towards her and began to play with words.

The day flew by but still no sign of Lucas. Jessica went around in a state of permanent anxiety. She was fielding awkward questions about appointments from Lady Grace without actually telling a lie.

The evening was melting into darkness before she heard the sound of his Porsche Boxster coming into the drive. He had been gone almost twenty-four hours. He came into the house, dishevelled and rubbing the dark stubble on his chin.

Jessica flew to him. She could not stop herself. For a few seconds, he was hers alone. They stood together and he rested his head against hers in complete exhaustion. Jessica was silent with delight, a fine flame running under her skin. Then both the children arrived and even Lady Grace hobbled into the hall. They moved apart, unsteadily.

'How's Maggie?'

'She's all right,' he said, wearily. 'We saved her. But we nearly lost her.'

'Thank goodness. I knew you would save her. I knew she would come through. You must be so relieved.'

'It was a fight. Touch and go. At one point, we thought—'

Lady Grace pushed herself forward on Fred, interrupting. 'I've been trying to phone you all day, Lucas. Your phone must be out of order. I couldn't get an answer.'

'I switched my phone off, Mother. They are not allowed in the operating theatre. I had major surgery in my own theatre, and was supervising my senior registrar in the theatre next door. And when I had a moment, I popped into theatre three to help out with the odd minor procedure. Hardly time for social phone calls.'

His voice was cold, distant, without feeling.

'Not even from your own mother?'

'Not unless you had fallen down the stairs.'

'I could hardly call you if I had fallen down the stairs,' Lady Grace said curtly. 'That's obvious.'

'But the angelic Jessica would have called the main switchboard and they would have got a message through to me. Though by that time, knowing how efficient she is, Jessica would have you in an ambulance taking you to the Royal Sussex in the fast lane.'

'Daddy, Daddy, I think Floppy Ears will have to have an operation,' said Lily, holding up sick rabbit. He did look pretty sick after the frantic day he'd had.

'Oh dear, that's very serious. Shall I have a look at him after I've had some supper? Meanwhile keep him warm and sedated.'

'Seat-dated.'

Lily rushed off to wrap Floppy Ears in numerous blankets and shawls. She thought sedated meant sit him in a chair near a calendar. He sat, propped up, for the rest of the evening, exhausted by all the fuss.

'One of my legs is definitely shorter than the other, Lucas,' Lady Grace said, trying again to catch her son's attention. 'I insist on seeing my consultant immediately.'

'If you say so, Mother,' he said, his voice as dry as sandpaper. 'I will make an appointment for you tomorrow. Now, I should like some peace and quiet.'

Lucas stood still and quiet. He was ready to drop, drained by the day.

Daniel had not said a word in all this. But now he came up to his father, serious and confiding. 'Peace and quiet,' he said in agreement.

'That's it, Son,' said Lucas, smiling at him. 'At least you understand.'

'It's not good enough,' said Lady Grace.

'Tomorrow,' he said firmly.

Lucas went into the sitting room, taking off his coat, dropping it onto the floor. He threw himself down onto the sofa with a groan, stretching out his long legs. Jessica saw how tired he was and, without a word, knelt down to take off his shoes. His socks were damp with green sweat from the theatre boots. She took them off too, and began to massage his feet with firm and gentle movements.

She could look at his face, drink in all his features, print them on her mind. His eyes were closed and those absurdly long lashes fluttered on his cheeks. His mouth was lightly parted and she glimpsed the white of his teeth as he breathed out. Any moment now he would be asleep.

She lifted his legs up onto the sofa and he settled into a more comfortable position. Her hand brushed the roughness of his chin as she shifted a cushion under his head. The temptation to touch him was almost too strong. She wanted to kiss his love-soft face, to breathe in his breath, lay her head on his chest and listen to that strong heart beating.

There was a fleecy throw on one of the chairs and she covered his bare feet with it. Jessica stood back as daylight flickered and faded from the room. She switched on a nearby lamp and left him in the rosy gloom. The moment was too precious to lose. If she stayed a moment longer, she would have knelt by him again and whispered three words into his ear.

She realized that she did love him. It was a strong, passionate feeling that swept aside all previous doubts. But she could not tell him. She would never be able to tell him.

That would not have been wise. Even if he couldn't hear.

EIGHT

Jessica never heard Lucas crawl into his own bed, somehow remembering the way to the stables. He disappeared from the couch, only a dent in the cushion to remind her of his presence.

The children had long gone to bed, including the now mortally sick rabbit, so she let Mrs Harris go home.

'I can do myself some supper and a snack for Lucas if he wants it,' she said. 'There's no need for you to stay.'

'If you don't mind, miss. There's a programme I'd like to watch on the telly.'

Lady Grace was climbing the stairs quite well, although Jessica always made sure she was close at hand. Her ladyship was in a better mood now that an appointment was promised.

'My son knows best, you see,' she said. 'You don't know anything.'

'That's why he's a surgeon and I'm a nurse,' said Jessica.

'I think I'll read for a bit. Hot milk at nine o'clock, please. This is quite a good book. I'm surprised that you found such a good writer. Perhaps you'll remember the author's name for the future.'

'I certainly will. I've read all of his books,' said Jessica, as she closed the door. She leaned against it for a moment. She was learning to maintain a calm composure in the face of all verbal assaults.

It was warm and cosy in the kitchen. She dragged the old rocking chair closer to the Aga, and settled herself with an egg, tomato and lettuce sandwich. This was her peace and quiet. Somewhere warm with a book and a sandwich. She seemed to live on sandwiches. The warmth spread through her and all the worries of the day faded. Lucas was safely home and that was all that mattered. He was here, somewhere, sleeping alone in his room in the stables. A room which she had never seen.

He had not mentioned this ill-planned marriage arrangement again. Maybe he had accepted her decision. She regretted nothing. Marriage was for two people deeply in love, who could not bear to be separated, who were twinned together in mind even when they were miles apart.

But she had to let him go. Lucas should go back to his medical environment and find a suitable woman to love. Perhaps another surgeon would set him afire. A woman who was perfect in every way, mind and body and soul.

Jessica let the book fall to the floor. She could not stop the tears coming. The thought of Lucas making love to another woman was shattering. She entered a world of excruciating pain. The night air was deep in dust and grit. She wanted to feel his hard body against her but it could not happen. She had to isolate herself from the situation Lucas had created.

'Guess what, everyone? We are going on a secret drive today, a mystery tour,' she announced at breakfast. It was the announcement of the day. 'All of us. Lady Grace as well if she wants to come.'

'A secret drive, how lovely!' said Lily, munching her way through a bowl of muesli with nuts and sliced banana. 'Where are we going?'

'It wouldn't be a secret if Jessica told you, would it?' said Lucas, sauntering into the kitchen. Jessica wondered if his hair ever saw a brush or a comb. But he had showered and the dark hair was glistening wet. He smelled of a sharp after-shave. He had also changed his clothes, was wearing ancient blue jeans and a white T-shirt. What did it matter? He'd be in greens in the theatre. 'What about school? Is it half-term already?'

'It's an inset day,' said Jessica. 'I'm not entirely sure what that means but the teachers do some sort of bonding and training exercises and the children have the day off. So we are going to do some bonding and training.'

'Sounds fun. The bonding bit. Perhaps I should suggest an inset day at the hospital. It might go down really well with the younger members of staff.' Lucas was already on his phone, asking the switchboard to put him through to Intensive Care. He was enquiring about yesterday's patients and seemed satisfied with the information. 'I'll be in later this morning.'

'Can Floppy Ears come on this secret drive?' asked Lily, wide-eyed with excitement.

'Is he feeling better?'

'Yes, Daddy made him better.'

'He can come,' said Jessica. 'But only if he behaves. No shouting, noisy squealing, or hopping about. One noisy hopping commotion from him in the car and he'll be out of the window, feet first.'

Lily looked horror-stricken. 'You wouldn't really throw Floppy Ears out of the window, would you, Willdo?'

Jessica saw that she had alarmed the little girl. 'It was only a joke, sweetheart. You'll put a seat belt on him, won't you?' she reassured her. 'Of course I wouldn't throw him out of the window. I'd put him in the boot to cool off.'

Lady Grace resisted the idea of a secret drive. She had on her stubborn face.

'I have no intention of going on a secret drive,' she said. 'I'm not a child and anyway I know every road around Upton Hall. There's nowhere that I don't know.'

'Want a bet? I bet you three games of cards that you don't know this secret place that I am taking you to. If I win, you can pay for tea out at a café.'

'Tea at a café!' Lily shrieked. 'Cakes?'

Lady Grace liked betting when she was confident she would win. 'That's a bet. And you will lose. We shall set a time limit. Midday. If I don't know where we are going by midday, you win. If I do, I win.'

'Sounds fair,' agreed Jessica. 'I'll get everything ready. No one needs to rush or panic. Take your time. It's not very far.'

She gave Mrs Harris the rest of the day off. 'Don't worry about making any lunch, I'm not sure of our plans,' said Jessica. 'Just leave something cold in the refrigerator and I'll serve it when we get back.'

'I'll make a sherry trifle before I go and some coleslaw, a rice salad, and a cheese and onion quiche.' Mrs Harris was determined to do her bit.

'That sounds quite a lunch. So kind. Thank you.'

It was a bit of a panic but only for Jessica. She had to pack everything they would need without anyone noticing what she was doing. It was more difficult in Lady Grace's bedroom as Jessica did not want to be caught snooping. But she found what she wanted, hidden in a box, on the top of a wardrobe.

Daniel was his usual uncommunicative self, but he was waiting outside, wearing his cowboy hat, so the idea of a secret drive had appealed to him even if he said nothing. Jessica winked at him. 'Help me put these bags in the boot, please, Daniel. They are all part of the secret.'

He nodded, but still said nothing. He was strong, at almost eight, and heaved the bags in. He showed no curiosity.

Lucas had already left so there was only Mrs Harris to wave them off. She stood on the porch steps, a forlorn figure in her flowered overall. She privately thought that they would be back in half an hour, with Lady Grace demanding a dry sherry or her first gin and tonic.

Jessica knew that her driving was under scrutiny. She was ultra careful with the automatic gears. Lady Grace was a back-seat driver, especially when sitting in the front and criticized every move that Jessica made. She had dressed smartly in a soft sage-green tweed suit and pearls. Jessica had checked the route beforehand and knew exactly where she was going. It was to a private estate of big houses facing the sea, past Goring, between Ferring and East Preston, where a lot of pop stars and football stars lived in walled seclusion.

Mrs Harris, who was in on the secret, had given her directions. 'They don't have a road in front of the houses,' she said. 'There's a wide stretch of grass and a path and then the sea. No traffic at all, so quiet. I've walked it many times. So the only access is from the back road. That's why all these stars go to live there. I believe one of the Beatles, or was it the Rolling Stones, lived there once.'

'I know where we are,' said Lady Grace triumphantly, peering out of a window. 'This is the Kings Mead Estate, very exclusive. Not a secret drive any more. You owe me three games of cards.'

'Yes, you are right there but that's only half the answer. You don't know exactly where we are going.'

The backs of the big houses were not so imposing. The usual range of garages and dustbins and car ports as anywhere else. The house she was looking for had a wide curving in and out drive. It was a classic white house, in a sprawling hacienda style, very Spanish with lots of balconies and shutters and iron grille work, dozens of terracotta pots spilling with late summer flowers.

Jessica drove in and parked near the back entrance or was it the front? She had managed to get here safely without an outbreak of fighting in the car.

'Is this the secret?' Lily asked dubiously. 'It doesn't look like a secret place. It's only a big house.'

'Not yet,' said Jessica. 'We are not there yet. The house has a secret. A very special secret.'

The back door open and a Filipino maid in uniform stood there smiling. 'Miss Harlow?'

'Yes, Miss Harlow and extended family,' said Jessica, smiling back.

'We are expecting you. Please to come this way.'

'And I'm Lady Grace Coleman,' said her ladyship, not wanting to be left out of any introductions.

'Welcome, Lady Grace,' said the maid. 'This way, please.'

Jessica heaved the bags out of the boot. Without being asked Daniel took two of the smaller bags. He kept up with the party going indoors.

They followed the maid through high, spacious white rooms and along wide white plastered corridors. Everything seemed to be white with minimal furniture, a few sofas and tables and drapes. They went down some steps and the maid opened a double door. Lady Grace held onto the handrail.

'There is no one using it today,' she said. 'You will not be disturbed. Please ring the bell when you wish to leave.'

A wave of warm heat washed over everyone. In front of them was a beautiful sight. A sheet of tranquil aquamarine blue water, perfectly still, not a ripple in it, set in white marble tiles. Round the edges were lounge chairs, deep with blue cushions, and at the far end, floor to ceiling windows that looked out onto the sparkling blue of the distant sea.

'Good heavens,' said Lady Grace, for once lost for words. 'What a place.'

'A pool,' breathed Lily. 'It's an indoor pool.'

'Pool,' said Daniel.

'And it's ours for the morning,' said Jessica. 'You can swim or not swim, Lady Grace. I'm going swimming and Daniel and Lily are going to have swimming lessons with me. But it would be wonderful for your hip. Even walking in the shallow end of a pool is an outstanding exercise. It places so little stress on your knee and the water is buoyant.'

'But I don't have a swimming costume,' she said, the slightest tremble in her voice. 'I'll just watch.'

'There is everything you need in this bag,' said Jessica. 'Those look like changing rooms over there. No steps to go down, only a very shallow ramp and rail.'

'I don't have a swimming costume,' repeated Lily, near to tears.

'Guess what's in this bag for you both.' Jessica waved an M & S bag from Brighton. 'Brand new swimsuits.'

'But Floppy Ears. . . ?'

'Floppy Ears doesn't want to get wet. He's going to sit this one out and watch.' Typically awkward rabbit.

Jessica had never worn her swimsuit before. It was a relic of the humiliation. Fraser had planned a romantic weekend in the Balearic Islands, somewhere warm and sunny, he said. She had begun putting together holiday clothes, endless lunchtime shopping. But the romantic weekend had never happened and the swimsuit had never been worn. She tore off the price label and wriggled into it. The sleek blue and pink striped one piece swimsuit still fitted even though she had lost weight.

Lily's swimsuit was bright pink and frilly, covered in polka dots. She loved it instantly. Jessica had played safe with Daniel and bought him plain navy trunks. He went straight into the water, splashing, disturbing the glassy surface with ripples of movement. Daniel could swim of sorts. Lucas had taken him twice last summer to the public pool in Littlehampton during the holidays, but it was so crowded and noisy. Daniel had hated it. Lucas had not tried again.

But this was different. There was no one here, no one to splash him or get in the way. Daniel struck out with confidence, remembering all that Lucas had taught him. He could see the end of the pool by the sun streaked window and it was not far away. It looked like a heaven beyond him.

Jessica put blow-up arm bands on Lily and guided her in, holding onto the side rail. 'You are going to learn to kick your legs first,' she said.

Lily decided that splashing Jessica was far more fun so no one actually saw Lady Grace emerge from a changing room. She was in a plain black swimming costume with wide shoulder straps and some sort of club shield in the centre. On her head she had a flowered swimming cap, very popular in the Seventies.

Jessica guided Lady Grace down the ramp into the shallow end. 'This is a bit warmer than the sea,' she said grudgingly. Jessica didn't know if this was a complaint or a compliment. She had no difficulty in getting Lady Grace to walk backwards and sideways, several times.

'You can do any kind of movement that feels comfortable,' said Jessica. 'The water is buoyant so less weight is placed on the hip and the knee. It will strengthen your muscles and make you feel more secure. Hold onto the rail. Or swim a few strokes, if you want to.'

'I can swim,' said Lady Grace with a sniff.

'I know you can,' said Jessica. The proof was there, embroidered on the front of the black swimming costume, the Brighton Swimming Club shield.

It was many years since those swimming days, but after a few hesitant starts, Lady Grace was breast-stroking the length, slow and stately. It was not possible to see her face but Jessica had a feeling that her usual expression of irritation had relaxed. No one could be annoyed in this peaceful water.

It was a beautiful pool. It must have cost thousands of pounds and yet it was hardly used. The house belonged to one of the girl singers in a pop group. They toured the world with sell-out concerts. She was very rarely at home. Then the house and pool would be humming with all night parties and beach barbecues.

Lily had no fear of the water and was splashing about with her arm bands. Jessica swam a few lengths alongside Daniel, slowly and easily. He was obviously in training to swim the Channel.

'All right?' she asked.

He nodded. But she could see from his face that he was enjoying it. This was another of his freedoms. Where he could be himself and no one would bother him. The water was endless and he could go on forever and ever.

No one noticed the maid coming in and placing a tray on one of the glass-topped tables. The sun glinted on the chrome fittings of a tall coffee pot. She smiled at Jessica and indicated the tray.

'Coffee and cold drinks,' she said. 'Bathrobes for your use over here. Please to enjoy.'

There was a row of bathrobes on the wall. Everything had been thought of. Lady Grace climbed out a little unsteadily, glad to put on a bathrobe and rest on one of the blue loungers. She was tired. She hadn't swum for years.

'Thank you,' said Jessica.

Lily, who would never say no to a drink and a biscuit, scrambled out. Daniel ploughed on, determined to beat some personal world record.

Jessica poured out the coffee, glad of a cup herself. Breakfast seemed a long time ago. It was excellent coffee. She had been worried in case this expedition was a failure. She might have fallen flat on her face. But it had been a wonderful morning despite the shaky start.

'So who won the bet?' asked Lady Grace. 'I knew where we were.'

'But you didn't know the secret,' said Jessica. 'Suppose we call it a tie? We could still play cards this afternoon.'

Lady Grace waved her hand round the pool and its surroundings. 'So, how did you arrange all this, young lady? You don't have a magic wand.'

They heard a discreet cough behind them. 'No, she doesn't have a magic wand, but she has a way with words and an inventive mind,' said a man's grave voice. He stopped suddenly in the doorway. 'Good heavens, if it isn't Grace Coleman. It is, isn't it? Grace Coleman, after all these years, well I never. What a surprise.'

Lady Grace had taken off the flowered cap and her grey hair was all mussed up but it was too late to do anything about it. The elderly gentleman walking carefully towards them was not looking at her hair. His face was one big beam.

'Well, I never thought to see you again. You just disappeared into thin air. We wrote and phoned but you never answered. We all missed you down at the club. You were one of our best lady swimmers.'

'Arthur Hopkins,' she said weakly, drawing the bathrobe closely around her body. 'After all these years. What a surprise.'

He sat down and Jessica saw there was an extra cup. She poured him some coffee. He ladled in sugar and milk, hardly taking his eyes off Grace.

'I'm not going to count the years,' he chuckled. 'I stopped counting long ago. It's only numbers after all. But we had some good times, didn't we? My goodness, that seawater was cold, but we didn't care, did we? The youngsters these days, they've got no stamina.'

'Some still swim in the sea,' said Lady Grace, always ready to argue.

'But they wear wet suits and goggles!'

'No stamina.'

Arthur Hopkins turned to Jessica. 'Grace Coleman was one of our best lady swimmers. Always the first in and the last out. Never mind the weather, even in winter. Championship material. Then she stopped coming, disappeared, not a word to anyone to say why.'

Lady Grace looked embarrassed and Jessica decided to come to her rescue. It was time to change the subject. She smiled at Arthur Hopkins and held out a warm but damp hand.

'I'm Jessica Harlow and I want to thank you and your granddaughter for letting us use this lovely pool. It's going to make such a difference even if we can only use it for a few weeks.'

'My dear young lady, you can use it as often as you like when Roxy is away. Roxy is my granddaughter. She sings with some pop group.'

'Miss Harlow is my nurse/companion,' Lady Grace said quickly, making sure he knew Jessica's status.

'What a nurse/companion! I wish I had such a pretty one. We're more than happy to see the pool used and to have your company, especially if it means that Grace comes along.' He chuckled again. 'We can talk over old times. This is Roxy's house, of course, and I'm her permanent house-sitter. It's a bit lonely at times. I'd like a bit of company.' He put down his coffee and clapped his hands. 'I could look out some old cine films, see if the projector is still working.'

'I think it's time for another lesson, Lily, and then we must go. Let's see if you can remember how to do the doggie paddle,' said Jessica, tactfully leaving the two old friends together.

'Woof, woof,' said Lily, grinning, waving her arms about. 'I'm a doggie paddling.'

'What a bonnie lass,' said Arthur, pouring out more coffee for Lady Grace. 'I'm so glad to see you, Grace. We've a lot of catching up to do.'

It was difficult to drag everyone away. Lily didn't want to come out of the water. Daniel also kept on swimming, pretending not to hear. Grace was deep in reminiscences about old friends with Arthur and the colour had returned to her face. But Jessica was determined that they should not outstay their welcome.

At last everyone was in the car, Lady Grace more composed now that she was neat and tidy in her suit and pearls and her hair combed up. The children were dressed but damp. Arthur and the maid stood waving them out of the drive, making sure that no cars were coming and the way was clear.

'Come again soon,' called Arthur. 'Any time. Look forward to seeing you.'

Lady Grace waved from the window like the Queen.

Now that Jessica knew the way, it seemed no time at all before they were on the road to Upton Hall. It had been a morning without thinking of Lucas and her mind had cleared. She couldn't live without him. But she couldn't live with him either. It would be an agony to be his wife in name only, while he took his pleasure elsewhere. It was like a door slamming in her face. It was as if he had told her that he did not find her attractive enough to bed, only to wed. She would have to start the process of getting over him.

She had got over Fraser, hadn't she? She could do it again. It would be a big loss at first, but then the sense of loss would get smaller and smaller.

'So how come this pool event happened, young lady,' began Lady Grace in her most dictatorial tone. 'We are allowed to swim in a famous pop singer's pool? Have you sold your soul to the devil?'

Lily's ears perked up. She always listened to everything.

'No, nothing so drastic. I value my soul more than that. I put a quarter-page advertisement in the local newspaper. I phoned it over and let them design the display. It came out the next day, looked really nice, with dolphins leaping about all round the edge.'

'And what did this advertisement say?' Lady Grace asked grimly.

'Lady and two small children desperately need regular swimming for medical reasons. Public pools unsuitable. Please can anyone help?'

'That's quite appalling. A vulgar newspaper advertisement. Most improper,' Lady Grace snapped. 'You should have asked my permission first. Our address, our phone number in a newspaper. This is really unforgivable. You have overstepped the mark this time, Jess.'

Jessica nearly stepped on the brake. Hard. She was astounded. They had all had a wonderful morning and she was being reprimanded, told off as if she had committed a crime. She could not believe her ears. It took all her self-control to keep her voice level and continue driving. She did not want Lily and Daniel to be alarmed.

'If you have any complaint to make, Lady Grace, I suggest you make it to your son,' said Jessica. 'And you will no doubt want to rest all this afternoon after such a strenuous and upsetting morning, instead of playing cards with me.'

Lady Grace snorted, not answering.

Jessica was so angry she could barely speak to Lady Grace. She gave the children their late lunch in the kitchen, and let Lady Grace eat by herself in the dining room. There was no way she was going to join her and have her head bitten off again.

'Mrs Harris has left us a lovely lunch. I'm sure you are really hungry,' said Jessica, laying the kitchen table. But she couldn't eat. Her appetite had fled. She rinsed out the swimsuits and hung them in the garden to dry. She took the children for a walk in the afternoon and then let them watch some television. It was a treat. Television was not allowed on school days. Daniel didn't watch anything. He didn't connect with television. He was busy drawing in his exercise book.

Lady Grace was still not speaking to her when Jessica took in her tea tray. She simply nodded her thanks, barely looking up from her book.

There was time for reading and writing with Daniel while Lily played with Floppy Ears. She was teaching him to swim in the air. Jessica's anger cooled and left her feeling sorry for the disgruntled woman. Nothing pleased Lady Grace. Lucas could sack her if he liked. She'd get some temporary job somewhere, washing up in a bar, but she would be sorry to leave the two children. Even Daniel was showing a fraction of movement towards her now, some fragile awareness that hadn't been there before.

She heard the Porsche turning into the drive. Her ear was tuned to the sound of his car now and she could recognize it from other cars. Animals could do that. They recognized a car sound. Knew when their owner was returning home.

But Lucas didn't own her. She went to meet him, driven by a basic and primitive force. But she made sure it didn't show. She didn't care what happened to her now.

'Hi,' he said, his coat flung over his shoulder. 'I see you've all been swimming today. I counted the swimsuits. Great idea. Excellent exercise.' His eyes were riveted on her, daring her to give a plausible explanation.

She read war declared on his handsome face. She turned away in bafflement. How could he have changed so suddenly? He looked as if he despised her.

'I suppose Lady Grace has spoken to you on the phone?'

'She has indeed. She wasted no time. She has told me all about the newspaper advertisement. Your public advertisement from Upton Hall for all the world to read. Not exactly to my mother's liking. Did it not occur to you to ask someone first? Perhaps even me?'

He was staring over her shoulder into the garden, not looking at her at all. Jessica felt the first taste of ash and fear.

She took a deep, steadying breath. 'Was that so bad? There's this beautiful indoor pool and we can use it, any time. Your mother needs to swim, as well as Lily and Daniel. It will improve their health. Daniel loved the quietness and the space. Your mother will get the vital exercise that she needs.'

'Well done, Jessica,' he said, coldly. 'You have got what you wanted. Very nicely done. Am I supposed to pay you a bonus? How would you like it? Cash or a cheque?'

'Got what I wanted?' Jessica faltered. 'I don't understand. What have I got that I ever wanted?'

He turned away and marched indoors. Jessica followed him, bewildered, almost stumbling over the porch step.

'Please, Lucas, don't treat me like this. I don't know what you're talking about. I accept that I should have asked someone about the advertisement, but you were busy at the hospital, never here and I didn't think. It seemed like a good idea at the time. Everyone had a lovely swim.'

'I don't give a damn about the advertisement,' said Lucas, his eyes cold as steel. He touched her jaw with a fingertip. It was not a gentle touch. 'I'm far more concerned about the way you have betrayed me and my family.'

'Betrayed? You're talking in riddles.'

'You're a scheming little hussy and I confess, I was completely taken in.'

Jessica's composure collapsed around her feet. She was devastated. She felt crushed into defeat. She shook her head.

'I don't ... understand, Lucas. This is all wrong. What are you talking about?'

'Your doctor lover-boy turned up at the hospital today. What's his name? Fraser Burton? Very good-looking, blond chap. Apparently you are engaged, have been for several years, and he is about to claim his bride. He seemed very eager. And, no doubt, you are too.'

Lucas stood back at a distance, his mouth set into a hard line.

Jessica staggered, dumbfounded. She couldn't even feel her own feet. They had gone to sleep. She didn't own any, feet or legs. She leaned her weight against the door, unable to stand without support. Fraser. That damned man. Surely Fraser hadn't come into her life again, to destroy all she had fought for in these last years?

'Fraser? Oh God, not Fraser. It's not true,' she whispered. 'Whatever he said, it's not true. I've never been engaged to him.'

'He certainly talked as if you were. He said he had been looking for you after some unfortunate misunderstanding.' Lucas was standing, legs astride, tapping his side with impatience. He looked at her coldly.

'The man is a cheat and a liar. You have got to believe me. He'll say anything about anyone, whatever suits him.' She felt her world spiralling away into an abyss.

'He seemed pretty pleased to know that you were here. He's coming to see you. I'll make sure I'm not around to spoil the lovers' reunion.' He turned his back on her as if she did not exist.

Jessica felt her heart thudding fiercely. She heard the pattering of small feet. It was Lily carrying Floppy Ears by his ears.

'Floppy Ears has got earache,' she said. 'From swimming.'

'Oh dear,' said Lucas. 'Do you want me to have a look at him?'

Lily looked at Jessica and then back at her father. She was an angelic pickle, all sunny smiles and mischief.

'Willdo has sold her soul to the Devil,' she said innocently.

'So I gather. And the Devil has come to collect.'

NINE

It was a thunderous grey sky, leaves skittering in a mischievous wind, long dark branches swaying in time to incantations. The atmosphere was close and humid, warning the world that the skies were about to explode.

Jessica wondered if she could cope with a storm on top of everything else that had happened this evening. She wanted to run away and hide from everyone. The thought of Fraser back in her life, disrupting her peace of mind, causing trouble with his demands and selfishness was too much. It was enough to send her packing and buying a one way ticket to Aberdeen.

Lily was tugging at her T-shirt. 'You haven't lost your sole, have you, Willdo? I can see both of them on your feet.'

'No, of course not. Your daddy was joking,' said Jessica, swinging the little girl up in her arms. She felt quite a bit lighter than the first time Jessica had tried this manoeuvre. 'I don't think you need a bath tonight,' she went on. 'All that swimming, then a shower. You'll turn into a fish with any more water and we don't want that, do we? How about two stories instead of one?'

'One for me and one for Floppy Ears.'

That rabbit was turning into a tyrant.

Lucas had disappeared into the library downstairs and she had heard the sound of a bottle being opened and the television being switched on. He was going to drown his sorrows. So what? Why should she care if he believed anything that Fraser told him?

Daniel was in his bedroom, reorganizing his rows of shells. They were now in a different rigid line which had a new meaning to him. Jessica had never quite worked out if it was by size, colouring, contours, texture or shape. He knew exactly what he was doing even if no one else did. She felt a split second of softness for him.

'Did you hear what I said about baths tonight, Daniel?' she called out.

He nodded, not looking up.

Somewhere in the distance there was a clap of thunder. The storm was a long way off but it was approaching, like some monster.

'What's that noise?' Lily asked.

'It's the clouds bumping into each other.'

'Does it hurt?'

'I don't suppose so. Clouds are full of rain so it's only water.'

By the time both children were tucked up and stories exhausted, the rain was beginning to hammer the windows. Lightning flashed across the sky in jagged peaks, followed by the rolling crashes of thunder. Daniel, with his intolerance to loud noise, hated the thunder and put his hands over his ears. But as long as they children were dry and warm and Jessica was with them, they were not frightened.

'Only silly old clouds bumping into each other,' said Lily, yawning, her eyes drooping. She was asleep in moments.

Daniel had elected to go to bed, to put the pillow over his ears. All that swimming had tired him out. Jessica put on one of his CDs of soft sounds, bird song or waves. They always lulled him to sleep.

'You must have done at least twenty lengths today,' said Jessica.

'Twenty,' he mumbled.

'Pretty good. Would you like to go again?'

The pillow nodded.

'No noise, no crowds, no bright lights. It was perfect for us all, wasn't it? That's what you like, isn't it, Daniel? It was a beautiful pool and so near the sea. Almost like swimming in the sea. Goodnight, then. Sleep tight.'

He nodded again, more sleepily. In moments he was asleep. He looked so like his father. It was like seeing Lucas as a child.

At least she had done something right today, even if everything else had gone wrong. Surely Fraser didn't think he could come marching back into her life as if nothing had happened? That humiliation had not been in her imagination and she still remembered the red dress to prove it.

She took some hot milk and two digestive biscuits up to Lady Grace. Her ladyship was as usual, sitting up in bed, reading, wrapped in a lace bedjacket. She actually looked a little more human than usual, her hair braided into two pigtails like a schoolgirl. It was normally rigidly stuffed inside a hairnet. Relic of the Sixties.

'I hope you are not feeling too tired after your swim,' said Jessica, putting the tray on the bedside table.

'I actually feel very well,' said Lady Grace. 'It was a nice surprise, thank you,' she added, as graciously as her name. 'Even if I strongly disapprove of the method.'

'How else would it have happened? I could hardly go round knocking on people's doors, asking if they had an unused pool.'

'Quite. Quite. However, don't do it again, without my permission.'

'It's not likely to happen. I shall probably be leaving soon. Not sure when, probably tomorrow. I think Lucas has changed his mind about employing me. He is going to sack me.'

Lady Grace's hand stopped halfway to her cup of hot milk. 'Oh no, definitely not. He can't do that. I won't allow it. I like arguing with you and having you here. You give me as good as you get. It's more stimulating than all those silly little ninnies we've had in the house these last years. And you're not scared of me.'

'No, I'm not scared of you, Lady Grace.'

'Everyone has always been scared of me. Can't understand it, really.'

Jessica paused, drawing the curtains. It was the first time that Lady Grace had spoken to her in a normal, pleasant way. A bit late for civility now. Jessica smiled as she drew the curtains together against the storm lashing outside. A zigzag of blinding light split the sky, lighting up the forked branches of trees. In a flash it was gone and in a few moments there came the rumble of thunder, louder and louder. The storm seemed to be right overhead.

'Are you all right with storms?' Jessica asked. 'Would you like some music on? We could find some late night music on Radio 2.'

'There was a terrible storm the night that Sir Bernard, my husband, died,' said Lady Grace, her face changing again, after a moment of silence. 'It was one of the worst storms of the year. He collapsed at the hospital, you know. Quite suddenly. They couldn't save him. He was always working too hard and took no notice of anything I said. I told him to slow down. The storm gave me the most terrible migraine. They brought him home to Upton Hall and I couldn't even look at him. My head was splitting in half. I was in bed with an ice pack on my head. Mrs Harris saw to him. She was wonderful, looking after us. I don't know what I would have done without her.'

Jessica listened to the other half of the story. There were always two halves of any story. If only Lucas would listen to the other half of her story. Fraser was a liar and a cheat. He had lied to her. Now he was lying to Lucas.

'How sad and what a shock for you that your husband should die so suddenly. I'm really sorry. It must have been a dreadful time,' said Jessica. 'But now that you have met one of your old swimming club friends and gone swimming, and your hip is getter better, perhaps lots of things will improve and good things will start happening.'

'Arthur has already asked me if I'd like a game of bridge sometime. Nice old chap. Would you be able to drive me over? You don't play bridge, do you?'

'Never got the hang of the bidding.'

'It does take a lot of concentration. I could teach you.'

It was the first time that Jessica had detected a chink in Lady Grace's iron-clad armour. She smiled again. 'I'd like that, thank you. But if I'm getting the sack . . .'

'What nonsense. Of course you are not getting the sack. I won't allow it. Lucas is overtired. He doesn't know what he's saying.'

Jessica went downstairs with a lighter step. Lady Grace was actually on her side. It was amazing. But it didn't change the situation. Lucas would get rid of her because she was not available as wife material. Fraser had said she was spoken for. She was no longer in the meat market. She had been surgically removed.

Jessica had not eaten. Nor had Lucas. She put a variety of cheeses and biscuits, celery, olives and chutney, on a tray and carried it through to the library. Lucas was sprawled in an armchair, eyes closed, the television twitching with goodies and baddies chasing each other, but no one was watching. She turned it off. He didn't move. Dead to the world.

The storm was still clashing with the universe outside, rain pouring down the windows, lightning and thunder in dangerous pursuit. Thunder still made her jump. She knew it was coming but never expected it.

No one had drawn the curtains and she stood watching the turmoil in the garden. Lady Grace's roses were being flattened. Leaves were torn from trees and scattered to the four winds. Branches were strewn over the drive. She hoped Lucas had put his posh car away. The Austin was safely in a garage.

Fraser would not come out to Upon Hall in this weather. Thank goodness for a small mercy. He only liked driving when conditions were good. Once he had made her drive home from a dinner party when it was snowing heavily. He'd pretended he'd had too much to drink but Jessica knew that he hadn't. It had been a nightmare journey, snow clogging the wipers, and one she would never wish to repeat.

'The Porsche is OK,' said a languorous voice from the armchair. Lucas was reading her thoughts again. 'I put it away in the stables. My first thought.'

'Good, I was wondering if it was still outside. It's a dreadful storm. I've brought you some cheese for supper,' said Jessica. 'I don't suppose you have eaten.'

'Is this the Last Supper before I am crucified?' he asked, eyes still closed.

'Don't be silly,' said Jessica. 'I'm not a vindictive person. But I wish you'd let me explain before you jumped to conclusions.'

She sat down opposite Lucas, not looking at him. She could not bear to see that accusing look on his face again. There were biscuits to butter and top with cheese, as if he were another help-less child. She put chutney on the mild cheese, nothing on the strong Stilton. There were sticks to spear the olives and celery.

'When do you want me to leave?' she asked. 'I can pack quite quickly. There won't be any trains at this time of night, but I could leave first thing tomorrow morning, catch the first train. I won't be any trouble. I'll order a taxi.'

Lucas leaned forward and took her hands, removed the butter knife and laid it down. He looked down at her, his eyes smiling with some secret memory.

'I don't want you to leave, Jessica. I don't want you to go. How are you ever going to forgive me? How am I ever going to explain my stupidity? I've done you a great injustice and you have behaved with the utmost dignity and carried on with your work. Anyone else would have flounced out in a rage and sued me in court.'

Jessica felt the warmth of his hands. She did not understand what was going on. This was another nightmare like step-ping into Alice in Wonderland, she was shooting down chutes, changing size. Now she was very small, very small indeed.

Lucas was actually smiling, an apologetic smile of sorts, as if he had forgotten how to do it naturally.

'I don't understand,' she said. 'Fraser told you a pack of lies today and you believed him. You were furious. You didn't give me a chance to explain. Now you are saying something totally different.'

'I was mad with rage. I was consumed with jealousy. This man said you were engaged to him, promised long ago. How could I know what was true? He sounded so plausible. You had worked in the same hospital. You refused my offer of marriage. Perhaps it was because you were already engaged to him. How could I know what was the truth?'

'Do you really want to know what happened with Fraser and me? I'll tell you all about it. It's something I've been trying to forget and since I have been here at Upton Hall, I have managed to forget because I have been happy.'

'You've been happy at Upton Hall?'

'Really happy. Even your mother and I have agreed to disagree. I love Lily and Daniel, they are super children.' Jessica nearly said and I love you, but she held back. His name might be stitched to her heart but he need never know.

'Tell me about this Fraser Burton person.' Lucas took a cheese-topped biscuit and crunched on it. 'This is good. There was only days' old shepherds pie in the canteen today.' He was not drinking malt whiskey but another bottle of New Zealand white from the vineyard called Oyster Bay. There was only one wine glass beside him. He held it to Jessica's lips and she took a sip. It slipped down like silky nectar. 'Tell me, Willdo, tell me all your secrets, please. I want to know everything. Don't leave out a word.'

Jessica did not know where to start. She had tried so hard to forget.

'It was when I started my nursing training. I was very young and inexperienced. I'd never had a proper home or family since my parents died, shunted around between relatives who didn't really want me. So I became a student nurse who hadn't been anywhere or done anything, or lived in London, let alone have a serious boyfriend. My future career was nursing and I was working hard. It is hard work and I was studious. There's a lot to learn. But I loved it. I knew I had made the right choice. Then Fraser appeared, a young, handsome doctor who had been everywhere, done everything. He was so smooth, so charming.

He bowled me over and he liked that. I was a young and adoring slave, ready for the picking.'

'And growing into a very beautiful woman,' said Lucas.

'We went out, on and off, for two years, mostly hospital parties and pubs. Not regular dating. Fraser was always going away to some conference or medical faculty. Sometimes I wouldn't see him for weeks. It was an endless round of engagements. He was important and climbing the medical ladder fast. I was totally out of my mind, bowled over by his attention. Nothing like this had ever happened to me before. I thought I was in heaven and he was the angel Gabriel.'

'So what happened?' Lucas asked, putting the wine glass to her lips again. She took another sip. She began to like New Zealand. 'You must tell me everything, Jessica.'

'We were going to the Balearics for a weekend in the sun. It was the first time that he'd asked me to go away with him. I was ecstatic, innocently thought that this was it; we were finally going to be a romantic item. I bought loads of holiday clothes. There was also a big party in a posh hotel for some top consultant who was retiring. Fraser had invited me to go with him. Wear something special, he said, it's very important. You'll meet lots of people. So I went out and bought this red dress.'

'You would look wonderful in red.'

Jessica paused. It was still so painful even with Lucas feeding her wine and listening to every word. She remembered every moment of getting ready for this important party. This was Alice land again. The Red Queen was about to arrive.

'It was a lovely soft silk dress that cost far more than I could afford on a nurse's salary. I went to the party on my own as Fraser, for some reason, couldn't pick me up. I went by taxi to the big hotel. There were so many people wandering about, I was completely lost. The reception was being held in the ballroom. I remember the chandeliers, all sparkling lights, the mirrored walls. Waiters wandering around with trays of champagne and wine. Then I saw Fraser and went over to him. He was standing with a woman, a sleek brunette who was also wearing a red dress. She was lovely. But her dress was couture. Mine was best Monsoon.'

'What happened?'

'I went over to Fraser, pleased and relieved to see him. There were a lot of people milling around and I was feeling more than a bit nervous. He brushed away my hand, hardly looking at me and turned to the elegant woman beside him. He drew her closely to his side.

"Let me introduce you to my fiancée, Dr Amanda Morgan", he said flamboyantly. Then he turned her and kissed this woman in front of everyone. In front of me. Can you imagine how I felt? "And this is Jessica Harlow", he went on, laughing, "one of the student nurses who thinks the sun shines out of my arse. She never leaves me alone. Follows me around like a pet puppy".'

'There was a stunned silence and then Dr Amanda Morgan, the sleek, elegant brunette, for no good reason, pretended to trip and her drink, whatever it was, went over my dress. "Down, doggy, down", she said, in a spiteful voice and turned away, laughing. As she turned away, her bag, a beaded evening bag, caught in the folds of my beautiful dress and tore the silk. The dress was ruined. The evening was ruined. I was shattered. She was his fiancée?'

'What did you do?' Lucas was quite still, listening.

'I hardly remember. I believe I ran down the stairs, out onto the street, a bit like Cinderella at midnight. No coach waiting. It was cold and windy. I got home somehow, in another taxi. Cried all the way.'

Lucas caught his breath, ran his hands through his hair and took a deep breath.

'Do you believe me?' she asked.

'Of course I believe you,' said Lucas. 'You've always told me the truth. I know that now.'

'But today, Fraser arrived at your hospital, and said he was looking for me.'

'He wasn't looking for you. He was checking on a private

patient, who had been moved to us, and someone in the staff-room happened to tell him about Lady Grace and my children and the wonderful nurse from London, from the same hospital, who was looking after them. When he discovered your name, he sought me out. It was not pleasant, I can tell you. He said you were engaged to him, that you had disappeared without a trace, that he had been looking for you for months, and that he feared for your sanity.'

Jessica shook her head, began to weep. 'All lies. He made it all up. Clever people can be cruel.'

'I know that now. But I didn't then. In minutes he destroyed all my dreams of you becoming my wife. It seemed to make sense of why you were always turning me down. It became obvious. You couldn't marry me if you were already engaged to someone else.'

'I'm not engaged to anyone and certainly not to Fraser. I hate him. It took me months to get over that humiliation in front of everyone. The word raced round the hospital like a flu epidemic. Other nurses used to come up to me on the ward and ask me where was the sun shining from today? It was horrible. It took me ages to get over it. Only work helped. So, how did you find out the truth about Fraser? What made you change your mind?'

Lucas stretched out in the chair, suddenly bone weary. 'My registrar phoned me half an hour ago. He said that he overheard Fraser asking one of the nurses out for a late dinner and saying that he would drive her home. He said that his wife was at their flat in London and she wouldn't mind. They had a very open marriage.'

'His wife? The woman who ruined my dress?'

'I have no idea, Jessica, who she is. It doesn't matter, does it? He is married apparently but it didn't stop him trying to make a dinner date with one of my nurses. She has been warned and has politely declined the offer.'

'A lucky escape.'

Jessica sat back, regaining her composure, a warmth flowing through her veins. 'I think I'll fetch another glass. Is that all right? I'd like some more of your lovely wine.'

'And I'll open another bottle. You deserve my best wine. Recuperation. You had a rough time with this bastard. I hope he doesn't come to my hospital again or he could find himself cornered in the car park on a dark night. Fortunately his patient is recovering and will be moved back to London tomorrow. We need the bed.'

'Thank you, Lucas. And thank you for believing me. I've never talked about it before. I couldn't. It was too humiliating.'

'Subject closed,' said Lucas, opening another bottle of wine. 'We shall never mention it again. I'm getting better at this opening lark.'

'It's all the practice,' said Jessica, breathing in the perfume of love, almost silent with delight.

'You're leading me down a slippery path,' he grinned. 'And talking about slippery paths. I hear you worked a miracle today. You got Lady Grace into a proper swimming pool. That was amazing.'

'She enjoyed it, eventually. Even if she did not approve of my method of finding someone who would let us use their pool.'

'Typical. She'll always manage to find something wrong. It's her occupation. If a guardian angel came to visit she'd complain about the draught from his wings. And the kids?'

'They loved it, both of them. It was perfect for Daniel, the quietness, the space, no people about. Daniel can already swim a bit, as you know, and Lily took to it straight away, splashing about with arm-bands on. And we can go again, which is wonderful. Lady Grace met an old friend, Arthur Hopkins, from her Brighton swimming club days. It was quite a touching reunion.'

'She used to swim a lot. I believe at one point, years ago, she was considering training to swim across the Channel. She took it very seriously.'

'So what happened to put her off? What made her stop swimming, and so abruptly? There must have been a reason.'

Lucas finished up the last of the cheese and biscuits. He liked Stilton. His appetite had returned. He was glad of her company and Jessica looked so relaxed and comfortable, so at home with him in the library. It was as if they had been together for years. The colour had returned to her fair cheeks as if a great burden had been lifted. Her story was out in the open now.

'No one knows. It happened, whatever it was, when I was a boy, so I never took much notice of what anyone in the family did. Mother was a private person. Father worked the same sort of long hours as I do now. I was always wrapped up in my own pursuits. All I can remember is that one day she came home from Brighton in a terrible state. Wearing clothes on top of her swimming costume, hair still wet, not speaking to anyone. She went straight upstairs to her room and didn't come down till late the next day.'

'And she didn't say anything?'

'She said nothing. She refused point blank to answer any questions. Dad and I gave up in the end.'

'How very strange. Something must have happened.'

'But I did remember something, although at the time it meant nothing to me, as a young boy. As she staggered up the stairs, I could see her ankles. They were torn and bleeding, skin shredded. I thought then that she had fallen on the shingle on Brighton beach, but now I realize that it was something more than a fall and a few scratches. They were quite serious cuts.'

'Jaws? Maybe there was a shark in the English Channel.'

'You may well laugh, but who knows what is on the floor of the sea, anywhere? There was a lot of activity along Brighton beach during the war. And there were fifty bombing raids. She could have stepped on some rotting barbed wire, or got caught up in it and panicked. The tides are high.'

'You may be right. I'm sorry, I shouldn't have laughed. I bet the beach was covered in barbed wire in case there was an invasion.'

'It was worse than that. There were concrete blocks, barbed wire and landmines all along the beach. They were prepared for the worst.'

Jessica finished her glass of wine. She was ready for bed now.

It had been an exhausting day, mentally and physically. She wanted to sail in the shallows of ocean sleep.

'Let's hope she can put the bad memories behind her now and enjoy swimming in this very luxurious private pool. Lady Grace did about three lengths today, very slowly, but she got there.'

'Three lengths?' Lucas pretended to look horrified. 'Good heavens. The Grand had better get in a few more crates of champagne. We're going to need them.'

Jessica started clearing the tray to take into the kitchen.

'What do you mean?'

'The Grand Hotel, Brighton. Remember? It was a wager we made. I bet you that you couldn't get Lady Grace to go swimming and you have. So you have won yourself a slap up dinner in the King's Restaurant at the Grand. I'll make sure we get a table with a sea view.'

'Surely that was only a joke?'

Jessica caught sight of the fire in his eyes and she moved away, coming briefly to her senses.

'You should know by now that I never joke about things that are important,' he said. Everything stopped, laughter, movement, even time. They stood, looking at each other, wondering if they dare break the spell.

The spell was broken by the smallest sound by the doorway. The door into the library had opened a few inches and they saw Daniel's face. He did not look fully awake but he had come downstairs in his pyjamas. He was standing in the doorway, stimming, tapping on the door which was his essential coping mechanism. As he moved forward, he continued tapping on his side.

'Hello, Daniel,' said Lucas, immediately aware of the stress signal. 'Is something the matter?'

Jessica put the tray on a side table, and lowered herself down to Daniel's level. She held out her hand but he did not take it, but went on tapping obsessively.

'Are you all right?' she asked.

He nodded, not looking at her.

'Do you want to tell us something?'

He was struggling. He didn't know the right words, couldn't find them, making small movements with his mouth. 'Floppy Ears,' he said at last.

'What's the matter with Floppy Ears? Has Lily lost him?'

'Lily,' he said, with relief.

'It's Lily,' said Lucas immediately. 'Something's wrong with Lily.' He was out of the door and up the stairs in seconds, straight into his daughter's bedroom. She heard him switch on the main light.

'Good boy,' said Jessica. 'You're a very good, clever boy to come and tell us. You did the right thing. Now I must go up to Lily. Stay here until I come back.'

'Lily,' he said again, more urgently. This was unusual for him to say anything twice with expression.

Jessica hurried up the stairs but she could already hear the wheezing. It was really loud. She didn't need to be told. Lily was having an asthma attack. She was fighting for breath through lips that were already tinged with blue.

'Chair,' said Lucas.

Jessica knew immediately why he wanted a chair. He sat the pale and clammy child on the chair, facing the back, her arms leaning over to help open the airways. Jessica opened a window so that there was some fresh air coming in, at the same time, draping a blanket round Lily so that she would not get cold. The storm was abating, the thunder more distant.

Lily was unaware of who was there or what was happening.

'Nebulizer and oxygen in the top cupboard,' said Lucas. The equipment was there. He was a doctor. He would be prepared for anything happening to Lily at home. Jessica plugged in the compressor to a wall socket, quickly washed and dried her hands, put the mask over Lily's nose and mouth and gave her a few whiffs of the life-saving oxygen. Lucas controlled the metered dosage of the nebulizer.

Lily breathed in the oxygen. The blue tinge went from her lips, her usual healthy pink returning.

'Adrenaline. The smallest dose. There's a hypodermic pack in the box.'

Jessica found the pack and broke the seal.

By now the terrible wheezing was easing and Lily's breathing was becoming more normal. It was a moment of relief. Jessica did not realize how tense she had become till Lucas took her hand and squeezed it gently.

His hand was firm and warm, the skin smooth, the nails clipped as a surgeon's hand would be. It felt reassuring. A man's hand. A hand you could trust.

'Well done,' he said. 'I wish all my nurses moved as fast as you do. Lily is going to be all right now. She'll be back to sleep in no time.'

But Lily had decided to wake up and pleaded for another story before she went back to sleep. And there was no editing out pages. Lily knew her favourite books by heart.

'Have the clouds stopped bumping into each other?' she asked.

Lucas gave his daughter some water to drink. 'No more bumping clouds,' he said. 'Shall I read you a story?'

'This story has got some long words,' said Lily dubiously.

'I can do long words.'

Daniel was back in bed. His bedroom had its usual soft, low lighting. Jessica put on another CD of natural sounds, wind and rain, the sea and bird song. She knew it was soothing and therapeutic. She stroked back his hair, wishing he would respond to her in some way. He kept his eyes firmly shut as if she was not there.

'Goodnight Daniel. Thank you for coming and telling us about Lily. That was the right thing to do. And you did it extremely well.'

TEN

Jessica was out in the garden, helping Lady Grace dead-head what was left of the roses after the storm. Her garden had been devastated but her ladyship had not been too dismayed. She had tossed away Fred and was using a stick.

'It's nature,' she said. 'But it will grow again. It always does. Next year. I'll show you how to prune next week. There's a skill, you know, with roses. You have to cut in exactly the right place.'

'If I'm still here,' said Jessica. She was not sure. It had been a good evening, talking to Lucas but her heart had steeled itself against more miracles.

'You will continue to be employed here for your contract, Jess. I'll make sure of that. I can see what you have achieved with the children. My son is an idiot if he doesn't see it. And the children need your kind of guidance. Of course, I would have got better on my own, but still you have been a useful and pleasant companion.'

Jessica hid a smile. There was no point in arguing with Lady Grace. She lived in a world that had moved on.

A fresh breeze combed the garden. Lady Grace shivered and patted down her hair.

'I'll go and fetch you a cardigan,' said Jessica. 'Which one would you like?'

'The royal-blue one, please. You'll see it folded on a chair.'

Jessica sped indoors. There was certainly the cool scent of autumn in the air. She knew how hard it would be to go when her contract ended. She found the cardigan and hurried down-stairs, out into the garden.

Her feet stopped in their tracks. Lady Grace was talking to a tall, blond haired man in casual jeans and leather jacket. He was looking at the house, taking in the graceful lines and big windows. Then he caught sight of Jessica, grinned and waved her over.

'Hiya, Jessica babe. Long time no see. You've done well for yourself. Upton Hall, no less, what a grand house, almost a mansion. You'll be setting your sights on the lord of the manor next. Always the one to grab at good opportunities,' he added with a smirk. 'You never miss a chance.'

Jessica's mind slipped down several notches into despair. How could she have ever thought this man was wonderful? It was Fraser Burton. He was a jerk. A nasty, malicious jerk. He had his hand on Lady Grace's arm, as if helping her, smoothing back his oddly long blond hair with his other hand.

'What are you doing here?' said Jessica coldly.

'Lucas invited me yesterday. He said drop in anytime. So I thought I'd call by and see how you are. After all, we were very close once. And maybe we will be again. You never know. You have grown into a beautiful woman.'

He dropped his hand and started walking towards her, but Jessica side-stepped his path and went to join Lady Grace. She was furious that he had dared to come to Upton Hall, pretend-ing that Lucas had invited him.

'Surely you are married to the delectable brunette, Dr Amanda? I distinctly remember you introducing her to every-one as your fiancée.'

'Well, it's a sort of marriage,' said Fraser with an easy laugh. 'Didn't last long. We are talking about parting, something ami-cable. And the first thing I shall do is give you a call, my sweet saucy Jessica. We could take up where we left off. I'd really like that.' He turned to Lady Grace. 'Jessica and I were very, very close once, intimately close, if you get what I mean.'

He was still handsome, but he had put on weight round the

middle. Too many parties. The longish hair did not suit him.

'I certainly don't, young man,' said Lady Grace briskly. 'I do not believe for an instance that my son invited you to call here to see Jess. He knows that she has her hands full looking after me and there is no time for visitors.'

'But he said that Jessica would love to see me. That she has been missing me, done nothing but talk about knowing me, and the fun we had together, since she arrived.' Fraser's eyes were feasting on every inch of her slim figure. Jessica wanted to scream, to run away, to hide somewhere that he could never find her.

'We were almost engaged, you see,' he went on, smoothly. 'Although, Jessica is a scheming young hussy and has probably set her sights on richer prey by now. I saw his car at the hospital. That beauty didn't cost peanuts.'

'It is none of your business, young man, how much my son paid for his car. He deserves every penny he earns. I don't believe a word of what you are saying about Jessica, and I suggest you leave. You are beginning to irritate me.' Lady Grace changed which hand she was holding the stick and began walking firmly back to the house.

Jessica closed her eyes for a second, half expecting something to happen. She did not like the expression she had seen cross Fraser's face. He was not used to being spoken to in that manner. He usually charmed every woman he met, whatever her age. Lady Grace could not be charmed.

'Well, well, fancy that,' he said, a flush rising on his cheeks. 'I'm beginning to irritate you, am I? I could say the same about your ladyship. Where's the famous Upton Hall hospitality? Don't I get a cup of coffee, a glass of Irish whiskey, a twenty-minute romp in a warm bed? I wouldn't say no to your bed, your ladyship, hip replacement or not, though of course a younger, slimmer body would be preferable. One without wrinkles or flabby bits.'

Jessica heard Lady Grace gasped at Fraser's audacity. She turned to confront him, her own sharp tongue ready to flail him for his impudence. At that very same moment, Fraser put out his foot and sent the stick flying.

Jessica ran forward at the speed of light and caught Lady Grace in her arms, seconds before she was about to hit the ground. She staggered for a moment with the weight, but managed to regain her balance. Lady Grace clung to her, her chest heaving, all colour gone from her face. She was fluttering like an injured bird.

'She's had a hip replacement, you fool,' Jessica shouted. 'A fall could have dislocated it. Don't you know anything? Get a chair for her.'

'Get it yourself,' said Fraser, kicking the stick further away. He got out his mobile phone and switched it on. 'Amanda darling? Quick message. Don't wait in for me. I shall be late. I have some unfinished business with an old flame of mine.'

His eyes were blazing. He turned to Jessica. 'Let the old woman go. I want what is rightfully mine and should have been mine, years ago. But you were always such a prude. Such a prissy. Well, I've waited long enough and now I am going to take what belongs to me.'

He moved towards Jessica, obviously about to pin her arms to her sides. Jessica felt control slipping away from her. Fraser was big and he was strong. He was also very angry. The odds were against her being able to fight him off and keep Lady Grace from falling at the same time.

Thank goodness the children were at school, thought Jessica, as her spine went into a spasm with a flash of pain. Her old back injury. Her throat constricted in fear at the sight of the savagery in his face. He grabbed at her shoulder.

Fraser's face was opaque with rage and desire. The weight of Lady Grace was tearing her shoulder ligaments. But Jessica hung onto the older woman.

A figure hurled from the house, a figure in a flowered overall, holding a wooden rolling pin. It was Mrs Harris. She went straight for Fraser and hit him firmly behind the knees, very hard.

He crumpled to the ground, groaning and swearing. He rolled over, clutching his knees in pain.

'I've always wanted to do that,' Mrs Harris said, breathing heavily. 'I saw it on the telly. Some detective programme.'

'Please help Lady Grace indoors,' said Jessica, still holding up Lady Grace. 'Sit her in the kitchen where it is warm and make her some tea. I'll get rid of this nasty piece of work.'

'Will you be all right, miss? Be careful. I'll stay if you like. '

'You look after Lady Grace. I'll be fine now.'

Fraser was clambering up and stumbling towards his car. He was covered in mud from the night's rain. He glared at Jessica as he fumbled for his car keys.

'I'll be back for you,' he said, spitting out mud from his mouth.

'Get out,' said Jessica. 'And don't you ever dare come round this way again. We've got a record of all that, you kicking away Lady Grace's stick and coming for me. You see we have a very elaborate security system here and you were standing right in the lens of one of the CCTV cameras. So it's all recorded. The Medical Council might take a poor view of your behaviour.'

'I don't believe you.'

'What's that camera up there? The one pointing straight at you now.'

He didn't look.

He started the car and drove away, very badly, driving over the grass and dragging a shrub out by its roots. He didn't speak, he didn't look back. He put his foot down on the accelerator and shot down the drive.

She could not believe he had gone.

Jessica was limp with pain and the weight of her disconnected thoughts. What was she going to say to Lady Grace? All the dreadful accusations that Fraser had made about her. She went into the kitchen reluctantly, wiping the perspiration from her face, longing for a drink. She went straight to the tap and poured herself some water.

Lady Grace and Mrs Harris were both sitting at the kitchen

table, drinking tea. The brandy bottle was out and Jessica could smell the fumes. Mrs Harris poured her a cup of tea and added a generous dollop of brandy.

'It's only cooking brandy,' she said. 'But you deserve it, my girl. A real young heroine. I saw him kick away Lady Grace's stick. I was at an upstairs window, dusting. It took me a few minutes to get downstairs. Then I saw him attacking you. So I came out.'

'Thank goodness you did,' said Jessica, putting her head in her hands. 'I couldn't have managed much longer on my own.'

'What a dreadful man,' said Lady Grace. 'However did you get involved with such a nasty person?'

'He wasn't always like that,' said Jessica. 'He can be quite charming. I was very young and blind, I suppose. But he was already engaged to this Dr Amanda, even when he was dating me.'

'A two-timer. Seen a lot of that on the telly,' said Mrs Harris, pushing the tea towards Jessica. 'Drink that now. It'll do you good.'

Lady Grace was looking much better. She had recovered her colour and was obviously not in pain. Jessica checked that she was unhurt from the fall. A dislocation would be a terrible set-back.

'He said some terrible things about me,' Jessica began. 'I don't know how to explain. None of it is true.'

Lady Grace stirred the last of her tea vigorously as if brewing some obnoxious potion. She had that gleam in her eye.

'Load of rubbish,' said Lady Grace, accepting a second cup of laced tea. 'I don't believe a word. It's the ranting of an ambitious and untrustworthy man. He is envious of Lucas, who is his superior in every way, at the hospital and at home. He just takes it out on anyone he thinks is weaker than him.'

'So you don't believe him?'

'Not a word. And he is mad with jealousy. He saw that you were happy here with us at Upton Hall and also, I might say, looking very attractive.' Lady Grace paused as if she had something momentous to say. 'I don't think we should mention this incident to Lucas. He might react very badly. He might go storming off to London to create merry hell in medical circles. Not good for his own career. Not good for his patients and they always come first.'

Jessica nodded, understanding.

'Thank you. I never want to see him again. The man is a menace. He cheated on me some time ago, humiliated me and made a fool of me in public.'

'Hard to do,' said Lady Grace.

'I agree,' said Mrs Harris. 'Doctor Coleman would be furious. He might even call the police, etc. We don't want that, people tramping about the garden, bringing in mud.'

'I told him it was all recorded on CCTV,' said Jessica. 'That his every action was filmed and recorded.'

'Very clever, my dear,' said Lady Grace. 'Perhaps we ought to get them installed. They might be useful. Well now, do you fancy a game of cards? Shall we play for money? Fifty pence?'

'So the odds are going up? We played for twenty pence yesterday.'

'It's all that exercise.'

ELEVEN

It was a strange end to the day, trying to act normally, to maintain a happy atmosphere for when the children returned from school. Lady Grace was made of sturdy stuff and her only frailty was to have an after-lunch nap.

Jessica went for a run in the gardens. She needed the exercise to relax her muscles. She was still tense after the morning's episode. It took a phone call from Lucas to wash away the last of the nasty taste.

'Supper tonight at the Grand Hotel,' he said. 'I owe you, remember?'

Jessica was unable to believe that she was going to have that promised dinner with Lucas at the Grand Hotel, Brighton. It had been a joke, a wild wager about getting Lady Grace into a swimming pool.

'Champagne, if you get her to do three strokes,' he had said, confident that he would win.

But Lady Grace had managed three lengths. Not Olympic lengths, but private pool lengths. Pop singer lengths when the sexy Roxy was at home. It all counted.

Jessica could feel her heart fluttering at the thought of time alone with Lucas, time to talk, time to know each other. It was what she had always been wanting, longing for. She knew that now. But would he feel the same way?

Jessica combed through her wardrobe earlier that day. There was nothing at all suitable for the Grand Hotel. She had not brought glamorous clothes, only working gear. That ruined red silk dress had gone to a charity shop, unwashed and torn. They had probably put it in the rag bag. Maybe it was even now being trailed round some dusty refugee camp, used as dressing up play clothes for children who had nothing. She rather hoped it was.

She would have to wear clean jeans and a white shirt.

Lucas had said be ready to leave by eight o'clock. It seemed a bit late to eat but then his work was unpredictable. She heard him come in, the front door of Upton Hall slamming. He was racing up the stairs, two at a time, and knocked on her bedroom door. His arm came round the edge of the door but not the rest of him.

His fingers were dangling a glossy white carrier bag with a fancy logo on the front. 'I've bought this for you, in case there was a wardrobe problem. It's probably the wrong size. I was using my surgeon's guess work measurements. We often have to make guesses in theatre. They are not always reliable.'

'What is it?'

'Something to help you forget that other red dress.'

'A kind thought. Thank you, Lucas,' said Jessica, taking the bag. 'I've got plenty of safety pins.'

'I'm off for a quick shower. See you downstairs in fifteen minutes.'

Jessica opened the bag. It was full of folds of pristine tissue paper. She would wear whatever he had bought, even if it was sack cloth and ashes, a carpet, a nurse's uniform. He would have an unerring feeling for the right clothes for her, she felt sure. Lucas seemed to know what she would like and wouldn't like.

She shook out the tissue paper and the dress fell over her arm in a cloud of diaphanous folds. It was the soft colour of raspberries, chiffon, with a silky petticoat lining. Stitched round the neckline were a hundred tiny roses made of the same material, cleverly folded and bunched, more stitched onto the narrow shoulder straps and edging around the low back. The length was not formal. It flowed down to mid-calf with an uneven hem that would swish around her legs as she walked.

Raspberry chiffon. It was a dream dress, casual, elegant. All memories of the strident red dress were washed away into oblivion.

'It's perfect,' she whispered, holding the dress to her face, breathing in the fragrance of the material.

The dress fitted because it was loose and unsculptured. No safety pins necessary. Jessica had some spiky heeled sandals with light coloured straps and a small handbag as a perfect accessory.

Her hands were shaking as she finished her make-up. She had pinned her hair up in a crazy arrangement with tendrils falling round her face. Nothing in her scant wardrobe was suitable to wear as a coat. She would have to freeze in the car, whatever the weather. No top down tonight, she hoped.

She went out onto the landing. Both young monkeys were still up, aware that something special was going on. Lily's eyes lit up with amazement at Jessica's appearance, the lovely dress, the high heels, the immaculate make-up.

'You look like a princess, Willdo,' she breathed. 'So beautiful. A fairy princess.'

'Maybe I'm going out with a prince,' said Jessica with a wink.

'She does indeed look like a princess, but he's not a real prince,' said Lucas. He was coming up the stairs, and drinking in how lovely she looked. The dress was perfect on her, the folds clinging to her slender figure, her slim ankles in the high heels, strands of tawny hair in disarray. How he longed to let his fingers disarray her hair even more, to crush her to him. Though Jessica smiled at him, she was keeping her usual distance.

'Thank you,' she said. 'The dress is a dream.' She didn't add that the evening was a dream coming true.

'You're going to be stone cold in that slip of a dress,' said Lady Grace, peering from her doorway. Her curiosity had got the better of her. 'Not much of a top; doesn't cover much. Haven't you got a proper coat, girl?'

Jessica shook her head. 'Nothing suitable, more's the pity. An anorak would certainly spoil the look.'

'Ridiculous. Young women don't know how to dress these days.' She went back in her bedroom. 'No sense at all.'

'You look beautiful,' said Lucas, taking her hand. 'Are you ready? Shall we go now? The car is outside.'

Lily was in her pyjamas and confronted her father, arms akimbo, Floppy Ears under threat of being strangled. 'Is this a date?' she asked suspiciously.

'Yes, I suppose you could call it a date,' said Lucas, hiding a wicked grin.

'Are you going to bring Willdo back? You've never brought your other dates back. None of them ever came again.'

Jessica looked at Lucas. What a revelation from his small daughter. He was wearing slim black trousers, an open-necked black silk shirt and white jacket. She had never seen him look so immaculate. Even his unruly hair had seen a comb. He had made an effort, for her sake. All that extra clothes shopping. It must have taken him at least half an hour.

Jessica hugged the little girl. 'Of course I'm coming back, sweetheart,' she said. 'It's Daniel's birthday tomorrow, isn't it? I wouldn't miss that for the world.'

Lady Grace came out of her bedroom. She had a silvery pashmina in her hands. 'You'd better borrow this shawl of mine before you catch your death,' she said, grumpily. 'Mind, I want it back.'

'Thank you, Lady Grace,' said Jessica. 'That's a very kind thought. It's perfect. I'll take great care of it.'

'You can take Floppy Ears with you, if you like,' said Lily, not to be outdone in the sacrifice stakes. 'He could keep you company.'

'That's very kind as well,' said Jessica. 'But I think it's past his bedtime. We don't want him to be worn out for tomorrow.'

Lily looked relieved and held up her face for a kiss.

'Goodnight, Willdo. Have a lovely date.'

'Goodnight, sweetheart. Goodnight, Daniel.'

'Night,' he said.

*

The King's restaurant of the Grand Hotel, Brighton, was their destination. Jessica felt like a celebrity with the graceful dress swishing around her, her heels sinking into the deep carpet as they walked through reception. The great green carpeted staircase swept upwards, round and round, to all the floors above.

'One hundred and twenty-three steps apparently,' Lucas whispered, as they were ushered towards the restaurant. 'It also has the first mechanical elevator ever in a hotel. Do you want to try it?'

'No, thank you.'

The restaurant was grand indeed. Slender pillars in red marble held up the ornate ceiling. Tall windows were draped in pale green damask. Chandeliers shed twinkling light in every direction. Beautiful pieces of antique furniture around the room. It was sedate and impressive.

As Lucas promised, they had a table by a window. There was hardly much of a sea view at night, but the road was lit with strings of lights, luminous waves washed the shore in the distance. They could be in fairyland.

'Does this feel very strange?' Lucas asked. 'We've never done this before. Life has been so busy, there has never been time for the two of us.'

'Very strange,' said Jessica. 'Not real at all. I'm not used to seeing you looked so smart and. . . .' she paused, lost for the word. She didn't know what to say. 'Sophisticated.'

'I know,' he said, as he pulled out the chair for her to sit down, beating the waiter to the duty. 'I'm usually shredded, unkempt, dead tired and useless in the conversation stakes. But tonight is going to be totally different. We are going to have a civilized meal. Put the world to rights.'

The table was laid with a starched white linen cloth, gleaming silverware, glistening glasses, a vase with real red roses. Nothing like meals in the kitchen or supper in the dining room, trays in the library. This wasn't real life but she was prepared to enjoy it for one evening.

'How come you have the evening off?' Jessica asked, as the waiter shook and spread the linen napkin over her lap. As if she couldn't do it herself.

'Lots of arm twisting. I've lost count of how many days I'm owed, holiday time that I haven't taken. It's never possible. There's always someone who needs my assistance.'

'How do you fit in time with Daniel and Lily, when you haven't got anyone to help?'

'I've always spent as much time as possible with both of them. I used to drive back from East Grinstead to spend some afternoon or evening time with them, and then drive back to the hospital when they had gone to sleep. It's been marvellous having you with them this last month, knowing they are happy with you and that I am not needed so much.'

'Are they happy with me?'

'Jessica, I've never seen them so happy. As I am, believe me. I've never been so happy. You have brought joy to my family, and to me.'

A warm feeling swept over Jessica. Lucas meant what he was saying. He was looking at her with intense awareness, as if he never wanted to stop looking. He was devouring her with his eyes. They could have been alone in the big room.

The waiter planted leather-bound, book-size menus in front of them. They would take half an hour to read. Jessica looked at Lucas over the top of her menu, her eyes twinkling.

'Supposing I ordered a tuna and iceberg sandwich?'

'The chef would have a fit. I should have to go into the kitchen to resuscitate. Start reading the small print.'

Jessica ordered a Waldorf salad, which she knew would be delicious, followed by lemon sole cooked in some special way and served with a selection of locally grown tender vegetables. Lucas went for heartier food, a steak. But she knew that the wine he ordered would be perfect. He knew his wines. She wouldn't look at his meal, pretend it wasn't there on his plate.

Their starters were both quickly served and devoured.

The lemon sole was served with style, a portrait on a plate. 'I am emptying the sea,' said Jessica, looking at the poor fish.

'But you couldn't have stopped it happening.'

'They say that even fish feel pain.'

'I read a paper about that, too. The cerebral cortex of their brain actually registers pain.'

'Perhaps I ought to have a cheese sandwich after all.'

Lucas leaned forward and put his hand over hers, his thumb gently rubbing her finger. 'My dearest young woman, you can't put this crazy world to rights with one sandwich.'

A waiter lit a candle on their table and the soft light was perfect. Lucas's dark features were a series of contours, slanted, long lashed, strong jaw jutting, eyes gleaming. The tension melted between them.

Jessica felt herself trembling. She knew that she would always love him, even if they parted at the end of her contract. It could happen. She would go to Sheffield Hospital, take up her duties, try to forget him. But she would always keep in touch with Lily and Daniel. They were part of her life now. There was no way she could walk away from them, what ever happened.

It was the same with Lucas. The candlelight was perfect for Jessica. She looked so beautiful in the soft raspberry dress, her shoulders bare and enticing, her skin luminous. She had no idea how tempting she looked.

If only he could make her believe that his wife's accident was in the past. That the hurt and pain was all over. His wife had left him for another man and that was more hurtful than the dreadful accident. Lucas longed for Jessica to believe him, to let him love her as he wanted to. It was like a fine flame invading his brain.

Neither could say the right words. Time was suspended in the air. The evening was full of light and laughter. They looked at each other and longed for each other's touch, never saying what they should say. Letting the time tick by with measured strokes.

They chose raspberries and cream. There was no question. It was the only dessert for them both. Lucas despaired of the time passing and he had not even begun to say what he wanted to say. Why were words so difficult? He was like his son, Daniel, unable to find the right words.

'I'm like Daniel sometimes,' he said suddenly. 'I can't find the right words to say, even when I know they are inside me.'

Jessica caught her breath. She wanted the words to come.

A wave of seagulls flew passed the window like pale ghosts, wheeling and dealing in the thermal air. The sky was the colour of dark slate, the moon lost behind shifting clouds.

'It happens to all of us,' said Jessica, slowly. 'We are out of touch with words. We are scared of words. It's today's mania for computers and games consoles and texting.'

It was coffee time already before Lucas forced himself to say what he wanted to say. He saw the time and panicked. He forced himself to speak.

'Jessica, we have to get this right between us,' he said. 'We need to get this sorted out. You have been so marvellous with Daniel and Lily. I could not have wished for someone who has taken more care of them, who understands them so well. And Lady Grace, what can I say? Somehow you know how to deal with her and she likes you. She actually likes you. It's a miracle!'

'She likes arguing with me,' said Jessica. 'It sharpens her mind.'

'At some point, when I was totally stupid and inept, I asked you to marry me. And you said no. Quite rightly, you refused me. I was being a complete idiot and yet if I had said what was really in my heart, your answer might have been quite different.'

Lucas wasn't making any sense, yet she wanted him to go on. She was still mesmerized by the sweetness of his voice. She was recognizing the honesty of every word he said. They were basking in the wonder of being together. She could not bear the thought of losing him. There were no halves, only wholes. She would give him her all, without thought, without reservation.

'I don't know what you mean.'

'When I saw you there, standing in the pouring rain outside Eastly Station, it was as if I had been hit by a thunder bolt. You bowled me over. Your beautiful blue eyes spat fire at me. Yes, that was it. Fire and ice. You were the fire, and yet you were frozen. That was the ice. I hardly knew what I was saying. I knew that you were the only woman in the world for me.'

'I don't think you know what you are saying now,' said Jessica, stirring what was left of raspberry juice into the cream. It was a satisfactory pink. She dare not look at him, in case his eyes contradicted his words.

'What I am trying to say is that I fell in love with you then, that very first moment, and I have loved you ever since. I've been waiting for you to fall in love with me. Is that so impossible? Even though I have made lots of mistakes, and said all the wrong things. I want to know. Could you ever begin to love me?'

Jessica's knew she was trembling. She could barely look at Lucas. They were both so careful and guarded. It was like music that never stopped. She couldn't answer his question without giving away all her thoughts and feelings.

'When you asked me to marry you, I knew it was impossible, because I wanted to marry a man who loved me, the real me. You only wanted me for the children's sakes, and for your mother. You even said that you would take your pleasures elsewhere. That's what you said.'

Lucas sighed. 'That was tactless of me and I don't know what I meant. It was unintentionally cruel. I think I meant that I wouldn't force you into anything you didn't want. Our pleasure together would come later as we grew closer. I knew the moment the words came out, that I had said it the wrong way. The only woman I really want is you. Jessica Harlow, I want you as my wife, my lover, my sweetheart for the rest of my life. I love you and I always have, since that very first moment in the rain.'

The waiter hovered with coffee refills but had the sense to fade back into the shadows. He could feel the surge of emotion eddying round the table, strong enough to blow out the candle. The man and the woman were wrapped in a trance. The coffee could wait.

'You love me?' Jessica whispered, hardly daring to voice the words. 'You really do? You always have?'

'Dear heart, how am I going to make you believe me?' said Lucas, reaching into his pocket. 'I wonder if this will help you.'

He brought out a small dark-navy leather box and pressed open the lid, turning it to face Jessica. 'Jessica Harlow, will you do me the honour of becoming my wife? I will love and honour you, but I can't promise to obey.'

Jessica felt the world spinning round her. Lucas loved her. She saw the warmth in his eyes and the apprehension. He was not sure of her. Yet she loved him and need not hide her love any more.

'And I love you, Lucas,' she breathed. 'I really do and I always will. It happened ages ago. I fell in love with you, not meaning to but it happened. I want to be with you for the rest of my life. I want to share in everything that you do, and the crazy way you live, those dreadful hours you work. I want to wait up till you come home, scrub your weary back. To help make life easier for you, if I can. Yes, I will marry you. I love you so much.'

He was looking at her with such tenderness, her heart went into a spiral. Nothing else in the world mattered at that moment. He touched her chin with a fingertip. His surgeon's fingers were so light, so delicate.

'I can't believe it, you've agreed, at last. My sweet one, my darling. Just you being with me will make life easier,' said Lucas earnestly. 'To know that you are at home, waiting for me, ready to take me into your bed. You will take me into your bed, won't you, Jessica?'

'I think we might need a bigger bed,' Jessica murmured, her coffee growing cold. 'We are both rather tall.'

'It'll be the first purchase for our home together,' Lucas promised. He moved the opened box closer to Jessica. She looked down at it for the first time. 'Do you like it?'

It was a ring, nestling in white satin. The sapphire winked at her from among a circle of diamonds. It was a magnificent ring.

'It's beautiful,' Jessica breathed.

'A beautiful ring for a beautiful woman. Sapphire to match your eyes. Will you wear it for me, Jessica?'

She slipped it on the ring finger of her left hand. It fitted perfectly. Surgeon's eyes or a lucky guess? The diamonds flashed in the light from the chandelier above and the flickering candle flame on their table.

The head waiter nodded across the room. Another waiter disappeared and returned almost immediately with a bottle of Dom Perignon champagne, wrapped in white linen. He took it over to their table and bowed.

'With the compliments of the management,' he said. 'And may we offer our congratulations to you both, with best wishes for your future happiness.'

He opened the champagne and the cork flew across the room with a sharp, dizzy burst of fine spray. He poured the champagne into tall crystal flutes, the tiny bubbles rising to the rims.

'To you, my darling,' said Lucas.

'To us,' said Jessica, smiling.

They were very late driving back to Upton Hall so it was already Daniel's birthday morning. They could not stop laughing or holding hands, touching each other, to make sure that the evening was still real. They did not want it ever to end.

They went reluctantly to their own bedrooms. His goodnight kiss sent her pulses racing. They clung to each other, arms wrapped in a close embrace, their lips warm and seeking. Jessica had never felt this hunger for any man before. It was lust and liking and loving.

'We'll wait,' he said quietly, on the landing. 'We are both too tired and had little sleep last night.'

'We could just sleep,' said Jessica tremulously.

'I could never just sleep with you. The temptation would be beyond my mortal body. I should want you so much. You would have to fight me off. But we will marry, very soon? Do you agree?'

'Very soon,' said Jessica, every nerve in her body clamouring

155

for him. His arms were still round her and she could smell the manliness of his skin.

'We'll make all our plans, when we have come down to earth.'

'I'll never come down to earth with you. I'll always be in some kind of heaven.'

'Dearest love, sleep now. I'll see you at breakfast. I may shock Mrs Harris when I sweep you into an ardent embrace.' He grinned.

'I think she would enjoy it. Your mother is more of a worry.'

'Leave Lady Grace to me.'

They drew apart, laughing quietly. Jessica went into her bedroom and twirled around the room, the chiffon floating round her like a pink cloud. They were going to be married. He loved her. Her dream was coming true.

Daniel's birthday tea was a picnic in the garden. September had decided on one more spectacularly sunny day. It was warm enough to spread a rug on the lawn and Mrs Harris had gone to town with birthday tea treats and the garden table was laden with goodies. Lady Grace had a garden chair, padded with cushions. Lucas had raced back from the hospital to be there for his son's birthday.

It was difficult to know if Daniel understood that it was his birthday. Birthday, years and age may not have any concept for him. A party was out of the question because he did not have any friends and would hate all the noise and confusion. But he seemed to like having tea in the garden.

Jessica had spent half the morning blowing up balloons and hanging them from the trees. They hung from low branches, swaying and bobbing in the gentle breeze. Daniel loved them because they made no noise. He started to help, putting them in lines, from low shrubs and bushes. The garden began to look full of globes of colour. Although Daniel's face did not change much, his body looked relaxed and carefree. His shirt had come un-tucked and he did not seem to notice.

Lily raced around creating total confusion. That was her contribution.

'When is it my birthday?' she shouted. 'Can I have balloons in the garden and a picnic tea?'

Jessica didn't know. How awful. She didn't know Lily's birthday. Mrs Harris whispered, 'February 21st.'

'It might be snowing,' said Jessica.

'Snowballs and snowmen?'

'Perhaps. A snow tea, everything white.'

Lady Grace came downstairs, wearing the silvery pashmina which Jessica had safely returned. It was her ownership statement. Jessica made her comfortable in a garden and brought her a glass of dry sherry.

'You might like something a little stronger than apple juice,' said Jessica.

'Glad to see you have more clothes on this afternoon,' said Lady Grace.

Jessica was in indigo jeans and her flame red shirt. She called it her Brighton outfit. And she had tied her hair back with a matching scarf.

'Last night was special,' she said, but added nothing more. They had not told anyone yet. 'What do you think about another swim soon? Would you like me to ring your friend, Arthur, and find a free afternoon?'

Lady Grace seemed to think about it, gathering her strength, finding it difficult to be unpleasant. 'Yes, I would like that.'

'No barbed wire in their pool,' said Jessica, without thinking.

Lady Grace went white, her hand trembling. Jessica took the sherry glass from her, cursing her own thoughtlessness. 'How did you . . . know?' she whispered.

'I'm sorry. Please don't distress yourself,' said Jessica, going down on her knees and stroking the old, veined hands. 'Lucas told me. He was there when you came back from Brighton on that awful day. He saw all the cuts and tears on your legs. We know that the beach at Brighton was heavily defended during the war, concrete blocks, landmines and barbed wire. There could so easily have been some barbed wire embedded in the sand, unseen, waiting for someone to tread on it, to become entangled.'

Lady Grace was gripping her hand tightly. 'It was barbed wire, Jess.' She choked on the words. 'My feet were caught up. I went down in the water to free myself but I couldn't do it. I ran out of air. I was struggling to come to the surface to breathe. The tide was coming in fast and the longer it took, the deeper it got. I panicked. Sea was washing into my mouth, choking me. I thought I was drowning and I nearly was.'

'You were so brave,' Jessica assured her.

'I took a great, deep breath and went down under the water again. I could hardly see for all the swirling water and sand. The barbed wire was twisted round my legs and my ankles. I had to drag them free or I would drown.'

'But you did,' said Jessica. 'You managed it. You are here now.'

'Someone helped me. I don't know who it was. There was someone dark and slim, swimming, tearing the wire away with their bare hands. Suddenly I was free and I shot to the surface. I was in such a state of shock, I never stopped to thank them or find out who it was. All I could do was somehow stagger home. I don't even know how I managed that.'

'And you never went back?'

'I couldn't face them.'

'So you don't know who saved your life?'

'My one regret is that I never thanked him. It's been a heavy guilt to carry all these years.'

'He must know,' said Jessica. 'He must know, in his heart, that he did a really brave thing and saved your life. He doesn't need your thanks. Because he knows that you are still alive.'

'Maybe he has gone, died, after all these years.'

'He will still know,' said Jessica. 'Thoughts travel. Send him your thoughts. What do we know about how radio and television work? It's all thoughts and words on invisible waves. Air that we can't see.'

The children were racing out into the garden with Lucas. Lily had dressed up for the occasion. She had added a net curtain train and tinsel in her hair. Floppy Ears was also wearing tinsel but not the train. Jessica gave Lady Grace back the sherry glass and stood to greet her family. For they were going to be her family now. Lucas, Lily and Daniel. Even Lady Grace.

Lucas came straight over and kissed her lightly on her cheek. It was all she needed. No one seemed to notice the gentle embrace.

'Hello, beautiful,' he said.

'Hello, Lucas,' she said, no need for more words.

The September afternoon swam into a sultry softness. Daniel loved his presents. He was in ecstasy with the pads of paper, the pencils, the books that he didn't understand yet. Mrs Harris gave him a big cake made in the shape of an eight. Lady Grace gave him money. He wouldn't know how to spend it.

And Lucas had another present for Daniel. It was a rocking chair. Daniel loved it instantly, climbed into it, rocking himself, a sketch pad on his knee, drawing leaves, the trees, the clouds. He was lost in his own world.

Lucas sat on the rug, eating everything in sight. He'd had no lunch. It had been a heavy morning. He shifted so that he was leaning against Jessica's knees. She had one of the garden chairs. He looked up at her and took her hand.

'I heard about yesterday morning,' he said. 'I want to thank you for saving my mother from falling and getting hurt.'

'How did you find out? We weren't going to tell you.'

'I know, but Mrs Harris told me. She changed her mind. She said the man had to be stopped from returning at some future time. And I was the only person who could do that. She was right. I have made quite sure that he will never bother you again. You can safely forget him now.'

'Thank you,' said Jessica, so tenderly. The afternoon became saturated with warmth and light. 'I'm glad you know. I never want to keep anything from you.'

Lucas tapped his cup for attention. Everyone looked at him.

'I think this is the right time to give you all some very special news,' Lucas said, swallowing his mouthful of cucumber sandwich. 'Last night Jessica did me the great honour of agreeing to become my wife. So we are going to be married. Jessica and me. Isn't that marvellous? Hasn't anyone noticed her ring? It's big enough.'

Jessica almost stopped breathing. Supposing everyone hated the idea? It was all so new. Lucas could change his mind.

But Lily hurled herself at Jessica, a bundle of excitement and joy. 'Are you going to be my new mummy?' she shrieked. 'Can I be a bridesmaid? And you will stay with us forever and forever?'

'Forever and forever,' said Jessica, taking the little girl in her arms. She was warm and cuddly and a little slimmer.

Even Lady Grace looked pleased. She managed a nod of approval. 'You can borrow my wedding veil,' she said grudgingly. 'It's very old, Brussels lace, but mind you, I shall want it back.'

'Of course, you'll have it back. Thank you,' said Jessica. 'I shall be delighted and honoured to wear it.'

Jessica turned to Daniel. He had tumbled out of the rocking chair and was standing near her, awkwardly, sketch pad dangling from his hand. He looked so like his father, it was devastating.

'Would you like me to be your mummy?' she asked softly.

'Mummy,' he said. Then he gave her one of his rare smiles.

TWELVE

Jessica had not been so happy for years. She could not remember the last time she had walked on a cloud. Her happiness was catching. Lily raced around the garden pretending to be a butterfly. Daniel drew a complicated picture of the close-up of a rose and gave it to her, without a word.

'Thank you, Daniel,' said Jessica. 'What a lovely present. I shall pin it on my bedroom wall.'

Even Lady Grace showed traces of a smile cracking her face.

'It's all right having you here, you know, permanently. I quite like the idea,' she said. 'But don't think you will be running the household.'

'As if I would,' said Jessica, shuffling the cards for their afternoon game of cards. 'I've more sense.'

Mrs Harris was far more astute. 'So you and Mr Lucas have been talking at last, have you?' she asked. 'Got things sorted out?'

'Just talking,' said Jessica, hiding a smile.

'Come to your senses, have you?'

'I don't know what you mean, Mrs Harris.'

'I wasn't born yesterday,' said Mrs Harris.

Lucas had asked her to wait but only for a short while. There were still a few loose ends to tie up before they could be married. Something to do with his wife's death. It had to be registered. Jessica did not understand. Surely after a road accident, her death would have already been registered?

161

Work never stopped and Lucas had been called back to the hospital almost immediately after Daniel's birthday. But he went with a lighter step, knowing that Jessica would be waiting for him when he got home, whatever the time.

Jessica realized that she would not be the sole mistress of Upton Hall when she married Lucas. Lady Grace would still want to think that she ran the household. But it had been a long time since her hands were on the reins, and it would be Jessica and Mrs Harris making the decisions. Even if Lady Grace thought she was in charge.

'We'll agree to everything she says and then do it our way,' said Mrs Harris.

'Mrs Harris! That is positively revolutionary. You must have taken part in the Peasants Revolt.'

'I'm not that old,' said Mrs Harris with a grin.

'When Lucas and I get married, we are going to have a honeymoon, but only a short one, somewhere warm and sunny. He doesn't think the hospital can function without him. We would like you to stay here, please, at Upton Hall, overnight, and we will also arrange for a girl to come up from the village to help you during the day. Would that be all right?'

'Perfect,' said Mrs Harris. 'I thought you would never ask.'

'And when we come back, we want you to have a whole week off as a holiday. I don't think you have ever had a holiday.'

'A holiday?' Mrs Harris looked taken aback. 'No, I've never had any holiday time. But my Bingo friend, May and I would like to go away together. We fancy one of those Shearing's coach tours.'

'As soon as we get our dates, you can book your coach holiday,' said Jessica. 'You are owed a lot of holiday time.'

Jessica made a note. She and Lucas would pay for Mrs Harris's coach tour. The woman was a saint. But it was loving Lucas's father that had turned her into a saint. And it hadn't happened overnight.

A few afternoons later, they were all in the garden, lolling about after tea, enjoying autumnal sunshine. Jessica was reading a new crime thriller, Lady Grace dozing in a cushioned chair, Lily was teaching Floppy Ears to do cartwheels. He was not getting on very well, a bit out of his usual orbit. Daniel was sketching as usual. No one was allowed to see what he was working on.

Jessica heard a car coming along the drive. It was not a car she recognized. Not Lucas's engine. Nor a delivery van. It drew up outside the front entrance, fired the engine again, and then it was switched off.

Jessica wandered round to the front to see who was disturbing their peace. A woman was getting out of a bright red sports car. The red was an over-bright colour against the mellow yellow and browns of the autumnal trees. The woman was slim, wearing a dark emerald green trouser suit, her hair ebony, cut asymmetrical with one side wing longer than the other. Very Posh Spice. Only it wasn't Victoria Beckham, it was Dr Amanda Burton.

The woman turned on her heel, grinding the spike into the gravel. She smiled at Jessica, but it was not really a smile. There was no humour in it.

'So this is where you are hiding out,' said Amanda Burton.

'I'm not hiding out. This is where I work,' said Jessica.

'Call it work, do you? That's a new one.'

Jessica refused to answer. She was remembering the last time they met when this woman deliberately spilt her wine down Jessica's dress and then her beaded bag caught in the frills and ruined it.

'What are you doing here?' Jessica asked. 'What do you want?'

'I was going to ask you the same thing,' said Amanda. 'What are you doing here? Up to some mischief, obviously. But one thing for sure, you are not getting my husband.'

'Your husband?' Jessica almost choked on the word. 'Fraser? I wouldn't touch him with a bargepole, or anything longer or shorter. He's the most repulsive creature I have ever had the misfortune to come across.'

'Come now, that's not what you used to think,' Amanda mocked. 'You used to think that the sun shone out of his arse.'

'I never said that.'

'It's what you thought. You adored the man. You thought he was a very fine catch for a student nurse.'

'I was very young and foolish. I knew nothing about men, especially ones like your husband.'

'Yet you spent the last two nights with him at the Double Cross Inn, outside Brighton. And I've got the receipts in my hand, and a photocopy of the registry book with your signature. You can't deny it. It's here in black and white.'

Jessica was speechless. It was all a total prefabrication. She had been here at Upton Hall, sleeping in the yellow bedroom. She would never go anywhere with the despicable Fraser. Yet, Amanda was waving bits of paper at her, and was now striding towards her.

'Don't think you are going to get away with this, trying to steal my husband. I'll make sure you are never employed anywhere, ever again. And certainly not at Upton Hall, looking after Lucas Coleman's children. You can't be trusted. You've no morals. Does he know where you were these last two nights?'

Lucas had not come home. There had been some awful flat fire and he had to deal with burned children, rebuild their skin, their faces. He had not been home for two nights. But they had spoken briefly, on the phone, reaffirmed their love for each other, knowing they would be together soon.

'You don't scare me,' said Jessica. 'I suggest you leave and go back to whatever miserable life you have with Fraser. I don't want anything to do with him or with you.'

'I've already faxed copies of these documents to Lucas Coleman. I'm sure he'll be interested to know what you do with your spare time when he is not here.'

'The way out is that way,' said Jessica, pointing down the drive. 'And don't come back here again, ever.'

'Don't think you are getting rid of me that easily. I know you are after my husband, but you are not going to get him. I'll fight you every inch of the way and I have a lot of weapons in my arsenal. I'll get you struck off the Nursing Register, so that you will never work again.'

Jessica felt an overwhelming tiredness. Amanda Burton was a vindictive woman and Jessica could not understand why she was acting this way. It was as if the nightmare had returned. Now it was Amanda who wanted to humiliate her for no reason at all.

'Willdo? Willdo? Where are you?'

She heard Lily's voice calling her. Jessica turned away and went through the rose garden. She heard the car engine start up and drive away with a burst of acceleration. It sounded as angry as its driver.

'Floppy Ears can't do cartwheels. His ears get in the way,' said Lily. 'Shall I get some ribbon and tie them up?'

'I don't think that would be very comfortable for him,' said Jessica. 'Would you like to have your ears tied up?'

'No, I wouldn't,' said Lily firmly.

'Why not try hand-stands? Floppy Ears could probably manage a few hand-stands if you help him.'

'Hand-stands! We'll do hand-stands all over the garden.' Lily raced away.

'It makes me quite tired just watching that child,' said Lady Grace, who had woken up. 'What do you feed her on?'

'Not sugar and spice, for sure. She's beginning to lose weight which is a good sign. But I think poor Floppy Ears is due for a relapse. I shall have to go to Brighton pier and win another one.'

Lady Grace's face changed with what occasionally passed for a smile. 'You might not be so lucky a second time.'

'I might come back with a camel. I suppose he'd be called Humpy.'

Daniel had been listening but said nothing. Jessica had lost her place in her book and she had lost interest in the plot. The unexpected visitor had upset her more than she cared to admit.

She wanted to see Lucas. She wanted to find out if Amanda had been bluffing.

It was a very tired and grubby Lily who went into the bath that evening. She hardly had the energy to do her brown inhaler. And she was almost asleep before Jessica finished reading a story.

'Floppy Ears v'good at hand-stands,' she said. 'Better'n me.'

Floppy Ears looked exhausted.

Daniel had already put himself to bed. He was old enough to wash himself now. He handed Jessica a sheet of paper from one of his new drawing pads. It was a perfect drawing of a camel.

'Hump,' he said.

Jessica waited up for Lucas returning from the hospital. It was almost midnight. Mrs Harris had long gone home, and Lady Grace was tucked up in bed with her hot milk and two digestive biscuits.

Jessica had a shower and changed into a clean track suit, her blue one. She knew Lucas liked the colour. There was a tray of sandwiches for him but he would probably be past eating. Maybe a glass of whisky and then he would be off to his bed, too tired to do more than kiss her goodnight.

She heard his car coming up the drive. He was coming quite slowly as if it was too much of an effort. The car went round the side of Upton Hall to the stable garages. Lucas seemed to be a long time coming into the house and she was beginning to wonder if he had gone straight to bed.

This was so unlike him that Jessica began to fidget around the room, unsettled by his non-appearance. Then Lucas came into the room and she was shocked by his appearance. He looked gaunt and haggard, shadows under his eyes.

She ran over to him and put her arms round him. His head sank onto hers as if he didn't have the strength to hold it up. She felt the weight of him against her and guided him to a big armchair. He fell into it with a groan, his eyes closed.

'You look terrible,' she said. 'What has happened?'

'We lost one of them,' he said. 'One of the children. Five years old, the same age as Lily.'

'Oh, how awful,' said Jessica. 'I'm so sorry. But I'm sure you did everything you could.'

'Of course I did everything I could.' His voice had a sudden sharp edge to it. 'But it wasn't enough.'

There was nothing Jessica could say to ease the guilt. She knew what it felt like, to lose a patient. She always wondered if she could have done more. If she had missed something, not been at a bedside when she was most needed.

She went to the drinks table and poured Lucas a glass of his favourite whisky. There were still some melting ice cubes left at the bottom of the ice bin. Mrs Harris had forgotten to fill it. She took the crystal tumbler over to him, knelt down and put it carefully into his hand.

'Maybe this will help,' she said. 'At least it will help you to sleep.'

He took a few sips and nodded. Then he opened his eyes, their usual brightness dimmed.

'You're looking very. . . .' Lucas seemed to search for a word. 'Very seductive,' he added.

Jessica rocked back on heels. It was such a strange thing for him to say. He had never called her seductive before. She had never thought of herself as seductive. Seductive was someone who wore black fish-net stockings and a plunge bra, not a blue track suit.

'Well, I don't feel it,' she said. 'It's been a busy day.'

'No, I suppose you don't. At least not with me. A worn-out and tired surgeon who is never at home. You should really find someone more lively and stimulating. Someone who will take you out and give you a good time.'

It was the second shock of the day, to hear Lucas speak to her in that way.

'I've never wanted "a good time", as you put it,' said Jessica. 'I'm very happy here with Lily and Daniel, and the occasional outing to Brighton pier.'

'Oh yes, I'd forgotten. You like Brighton, don't you? Is it one of your regular haunts?'

Jessica got up from her knees. Lucas must have been drinking and that's why he drove so slowly up the drive. If he had lost a patient, one he cared about, then perhaps he'd already had a few whiskies.

'I think you need some sleep, Lucas,' she said, trying to stop her voice from trembling. 'You'll feel a little more like yourself in the morning.'

'Perhaps I will,' he said, getting up clumsily. 'I don't know what to think.'

He went from the room, not stopping to kiss her, the whisky almost spilling in his hand. Jessica did not know whether to go with him or let him find his own way to the stables. It was his house. He must know the way.

'Goodnight, sweetheart,' she said, her voice still trembling. He had not kissed her. She followed him out into the hall. His coat was thrown on a chair. His briefcase thrown on another chair. It had come open. Some papers had fallen to the floor. She bent down to pick them up and froze.

THIRTEEN

Jessica could hardly remember how she got herself to bed. The pretty primrose bedroom seemed a foreign place and there was no comfort in it. She left her track suit on the floor and curled up in bed, the tears welling up in her eyes. Lucas had copies of the hotel receipts and the page of the hotel registry in his briefcase.

And there was her signature on a line, right below Fraser's. Jessica Harlow, her handwriting. And she had no idea how it got there. Amanda Burton had carried out her threat and faxed the incriminating documents to Lucas at the hospital.

No wonder Lucas was distraught. He had lost more than a patient. He thought he had lost her as well. Now she had another mountain to climb, to convince him that it was all some vile vengeance by a woman who would stop at nothing.

She did not fall asleep until the small hours, exhausted by a turmoil of thoughts and silent weeping. She wondered how she would get through the next day.

Lily woke her with her usual bounce and hug. Floppy Ears had come too. He did not look as if he had had a good night either.

'Willdo, it's morning. Wake up. Today is here. What are we going to do today? Have you got a surprise for us?'

'Yes, I might not get up today,' said Jessica. 'That's my surprise.'

Lily looked aghast. 'Not get up? Willdo, you can't stay in bed

169

all day. Daddy has already got up and gone to work. You must get up. We need you.'

Jessica heaved herself up. 'Lucas has already gone?'

'Yes, I heard his porch go very early.' She pronounced it like it was the front of a house. 'He has very sick children to look after, you know.' Lily looked serious and worldly. 'Daddy is a very clever man.'

'Yes, that's true,' said Jessica. 'He's a wonderful man.'

'Is that why you are marrying him?'

'Yes, because he's wonderful and clever and I love him.'

Lily's face glowed. 'He loves you too,' she said. 'We all love you.'

Jessica swung her legs over the side of the bed, feeling the softness of the carpet beneath her feet. She still had her job to do, whether Lucas threw her over or not.

'Washing first,' she said. 'You, Lily, not Floppy Ears. He needs another five minutes sleep.'

'Another five minutes,' she agreed, tucking him into Jessica's bed. 'Go back to sleep, Floppy.'

Jessica went into automatic mode. She got the children ready for school, breakfasted and onto the school bus. She ate no breakfast at all. Lady Grace received her usual attention, the exercises, the medication, a discussion of the state of the world.

Mrs Harris was as sharp-eyed as always. 'No breakfast, miss? Off your food, are you? Not pregnant, are you?'

'If only,' said Jessica.

'So what's the matter with you this morning? Not had a row, have you?'

'Not exactly.'

'A misunderstanding?'

'Sort of.'

Mrs Harris poured out a fresh black coffee. Jessica took it gratefully. It might keep her awake. She watched Mrs Harris toasting a slice of granary bread and spreading it with peanut butter.

'Get this down you, miss, before you pass out on us. Your

face is as white as a sheet. I don't like the look of it at all. It must have been something pretty awful.'

'You remember Fraser? The unpleasant fair-haired doctor who came here?'

'Tow-haired lout? The man I whacked with a rolling pin?'

Jessica nodded. 'His wife turned up here yesterday with a pack of lies about me. And she has sent so-called proof of those lies to Lucas.'

Mrs Harris looked up from her pastry-making, her fingers covered in flour. She looked enquiringly at Jessica. 'Proof? What sort of proof?'

'Documents. One with my signature on it. It's not true, of course. I didn't do what she is saying I did.'

Jessica nibbled at the toast, to please Mrs Harris. Mrs Harris continued crumbling the pastry. She was a light-fingered expert.

'I read a lot of books, you know,' Mrs Harris continued. 'Crooks can forge anything these days. They are pretty clever at it, make passports and identification tags. I'll see what I can find out. If the wife is as nasty as the husband, then they deserve each other.'

Jessica found a wan smile. 'Thank you, Mrs Harris. It's Lucas I'm worried about. He seems to believe the implications.'

'He ought to have more sense, not take the word of a pair of scoundrels.'

'He was very tired last night,' Jessica added. 'Too tired to think.'

'All the more reason for him to come home now and sort it out with you. Before it gets worse. And before you pass out for want of any decent nourishment. Look at you, skin and bone.'

'Don't worry about me. I shall certainly have some of that apple pie you are making. Your apple pies are famous.'

Jessica spent the morning walking Lady Grace round the garden. They did a little dead-heading. The flowers were coming to an end. Autumn was on its way, with more rain and cold fingers. Her patient was gradually becoming used to walking with a stick, sometimes quite briskly. She only used

Fred upstairs now, preferring to lean on him while she got her bearings first thing in the morning.

'Pity he's not better looking,' she said once. 'I might take a fancy to him.'

Jessica had to laugh. It was the first time Lady Grace had said anything that was almost flippant. She had a smart reply on the tip of her tongue but thought better of it. She still had to tread warily with Lady Grace. No crossing the social boundary without permission.

They had a light lunch together in the dining room but Jessica still could not eat. She was racked with worry about Lucas and wanted desperately to talk to him, to tell him her side of the prefabrication.

Lady Grace said very little during lunch. But while she was stirring cream into her after dinner coffee, she looked at Jessica with a piercing glance.

'I have perfect hearing you know,' she said.

'Lady Grace?'

'I can hear a pin drop. Yesterday afternoon, I heard that woman berating you. Of course, I couldn't hear everything she said, but I got the general gist of it. What was she saying to you?'

Jessica was shaken that Lady Grace might have overheard what Amanda said. 'She was accusing me of trying to steal her husband,' said Jessica, barely able to get the words out. 'She said I had been cheating on Lucas.'

'And who is her husband?'

'Doctor Fraser Burton. The tall, blond man who came here, who kicked your stick away, who tried to grab me. That's him. He's her husband.'

'That piece of garbage? No woman in her right mind would want him, and certainly not you, Jess. What rubbish. What proof has she of this accusation?'

Jessica felt her face colouring. 'She has hotel receipts and proof of my registering at a hotel with him. My signature is on the line.'

Lady Grace snorted. 'And just when was this illicit rendez-vous, may I ask?'

'Sometime this week apparently. I don't know. I didn't see the dates.'

'Absolute nonsense. You've been here at Upton Hall for weeks now, every night. I can vouch for that. Who else brings me my milk and digestive biscuits?'

'I could have slipped out after you'd gone to sleep, driven to this inn outside Brighton,' said Jessica, making it worse for herself. 'It's not that far.'

'And been back in time for Lily to jump on you with Floppy Ears, first thing every morning? I told you I have very good hearing. It's not possible. The woman is an outrageous liar. Like her husband.'

'She is lying but Lucas believes what she has put before his eyes. He barely spoke to me last night. Left me without a word. It was awful.'

'My son is a fool. A clever surgeon but a fool when it comes to women. He trusted his wife so I suppose he is worried that it could all happen again.'

Jessica didn't ask although she wanted to know. The conversation had exhausted her. 'Shall we have a game of cards before the children come home from school?'

'Good idea. Whist or bridge?'

'I don't think my brain could cope with bridge today. A game of whist would be best.'

'I shall certainly beat you then.'

The afternoon raced by till Daniel and Lily arrived home from school, but Jessica barely knew what she was doing or what she was saying. All she could think of Lucas coming home, of having to talk to him, having to convince him that he had been sent a pack of lies.

'Don't you want any tea?' asked Lily at tea-time. 'Floppy Ears says you are not eating anything.'

'I had a big lunch,' said Jessica, lying. It was the first time she had lied to Lily. It was a horrid moment. But what could she say? Your Daddy thinks I've been cheating on him?

'You can have some of my tea. I'll save you some,' said Lily. 'You'd like that, wouldn't you? Then I wouldn't eat so much.'

'A very good idea,' agreed Jessica. 'I'd like that.'

'And Floppy Ears will save you some of his lettuce.'

'Wonderful,' said Jessica faintly. She didn't fancy twice-chewed lettuce.

Lucas came home early evening. She heard his Porsche coming up the drive with quite a determined sound. He didn't put the car in the garage but parked it by the front door. He slammed the door and strode into the hall. He went straight into the kitchen and poured himself some coffee from the percolator on the Aga.

He leaned against a wall, sipping the coffee, his eyes sweeping over Jessica coldly. 'So,' he said, 'what have you got to say?'

The kitchen was empty, apart from the two of them. Mrs Harris had gone home. Lady Grace was reading in her sitting room. Both Lily and Daniel were already in bed, drawing and crayoning. It was a treat.

Jessica had been clearing up the tea things and making a salad supper for Lady Grace. She was slicing tomatoes and beetroot before making a light dressing. She remembered the day she had arrived at Upton Hall when Lucas met her at the station in the pouring rain. She had stood up for herself then. She would do it again, even if it meant losing Lucas, the man she loved.

'What have I got to say?' she repeated. 'Good evening, Lucas, would be a polite start. Are you talking to me this evening? Or is this going to be more of the cold shoulder that I endured last night?'

'Don't you deserve the cold shoulder after the way you've been behaving? You really fooled me. The cool young nurse who is really a rampant sex-pot. Not exactly the right person to be looking after my children, and certainly not the right person I want to marry and to be my wife.'

Jessica started to lay a tray for Lady Grace's supper. She put a lace cloth on the tray and laid it with pretty china, the dressing in a jug, the cottage cheese salad on a plate. She put a fresh wholemeal roll on a side plate with some butter.

'It would be interesting to know why you have changed your opinion of me,' she said. 'I remember a dinner at the Grand Hotel, Brighton, quite recently, when you asked me to marry me, gave me a ring. A beautiful ring. A ring which you see, I am not wearing. I thought it was hardly appropriate after your behaviour last night.'

'My behaviour last night was that of a man who thought he loved you, who thought you loved him. Who believed you when you said this Fraser meant nothing to you, but then I find you have spent two nights with him, this week. In some inn at Brighton, of all places.'

He said it as if Brighton had some special significance. As if she could only go to Brighton in his company.

'Right on our doorstep,' he went on. 'Under my nose. When you knew I was working late, staying overnight at the hospital, because of the burns cases. You took advantage of the fact that I was not here. It's a wonder that Super Stud didn't sleep in the yellow bedroom with you.'

Jessica listened to the tirade, trying to keep her own temper. It wouldn't help if she lost her temper. She put a ripe peach and a little knife on a dish on the tray.

'If you'll excuse me a moment, sir,' she added the 'sir' deliberately. 'I'll give your mother her supper and then we will continue this conversation. If you can call it a conversation. It's more like an indictment, a charge of criminal wrongdoing. I believe it is my turn to say something.'

'I'm not going anywhere,' Lucas said bitterly.

Jessica took the tray in the sitting room, putting it on the sideboard while she arranged a side table closer to Lady Grace. She put the tray carefully on the table, making sure that Lady Grace could reach everything. There were such awful stories of elderly patients in hospital not being able to reach their meals, and starving to death.

'Very nice, thank you,' said Lady Grace, glancing over the tray. 'Would you approve of a glass of sherry before I have my supper? It would be civilized.'

'Of course,' said Jessica. She went to the decanter of sherry and poured out a glass of dry. Lady Grace always used exquisite cut glass glasses. 'Very civilized.'

'Bring over two glasses,' said Lady Grace.

Two glasses? Lady Grace was hitting the bottle this evening but Jessica did as she was asked. She put them on the side table.

'One of them is for you, Jess. Get that sherry down you and you might not look so peaky. Now tell me, how are you getting on that awkward son of mine?'

'Not very well.'

'He needs some sense knocked into him. Send him into me, here. I'll tell him that you never left Upton Hall for one minute.'

'I want to prove to him that the documentation is false. That none of it is genuine. That I have never cheated on him. That it is all some ghastly scheme cooked up by the Burtons. Some sort of revenge.'

Lady Grace sipped at her sherry. 'I have a plan,' she said in a voice that brooked no rejection. 'I phoned Arthur earlier today and he is coming over for a game of bridge this evening. You were hardly concentrating on that whist this afternoon. We can keep an eye on Daniel and Lily for a couple of hours, though I draw the line at reading them stories.'

'So?' Jessica could not guess what was coming.

'Lucas can drive you over to this hotel, or whatever it is in Brighton, and sort it out, once and for all. Someone must remember whether they saw you. Take the documents, see if they are genuine or not. Mrs Harris told me this afternoon that they can do wonders with photocopying these days. She read it in a book.'

'Well, well,' said Jessica, suddenly feeling a lot better. She was not sure if it was the sherry or Lady Grace's confidence in her. She had an idea.

'You know all those Sunday paper glossy magazines? Have you got any of them around? I need a photograph of someone famous,' she said.

'Take what you want,' said Lady Grace, finishing her sherry. 'You'll go?'

'We'll go,' said Jessica. 'I think it's a brilliant idea.'

'Well, thank goodness for that. You are doing something sensible at last.'

Jessica threw on a fleece. She explained to Lily and Daniel that there would be no story tonight, because she had to go out suddenly with Lucas. She explained that their grandmother would be in the house with Arthur, her swimming friend, the man they met at Roxy's pool.

'We could ask him when can we come over again?' said Lily, not slow at seeing an opportunity.

'I don't think that is very polite,' said Jessica.

Daniel rummaged through his drawing pad and opened a page. 'Pool,' he said.

It was a drawing of the pool, perfectly in perspective, even to the ripples on the water, and the robes hanging on the wall.

'That's lovely,' said Jessica. 'I think Arthur would like to see that.'

Daniel closed the page, saying nothing more.

Jessica strode into the kitchen, a batch of magazines under her arm. Lucas was eating cheese and biscuits at the kitchen table. He looked up.

Jessica was in fully fledged Boadicea mode, spear at the ready. 'We going out,' she said. 'Finish what you are eating. Lady Grace says she can look after Daniel and Lily for a couple of hours, and she has a friend arriving to play bridge.'

'I've had no supper,' said Lucas.

'Neither have I. Nor breakfast. Nor lunch. We are among the starving millions.' She picked up her shoulder bag. 'Shall we go in your car or mine?'

'Where are we going?'

'That inn of ill repute. The Double Cross Inn or whatever it's called. You may know where it is, but I certainly don't.'

'My car.'

They never said a word as Lucas drove towards Brighton. Jessica leafed through the magazines. It was not easy. She hated reading in a moving vehicle. It made her feel sick. But she found what she wanted, several of them, which was a big relief.

The Double Cross Inn was on the outskirts of Brighton. It was partly an old pair of farm cottages knocked together, with a modern attachment. A stark building like a Travelodge had been built on at the back. There was plenty of parking space in a tarmac yard.

'Bring back happy memories?' said Lucas sarcastically.

'Never seen it before,' said Jessica.

The bar was ancient, very pleasant, lots of old brasses and farm implements on the walls. It was full of customers, sitting around at booths and odd tables. None of the wooden furniture matched. Jessica went straight up to the bar.

'Can we see the manager please?' she asked.

'I am the manager.'

He was a sturdy man, grey-haired, worn out by years of pulling pints, his skin pitted with acne. 'Can I help you?'

'We'd like to ask you a few questions.'

'I'm a bit busy. But later on, when my help arrives. Do you want a drink?'

'A glass of house red, please,' said Jessica. 'And half a lager.'

She waited while the drinks were pulled. Even the wine was from a box. She paid for them.

'Why is this inn called the Double Cross Inn?' she asked.

'Because highwaymen were hanged here. Two at a time.'

Jessica shuddered. 'Happy times.'

She took the drinks over to Lucas. He was sitting at a rickety table with uneven legs. He looked ill at ease, brow furrowed. 'Why are we here?' he asked, taking the glass without a word. He folded a beer mat in half and put it under the shorter leg.

'Because I am going to prove to you that I have never been

178

here before, with or without a companion.'

'I suppose you've bribed the manager. Slipped him a couple of twenties.'

'It was fifties actually.'

'Makes sense.'

'It makes no sense at all,' said Jessica.

FOURTEEN

It was half an hour before the manager came over to their table. It was an uneasy thirty minutes when they hardly spoke, sipped their drinks, looked everywhere but at each other. The inn was busy and the noise drowned their silence.

Jessica had turned down the corners of the magazine pages she was going to show the manager. She let Lucas open the conversation.

'My name is Lucas Coleman,' he began. 'There has been a slight family disagreement which we are hoping you can resolve.'

Slight family disagreement. Jessica almost choked on his words but managed to contain her irritation.

'Nice to meet you, Mr Coleman. Jeff Draper's the name.'

'Mr Draper, thank you for your time. We have information that this lady,' Lucas went on, hardly looking at Jessica, 'stayed at your inn for two nights this week, probably in the Travelodge. She stayed with Dr Fraser Burton.'

Jeff Draper looked at Jessica. 'I don't rightly know,' he said. 'We get so many people at the lodge, coming and going. You see, it's convenient for Brighton. I can't keep track of them all. I'd better go get the hotel register and we'll have a look.'

The manager returned with a red leather-bound book under his arm, and opened it out on the table. There was hardly room for it on the small table. The page was crammed with dated entries, names, car registration numbers, home addresses, some readable, some unreadable.

'And that's only today,' he said. 'It's been busy.' He flicked a couple of pages back.

'That's yesterday's and the day before ... hold on, we're missing a page.' He did some quick checking. 'Well I never, there's a page missing.'

Lucas took the sheet out of his brief case. 'Is this the missing page?'

The manager took it from Lucas. Now it was Jeff Draper's turn to look annoyed. It was clearly a page from his register, same lists of information. 'I have to ask you where you got this page, Mr Coleman. I'm sure it is an offence to remove anything from a hotel register.'

'Be assured, I didn't do it. The sheet was faxed to me yesterday, to my ... office.' Lucas almost said 'surgery'. 'As you will see, Dr Fraser Burton signed in for two nights, there.'

'Room fourteen,' the manager confirmed. 'I remember it now. It was pretty late at night and he seemed in a hurry. They didn't have much luggage, just a bag between them.'

'And who was with him?'

'I believe it was his wife.'

'Did she sign the register?'

'No. We don't usually ask questions of that nature. We assumed it was his wife. I think he signed for her, put ditto marks. Yes, here are the ditto marks under car registration, address, etc.'

'But the name underneath his is my name,' said Jessica. 'Signed in my handwriting.'

The manager look mystified, out of his depth. 'Really, I don't know, miss. I know nothing about this.'

Jessica produced the glossy Sunday supplement magazines. 'Would you kindly identify the woman in this photograph and this one?' She turned a page. 'And again on this page. Do you know who this is?'

'Of course, I do, miss. Everyone knows who that is. That's Posh Spice, the model who's married to David Beckman. Always getting their pictures in the papers, regular like. I think her name is Victoria.'

'Does she look anything like the woman who booked in with Dr Burton? Do you recognize the hair, the black bobbed hair, with one side longer than the other?'

'Now you mention it, miss, that lady did have funny hair, cut different lengths either side of her face. I thought it was a mistake and she ought to go and have it tidied up. She was quite a bit older than this smart Posh Spice, but the same hair.'

Jessica sank back in the chair, relief washing over her face. 'Thank you,' she said. 'The lady with Dr Burton was his wife, Amanda Burton. It wasn't me at all.'

'Nothing like you, miss, if you don't mind me saying so. And she was in a right temper, demanding this and that and at that time of night. I told her there's a hospitality tray in the room to suit everybody's taste and I could do no more.'

Lucas was looking confused. 'I don't know what to think. But Jessica's signature is on the next line.'

'If you don't mind me saying so, sir, it's quite obvious to me. This page was torn out sometime, probably the next day, because there are more entries underneath. But it's not the same page because it doesn't have a ragged edge. It has a smooth edge. It's a photocopy of my page. If you look at my register, you can see bits that were left behind, as if it was torn out in a hurry.'

'That's what Mrs Harris said,' Jessica said triumphantly. 'She said crooks often photocopied things and you could never tell the difference from the original. Except in this case, there should have been a tiny ragged edge where it was torn out..'

'And where would he get your signature?' Lucas's voice was gruff now.

'From the hospital. It's in all the records. Nurses are always signing for things. He'd have no trouble looking in an old file. You should know that. He got my signature from somewhere, cut it out and put it over the ditto marks on the empty line below his signature, levelled it up, then photocopied it. No one would be able to tell at first glance.'

'And the credit card receipt is correct?'

Jeff Draper looked at it. 'Yes, sir. Room fourteen for two nights. Perfectly correct. I believe they had some extras but they were paid for separately. Now, if you don't mind, I have to get back to the bar. It's getting crowded and my assistant is looking harassed. Big crowd just come in.'

'I wonder if I could have another glass of your house red,' said Jessica, throwing caution to the wind. She felt like celebrating.

'Of course, miss.'

Jeff returned with a brimming glass. He was grinning. 'On the house, miss.' He was not daft. He'd worked it all out. He hoped the nice young lady would be happy now.

Lucas didn't say much on the drive home, but he drove carefully, not taking any chances. It was dark now and the flashing headlights lit up the road ahead, catching the eyes of rabbits sitting on the wayside grass.

'They are all going blind again,' he said.

'How sad. Poor things,' said Jessica.

A fox dashed across the road, his bushy tail streaming fiery red. He leaped into a hedge and was safe, bounding across a low-lying Sussex field.

'It's the badgers I worry about,' said Jessica. 'They are such slow old things. They don't stand a chance.'

'I see a lot of dead badgers,' said Lucas. 'Road-kill. Coming home late.'

Jessica clutched the magazines to her chest. She felt she ought to cut out all the photographs of Victoria Beckham and pin them round her room. Posh Spice had saved her though she would never know about it in her Californian castle.

They came slowly up the drive to Upton Hall. There were lights on as if Lady Grace and Arthur were still playing bridge. Arthur's car was parked neatly to one side.

Jessica got out of the car and went up the steps to the front door. She turned round. Lucas was immobile at the wheel of his car, gripping the wheel.

'I'll say goodnight, Lucas. I don't think we need say anything more. I'll make sure that Lady Grace gets safely to bed. I'm sure you need a good night's sleep.'

'Jessica,' Lucas began, hesitantly.

'Tomorrow,' said Jessica firmly. He had made her suffer. She was not ready to forgive him.

Lady Grace came out into the hall. She looked enquiringly at Jessica, dying to ask but good manners holding her back.

'All sorted, done and dusted,' said Jessica. 'It wasn't me at all staying at the Double Cross Inn. The manager recognized a look-alike photo of Fraser's wife, Amanda Burton. And the hotel register had been skilfully photocopied with my signature on a line.'

'That's good. Now we can have some peace at last around here. Daniel and Lily are asleep. Bert kindly escorted me up the stairs in case I had trouble, but of course, I didn't. I can manage the stairs quite well now.'

'You're a star,' said Jessica. She was mentally exhausted. She didn't want to talk any more. She wanted to sleep and sleep. But there was the nightly ritual to get through first. She was still employed at Upton Hall, for the time being.

'And did my son apologize to you?'

'No, not exactly. But he did stop biting my head off. I think it will take some time.'

'That damned Coleman pride.'

'He might get round to it,' said Jessica.

'He might be too late,' said Lady Grace shrewdly.

Arthur followed her out into the hall. He was putting his coat on. 'Time to hit the road. It's been a lovely evening, Grace. I'll beat you next time. Just out of practice,' he chuckled.

'Next week?' Grace was not slow.

'And swimming? Would it be convenient for you to bring Lady Grace and the children for a swim soon, Jessica? Roxy is touring somewhere in the world. She won't be home for at least three weeks.'

'We'll fix a date,' Jessica promised. It all depended if she was still at Upton Hall. She wanted to work out her three months contract. Daniel and Lily were almost like her own children. But Lucas might have other ideas. Their marriage was definitely off. She couldn't marry a man who didn't trust her.

Jessica went into the kitchen, leaving Lady Grace to see her guest off the premises. She heard laughter coming from the porch which was a good sign. She heated some milk and laid a tray with two digestive biscuits. Lady Grace was capable of seeing herself to bed these days.

Lady Grace was sitting up in bed, her hair plaited, her face relaxed and composed.

'So we both had a very satisfactory evening,' she said.

'So it seems,' said Jessica, putting the tray on the bedside table. 'Can I fetch you anything else?'

'No, thank you, Jess. Do the usual locking up, please. We don't want any intruders. Arthur suggested starting a bridge club for we old-timers. We've plenty of room here. Once a month, perhaps? What do you think, Jess?'

'What a great idea,' said Jessica. 'Old friends. Couldn't be better.'

'Goodnight, Jess.'

'Goodnight, Lady Grace.'

Jessica closed the door carefully. Daniel and Lily were both sleeping peacefully. Everything in Daniel's room was lined in rows, as usual, different rows to those the night before. Lily had Floppy Ears in bed with her. Even he looked more at ease for once.

She checked her emails. There was an email from Daniel. It said: Don't GO. The 'G' was the right way round for once, but she got the message.

Lucas had not appeared. She waited in the kitchen in case he came looking for a late supper, but there was no sign of him. That damned Coleman pride. What did Lady Grace mean by that? Lucas or her husband?

Jessica opened the door to the refrigerator. She knew she ought to eat. She could not exist on her nerves. It was not sensible, but all she could swallow was some set vanilla yogurt. It slipped down without any effort.

Bridge parties and swimming. They were setting themselves up for fun ahead in the future months when she would not be here. Once Lady Grace was fit enough to drive, they could take themselves over to Roxy's pool. They would not need Jessica any more. She could take up her post in Sheffield and try to forget them all.

But she knew that she would never forget them. She still loved Lucas. And she certainly loved the children. Mrs Harris was a good friend and Lady Grace had earned her affection. It was going to be hard to leave them all.

Jessica went through the usual routine of locking up and setting the alarms. She had cleared her name but the cost had been exorbitant. She had lost Lucas and he was the only man in the world for her.

There were murderous feelings in her heart that night as she went to bed. The Burtons had ruined her life. If either of them ever showed their faces again at Upton Hall, it would be hard to stop herself taking a kitchen knife to them both. She could not understand why they were both so evil-minded. They had good jobs, excellent salaries, plenty of money to spend. But they didn't have happiness.

Perhaps that was the answer.

FIFTEEN

Lucas was gone again, next morning, before anyone was down for breakfast. Jessica heard the Porsche driving away, the distinctive engine noise waking her up after a restless sleep. She did not know how to put things right between them.

The ball was in his court but perhaps he didn't know how to serve. She smiled to herself at this ridiculous analogy. Her brain was not yet in top gear.

Lily bounced into the bedroom, carrying Floppy Ears by his ears. 'We didn't get a story last night,' she said. 'Grandma can't read.'

'Your grandmother can read but only her kind of books. Your books are rather different. Shorter words and lots of pictures.'

Lily digested this information. 'OK, so when our books don't have pictures any more, then Grandma will be able to read them?'

Jessica laughed. 'You'll have to see. Now what are you hiding behind your back? Is that a book, I espy? Is it a book I will have to read before I get any peace?'

'Yes, yes, yes!'

The door was open so Daniel could also hear the story if he was awake. Jessica made sure she used her nurse's voice that would carry. Sometimes she had to use that voice if A & E was crowded with drunks and drug-addicts, occasionally on a ward if there was unexpected turmoil.

'This afternoon, after school, we'll go down to Worthing

and have a picnic on the beach before the cold weather sets in. Would you like that? There won't be many more days of good weather this year. It's your early afternoon, isn't it?'

'A picnic! Lovely, lovely. Without plates? Daniel will come too and we'll find more shells and paddle in the sea.'

'You might find it is too cold.'

'No, no, it won't be too cold.' Lily was pretty sure.

Daniel sent Jessica an email which said simply: *piknik*.

It required mammoth organization if Lady Grace was coming too. She would need a folding chair on the beach. Mrs Harris prepared a picnic basket of goodies, all easy finger food with two thermoses of hot water so that Jessica could make tea. Lady Grace would certainly require freshly made tea. It was always Earl Grey, of course, in the afternoon.

Jessica was determined that life would go on at Upton Hall even if Lucas cut himself off from her. It would break her heart, but then her heart was already broken, so how could it hurt any more? She had a shut-down look, shielding the pain.

Mrs Harris was delighted that her photocopying theory had been proved right. She was also interested in the highwaymen being hanged at the Double Cross Inn.

'Fancy that. There's so much history everywhere. And we don't know half of it,' she said.

'Does anyone know the history of Upton Hall?'

Mrs Harris shook her head. 'No one has ever had time to research the history of Upton Hall. The house has been here a long time. Look at the stone room, all those huge slabs of slate on the floor and the big timber post holding up the ceiling. That could tell a story or two.'

'Is it part of the original farmhouse, do you think?'

'I won't go in there at night, I tell you.'

It was the first time Mrs Harris had admitted to feeling any-thing unusual about Upton Hall. Yet the man she loved had been brought home here and she had laid him out. There must have been many deaths in the house and in the grounds over the centuries, but Jessica did not feel anything strange. And she had been up late many times, seeing to Lady Grace or to the children. Or waiting up for Lucas to come home in the small hours.

It was something she could do during her last few weeks at Upton Hall. She could research the history of the house on the Internet, find books in the library and records at the church. It would keep her mind occupied, so that she did not dwell on her unhappiness.

She had often told her patients the same thing, when they lost someone they loved. Keep busy, do something positive. Live each day for the day. Now she was telling herself the same, now that she had lost Lucas.

For Jessica felt sure that she had lost him. There had been no reconciliation, no words of apology from Lucas, not a single act of kindness. Last night had been a relief that she had cleared her name, but he had said nothing, done nothing to help ease the pain that she felt. Damned Coleman pride, Jessica thought. This was something over which she had no say. It was in his genes.

Everything was packed into the car when the children arrived home from school, earlier than usual. Lady Grace was sitting in the front passenger seat, while the children climbed into the back. She had decided that a picnic might be a pleasant change.

'Please wait. I haven't got Floppy Ears,' announced Lily, trying to get out again but Jessica had already put on the child door locks.

'He won't mind about being left at home for once. You know how he hates getting wet,' said Jessica. 'And we haven't really time to go back for him. The days are getting shorter and we want to have as much time as possible on the beach, don't we?'

Lily absorbed this information. 'If the days are getting shorter, where does the rest of the day go?' she asked.

'We get longer, darker evenings,' said Jessica, hoping this would satisfy the little girl's curiosity.

'So the day becomes an evening instead of being a day?' Lily went on relentlessly. She was trying to take this in.

'Why don't we play I Spy before I get a headache,' said Lady Grace quickly. 'Let me see. I spy with my little eye something beginning with T.'

'Tree,' said Daniel.

It was a shock. Daniel had actually contributed a word of his own that was not a parrot word. It was a moment of joy. But Jessica said nothing. She knew Daniel would not like the attention.

'It's your turn now, Daniel. You choose something for us to guess.'

But this was beyond him so Jessica took over his turn. It was simpler.

The game lasted the drive into Worthing but Daniel did not speak again although it was obvious that he often had the answer. Jessica found a place to park along the sea front and fed some money into the meter.

The tide was higher than she had expected, thrashing against the shingle shore, shifting pebbles. No running along on the sand this afternoon. They found a sheltered spot against a groyne, not too far along as Lady Grace found it difficult to walk even with a stick. She took Jessica's arm, hesitating. She was looking at the pounding sea as if she had never seen it before. She had not realized that it was going to be a picnic by the sea

'Are you sure this is safe for me to walk on?' she said.

'It will help with your balance,' said Jessica, offering her arm. 'Take your time, don't hurry. Feel each step. We've got all day.' She was also carrying a folding beach chair.

'We haven't got all day if the day is becoming the evening,' Lily informed them.

Lady Grace was glad to sit down when they reached the groyne. There was a blustery southerly wind and it sheltered them well. They had a good view of the long pier reaching out to sea on its spindly legs. There were several windsurfers making use of the southerly, their colourful sails like swerving butterflies. Jessica went back for the picnic tea and the folding table which was solely for making this cup of tea. Lady Grace had to have a certain amount of civilization, even for a picnic.

Lily and Daniel were soon down to the water's edge, throwing pebbles into the waves, escaping the wavelets that washed too near their feet. The tide was coming in slowly so they got caught several times with shrieks of laughter.

'The tide's coming in,' said Lady Grace. 'That's the blessing of a shelving beach, you can always see how far it will come in. We're all right here. This chair sounds a bit creaky. Where did you find it?'

'In the stables,' said Jessica. 'I don't think it has been used for years. Mrs Harris gave it a clean up.'

'I used to love the sea,' Lady Grace went on, more to herself. 'When you swim out past the fringe of seaweed, the water is lovely, so cool and deep. Ouch! I think I heard something. I think the canvas is splitting. It's probably rotten.' She got up quickly, holding onto the top of the wooden groyne.

'Hold on, lady. I'll soon sort you out. Got just what you need.'

A lean and sunburnt man in a fawn sunhat and khaki shorts was striding across the shingle with a folded deck chair in his hand. It was the beach deck-chair attendant, quick to spot a new customer.

'Your chair's had it,' he said. 'Look, it's splitting along the bottom seam. Another minute and you'd have fallen right through. You'd have got a nasty bump.'

'How convenient that I heard it going and got up when I did,' said Lady Grace in her don't-argue-with-me voice. She didn't care to be sorted out, as he had promised.

'These are really comfortable deckchairs,' he went on. 'Adjustable height, canvas new this season. I'll put it up for you. You can have it half price as it's the end of the day.'

'I think I might go back to the car,' said Lady Grace.

'What and miss this lovely bit of sunshine? The last of the season. It'll be cold and wet next week, mark my words. I'll be packing up my chairs for the winter.'

'That's very kind of you,' said Jessica quickly. 'If you would kindly put it up for Lady Grace. I can never sort these chairs out!' She opened her purse for some money, hoping a pound would be enough.

The man stopped in the middle of sorting out the mechanics of unfolding the deck chair. 'Grace Coleman? Is it Grace Coleman? Well, I never. You won't remember me. I'm Mark Adams, one of the members of the junior cross channel relay team. Don't do it now, of course, long past the age of any junior team. That was years ago.'

Mark Adams settled the chair firmly into the shingle and against the groyne. He held out his hand and Lady Grace let him help her into it. She seemed shaken by his introduction.

'No, I'm afraid I don't remember you,' she said.

'I was one of the noisy youngsters. You told me off a couple of times for not paying attention to the coach.'

'Did I?'

'We were used to it. You took your swimming very seriously. Quite right, too, because you were one of the champions. Of course, it's all changed now. Different committee, different rules. But they still meet early mornings.'

'It's been nice meeting you again,' said Lady Grace, recovering her composure. 'But if you don't mind, we are going to have our tea now.'

'Quite understand,' said Mark Adams. 'Don't worry about returning the chair to the stack. I'll do it for you. Got a couple of lively kids, you have,' he nodded towards Lily and Daniel and to Jessica. 'I like to see kids enjoying themselves.'

He turned to go, then turned back. He was lean and sinewy, arms muscled and burnt brown by the sun. He looked as if he worked hard all summer, running the deck chair business along the beach. 'Ankles got better, did they? All right now?'

Lady Grace looked even more shaken. 'My ankles? What do you mean? What do you know about my ankles?'

'Got torn to ribbons on that barbed wire, didn't they? Nasty business. The council ought to have cleared the beach. I reckon you could have sued them.'

'I – I don't remember. It was a long time ago. . . .'

'I thought you were a goner,' said Mark Adams. 'You were going to drown in that deep water. The barbed wire was twisted round your ankles, all rusty and rotten. And your hair had got caught in the wire when you bent down to try to get your feet free.'

'My hair . . .' said Lady Grace faintly. She had not mentioned her hair to anyone. No one knew that her long dark hair had been caught in the barbed wire. She'd worn it then, as she did now, in an elaborate French pleat, pinned up with combs.

'I had to cut your hair off,' Mark went on. 'It was the only thing to do and there was no time to waste. You were gasping for air. Had to get your head up somehow. Luckily I had a knife on me. I always carry a knife.' He patted his back pocket. It was buttoned down.

'You cut my hair off?'

He grinned. 'Sorry, it was more of a hack off job than a nice trim and style. I was a little out of practice in the hair depart-ment. Then I got your feet free of the wire. They were torn and bleeding. Pretty nasty.'

'So it was you who saved me,' said Lady Grace, pausing. 'I never knew. I never even tried to find out. I wanted to forget it all. This is the first time I've been to the sea since that day.'

'Not surprised. It was enough to put anyone off. You nearly drowned.'

'Did your feet get cut as well?'

'Right mess, they were. And they got infected. I wanted to go into the army but they wouldn't take me. All that marching, I expect. Still, I walk miles along the beach every day, no trouble. Well, I'll leave you ladies to your tea. Nice meeting you again, Mrs Coleman.'

He was gone before there was a chance to say any more, probably spotted another customer. He hadn't taken Jessica's pound coin.

'And I still haven't thanked him,' said Lady Grace. She looked desolate. 'What shall I do, Jess? I must thank him somehow. I could hardly give him a tip, could I? It would be most inappropriate.'

'I think he could see that you were really upset, being reminded of the accident again, remembering that awful day. It was enough for him to see that you were well and had recovered.'

'But it's not enough,' said Lady Grace, firmly. 'I must do something.'

'Let's think about it,' said Jessica. 'We may get a bright idea.'

The children came back, sensing teatime, scrambling up the shelving shingle, waving wet shoes in their hands. 'We're all wet,' said Lily happily.

'How fortunate that I brought some dry socks and trainers,' said Jessica, delving into her beach bag.

Tea was a success in every way, despite Lily's preference for eating out of a box to eating off a plate. Lady Grace enjoyed her cup of Earl Grey and even found an appetite for a home-made scone with strawberry jam and cream. She spent a long time just gazing at the sea as the waves pounded the shore, rising slowly higher, creeping up the steep shingle. She was remembering the days when she had been a champion swimmer with a promising future.

'I don't know what I could get that young man, the beach attendant,' she said, as they were on the drive home in the gathering dusk. Daniel had collected seaweed this time, and the inside of the car smelt of the stuff. For once Lady Grace did not complain.

'You could get him a bicycle,' said Lily. 'I saw him walking miles along the beach. And he was limping a bit. I expect his feet hurt with all that walking.'

Lady Grace was about to say that a bicycle would be a ridiculous idea, but stopped herself. It would be a start and she had to start somewhere.

'You might have something there,' she said quietly.

SIXTEEN

Lady Grace retired to her bed earlier than usual. The afternoon had been mentally tiring and the surfeit of fresh sea air had made her sleepy. She did not want any supper but required her usual milk and biscuits later on.

Daniel came into the kitchen and started wandering around, poking into things and opening drawers and cupboards, getting in Jessica's way. Mrs Harris had gone to her Bingo. He was carrying his plastic bag of seaweed.

'Do want somewhere to keep your seaweed?' Jessica asked.

'Weed,' he said.

'How about a plate or a jug or an old plastic container?'

He shook his head and went to the sink, turning on a tap. He let the water run, tipping his bag of seaweed into the running water, watching the strands curl and swirl into a dark mass. He had collected rather a lot.

Jessica went into the walk-in pantry, to the back where Mrs Harris kept her spare jam jars. She came out with several jam jars perched on her fingers. 'Would these be any good?'

He nodded enthusiastically, arranged the jam jars in rows on the draining board and began to fill each one with water and a few strands of seaweed. Jessica watched him from afar. He didn't like anyone close, leaning over him.

'You've got several different kinds there. Tomorrow we could look them up on the Internet so that we can give them names.'

'Names,' he said, without looking up.

Jessica left him absorbed in his task of tanking up the seaweed. She had Lily to put to bed, read a story, and then hope that Lucas would come home and they could talk at last. Surely that stubborn Coleman pride would have come to its senses by now. She couldn't endure this not-knowing for much longer. She wanted to be with him, to feel his arms around her again.

Lily had worn herself out on the beach so it was a quick bath and an even quicker story. Now that he was eight years old, Daniel stayed up a little later, needed little supervision going to bed. He preferred to wash alone.

Jessica made herself a cup of black coffee and took it into the library, turned on the television and flopped down in front of it. She did not want to watch any mindless programme, but hoped there might be a good drama or documentary. She needed something to take her mind off Lucas and the current predicament.

Perhaps she had made a mistake, searching for the truth. Perhaps he would have preferred to forgive her in a lordly way and make her pay for it in a marriage of misery. But that was surely not his way, not his nature and certainly not hers. His love had seemed so strong and so true. He had meant every word he said and his warm and passionate kisses had come straight from the heart. He had wanted her and the strength of his body close to hers told her how much.

Fire and ice, Lucas had once said to her. Had they had the fire and this was now the ice? Maybe the fire had consumed them for a while and now the ice froze over their love.

Jessica fell asleep in front of the television, her coffee untouched. The sea air had obviously brushed away the cobwebs that had prevented her from sleeping the last few nights. She dreamed she was in a boat, a small boat, but she could not see who was rowing. He had his back to her.

A shrill, strident bell projected itself through the dream. At first she thought it was a bell from a nearby lighthouse in her dream, then she roused herself and realized that it was Lady Grace's bell.

Even the bell sounded annoyed.

She shook herself awake and tried to stop herself from racing up the stairs. This was not the time for a careless accident. She'd seen enough falls downstairs at A & E.

'I'm sorry,' Jessica said. 'Your milk is late, I know. I dozed off.'

'It's very late,' said Lady Grace, who did not admit that she had also dozed off. She looked accusingly at her bedside clock. 'I'm not used to having it so late.'

'I'll fetch it straight away,' said Jessica, turning away before she got the nightly instructions about two biscuits - as if she had the brain of a peanut.

In the kitchen she noticed that Daniel's jars of seaweed were still on the draining board, but he had emptied the sink of water. She must remember to put them in a safe place before Mrs Harris came in. That good lady might empty them down the drain.

Jessica made the drink and carried the tray upstairs to Lady Grace. She put it on the bedside table.

'Thank you, Jess,' said Lady Grace. 'You know how to do this Internet ordering thing, don't you?'

'I can find my way around a bit.'

'Can you find your way around this Argos firm that sells things and order a bicycle, a good one mind you, to be sent to Mark Adams. No mention of my name. I want him to receive it anonymously. Don't you think that's a good idea? To send him an anonymous gift? After all, a bicycle hardly equates to saving a life, does it?'

Lady Grace seemed pleased with the idea and for remembering Argos, the mail order firm. She might get their catalogue and have a look through it.

'I think he'd like that. Surprise presents are always fun. I'll look Argos up on the Internet and see how you order online,' said Jessica.

'It could be addressed to him care of The Pier. I saw some of his deckchairs on the pier. They'd make sure he got it, wouldn't they?'

'I'm sure they know him. Goodnight, Lady Grace.'

'Goodnight, Jess.'

Jessica crossed over the landing and peeped into Lily's room. She was fast asleep, Floppy Ears on the pillow beside her. They both looked as if they had had a good day.

Daniel's bedroom was in the dark which was unusual. He had not switched on his glow lamps or put on a tape of soft sounds. Jessica hesitated in the doorway. She did not want to wake him by putting on the main light. The landing light shone weakly into the room. His shells were rigidly in rows. His drawing books, his shoes, his school uniform folded, everything in its allotted place.

She looked at his bed. The duvet was flat and untouched. There was no dark head on the pillow. The room was empty.

He must be somewhere in the house, curled up on a chair, or drawing on the floor, little monkey. He'd taken advantage of her falling asleep.

Jessica made a quick detour of the house, expecting to find Daniel at every turn. But he was nowhere. She could not find him anywhere. It was getting dark outside. Perhaps he was doing some mysterious errand out in the garden, drawing the moon?

His anorak had gone from the clothes cupboard by the back door. Jessica began to feel worried. Where on earth had the little boy gone? He was tall for his age but he was still only eight years old.

She heard the Porsche coming up the drive and ran outside. Daniel had probably gone to meet his father. That was it. What could be more natural than going down the drive to meet his father?

Jessica went onto the drive and waved at the Porsche. It slowed down. 'Have you got Daniel?' she asked, keeping any worry out of her voice.

'Daniel? No, why should I?'

'I thought perhaps he'd come out to meet you. I thought . . .' she faltered.

'Don't you know where he is?' Lucas said forcefully.

'No, I don't know where he is. I've lost him. I can't find him.'

'Have you made a thorough search of the house and the stables?'

'I didn't go into the stables,' said Jessica.

'Why not?'

Because she did not want to meet Lucas. He lived in the stables. She could not go in there, in case there were secrets.

Lucas swung the car round towards the stables and stopped outside. He raced into the building. Jessica began searching the gardens. The humidity was closing in on her, dark clouds gathering. The sky was the colour of dark slate. A storm was on its way. She could feel it in the air.

'Daniel, Daniel. . .' she called repeatedly. But of course he would not answer. He would not say anything. Nor would they be able to hear anything. How could they find an autistic boy in the dark who wouldn't speak?

She heard Lucas returning in his car. He pushed the passenger door open.

'Get in,' he shouted.

She obeyed, afraid not to. She was already very cold, with fear and with worry. But she steeled herself. She got in and strapped on the safety belt.

'I've searched the house,' said Lucas. 'But there's no sign of Daniel. I have told my mother that we are going out and will lock up when we return. I said nothing about the children. Have you any idea where Daniel might have gone?'

Jessica shook her head. 'We went to Worthing today and had a picnic tea on the beach. Lily and Daniel had a great time. Daniel came home with a bag full of bits of seaweed. I left him in the kitchen, filling jam jars with the stuff.'

'What else?'

'I don't know what else,' Jessica, desperately. 'There isn't anything else. Who knows what goes on in Daniel's mind? He could have decided to do anything, go anywhere. He has no idea of time or distance, let alone telling anyone of his plans. I know it's partly my fault for falling asleep, but I was so tired. I haven't been sleeping well lately. . . .'

She let her voice trail off into a landscape of quiet despair. She'd been thinking about Lucas, going over the situation again and again, wondering how she could put things right. Wondering if they would ever regain that heady happiness.

'We'll go look for him. He can't have gone far. I'll drive slowly, you look on the paths and near hedges. Here's a torch. I'm sure he'll keep to roads, something that he knows about from the school bus and drives with you. He doesn't like anything unknown.'

Jessica nodded. It was already starting to rain, a fine mist clouding the windscreen. Daniel had his anorak on but not much else. She shivered.

'You're cold,' said Lucas. 'There's a fleece on the back seat. Put it on.'

It was the first kind word he had said to her for days. Jessica reached into the back and pulled on his old navy fleece. It smelt of him and she breathed it in as if he was himself wrapping his arms round her. But the moment vanished as they turned out of the drive onto the roadway.

They drove with the passenger window down so that Jessica could flash the torch onto the paths and verges. Tatters of rain were coming down steadily and soon her sleeve and face were pitted with drops.

Finding Daniel became even more remote as the rain thickened and the windscreen wipers struggled to keep the vision clear. Branches swayed overhead, wailing like banshees.

'Daniel, Daniel. . . .' she continued to call. Lucas was watching the other side of the road, driving slowly and steadily. Moths collected in his headlights for their doom. They came to the village of Eastly, wondering which way Daniel might have chosen.

'Which way?' asked Lucas.

'I don't know.'

'Guess. Try to think as Daniel would think. You know him

better than anyone else.' His voice was dry and bitter.

'He had a bag of seaweed,' said Jessica. 'But he had brought home an awful lot of seaweed, far more than the few jam jars would hold.'

'So?'

'Perhaps he's returning the seaweed to the sea.'

'You mean, he's walking to Worthing, to put the seaweed back into the sea?' Lucas sounded incredulous.

'I'm only guessing,' she cried. 'He wouldn't like to think of it dying. It would worry him. He wouldn't wait till morning. He would have to do it now.'

Lucas turned onto the main dual-carriage way towards Worthing, his face set grimly. The rain was now torrential, almost blinding him. Jessica was soaked, her hair flattened against her head. The car heater was on but the heat flew straight out of the windows.

Then she saw him. A small figure, plodding on, head down, barely visible in the downpour. 'There he is,' she cried. 'Over there.'

Lucas spotted him too in his headlights, drew ahead and then slammed on the brakes. Jessica wrenched open the car door and ran towards the boy over the long wet grass. She clasped him into her arms, cradling him, her face against his wet hood.

'Daniel, you're all right! We've found you. Thank goodness. Thank goodness.' Jessica held him close, for the first time ever. He did not stiffen but seemed to lean into her, the fear of the night taking away his usual reserve.

'Get into the car, love. We'll soon have you home, warm and dry,' she said, guiding him towards the car. She somehow steered him onto the front passenger seat and then got herself in as well. Daniel ended up, curled on her lap, her arms still firmly round him. He did not resist.

'Hello, Son,' said Lucas, turning the car slowly at the next intersection. He realized that Jessica could not fasten the seat belt. 'Not a goodnight for a walk about.'

Jessica felt the boy's weight against her and she could smell the tang of the seaweed. Somewhere, on him, probably inside his anorak was the bag of seaweed.

'Were you walking to Worthing, Daniel?' she asked. She felt only the merest of nods.

'With your bag of seaweed?'

'Weed,' came his muffled voice.

'Were you going to put it back into the sea?'

'Sea.'

'We'll do it tomorrow,' she assured him. 'The tide would be on its way out by now and we'd never find the sea in the dark. Seaweed is pretty sturdy stuff, you know. It'll survive till tomorrow.'

Daniel was almost asleep by the time they reached Upton Hall. It was the first time he had ever allowed anyone to hold him or touch him. But he had almost fallen asleep in Jessica's arms and, for both of them, it was a milestone.

Lucas carried Daniel indoors, upstairs to the family bathroom. He took off the boy's sodden clothes and put them and the bag of seaweed on the floor. It was only a quick wash in warm water as Daniel was half asleep. In no time he was curled up in bed, warm and dry, part of him knowing how much he was loved.

Jessica was downstairs in the kitchen, making a pot of tea, knowing Lucas needed a hot drink too. She was still in the soaked fleece. Everything was wet. She knew she looked a sight but she didn't care. Daniel was safe and that was all that mattered.

Lucas stood in the doorway holding an armful of wet clothes. 'He's asleep.'

'Good,' said Jessica. 'I'll put the rescued seaweed in a bucket.'

Lucas came over to her, awkwardly. He was as handsome as ever, but there were lines etched on his face, as if he had aged. Rain was spiking his hair and his clothes were wet, but his eyes were smiling with a quiet hope.

'Are you ever going to forgive me, Jessica?' he said. 'I've been such a fool. A complete idiot.'

SEVENTEEN

Lucas was standing barely a few inches away from her. A lump formed in her throat. He was looking at her with an odd, searching look. Jessica refused to allow any romantic thoughts to flood her mind. Lucas had to say them. He had to heal all the hurt.

'Jessica,' he said, his voice gravelly and full of anguish. 'We must put this right. I don't want to lose you.'

Jessica was aware that she was very cold. One side of the fleece was soaked through and the rest almost as wet from holding Daniel in the car. But she had to stay and listen to what Lucas had to say.

'You almost have,' she said, trying to stop her teeth from chattering.

He groaned. 'I know. I don't know what devil got into me. I felt I couldn't go through intrigue and deception again, even when you proved to me that it was all lies. I hadn't the sense to trust you.' He bent and touched the lovely line of her mouth. 'Please forgive me. Please take me back into your life.'

'Take you back?' said Jessica. 'After what you've put me through? You expect me to fall into your arms and say everything is all right? Will it happen again? How many times will it happen? I don't want to be constantly living on a knife edge.' Her feelings washed over her body in a wave of pain. She had suffered so much in the last few days.

Her mind was teeming with angry, bitter things to say even

though she loved him. No way was he going to walk in and say he was sorry and everything would be back to square one. There was no way she could handle this now. The search for Daniel had drained her. She was exhausted. She was wet and she was cold. This was not the time for soul-searching.

'I've made some tea,' said Jessica, pouring out two mugfuls. 'Perhaps we should put some warmth inside ourselves before we talk any more.'

Lucas took a step back with his mug of tea. 'Always the nurse,' he said with a note of sadness. 'Where's my fiery, passionate woman?'

'Your fiery, passionate woman is soaking wet and close to hypothermia.'

It was the first time he had looked at her physical condition and it shocked him. He gulped down some tea and then put his hands lightly on her shoulders, turning her in the direction of the stairs.

'Bath and bed, in that order,' he said.

The terse words meant more to Jessica than any flowery declarations. Some sort of communication sprang up between them. She let him propel her out of the kitchen, taking her tea with her, sipping the hot liquid. She wanted to be looked after, to be taken care of as lovers took care of each other, whatever the world presented.

He turned on the landing towards her yellow bedroom. She was too numb to wonder what was going to happen. The swirling feelings inside her were all part of the trauma of the night's events. They had found Daniel. They did not have to worry about him for a while.

Somewhere on the way upstairs, she lost her sodden shoes. The soft carpet was bliss underfoot. Lucas steered her into the primrose bathroom, leaned over and put in the plug and turned on both taps.

'Get undressed,' he said.

But her fingers were to cold to obey. She struggled with zips and buttons and hooks. At some point Lucas took over, his face intently serious. He unzipped the fleece and removed it. Then he helped her out of her clinging wet jeans. He could barely keep his hands from stroking her long brown legs. He caught a glimpse of her white lace briefs and his desire was on fire.

He pulled her T-shirt over her head, his fingers skimming her skin, and her heart turned over as his touch became a sensitive delight. How could he know what he was doing to her? Stripping her of her clothes as if she was another eight-year-old?

Lucas could not hold back his feelings as she stood before him in lacy bra and pants. His lips parted in anticipation and he drew her to him, taking her mouth into his, drowning his feelings in an intimate imprisonment.

He ran his fingers lightly over her thigh, hip and waist, caressing her skin with a feathery touch, outlining her soft curves. Then he realized she was shivering, from cold or from passion, he did not know.

'Into the bath,' he said.

He helped her step in and lower herself into the warm water. His eyes were clouded with desire. He could not bear to look at her loveliness. A great wave of tenderness overcame him. Jessica was his woman, the only woman in his life and he wanted her for his wife.

He had not put on the light and only light from the bedroom shone into the bathroom. It was a softness that shadowed any flaws. He took the tablet of jasmine soap and rubbed the suds over Jessica's arms and shoulders. Then he found her feet and legs and gently soothed them with massage and kneading, each little toe receiving loving attention. .

Jessica began to relax, sliding further into the warm water. His hands were magic. She did not care what he did to her. She did not have the strength to resist him even if she wanted to. She was starved for this kind of attention. Tears stung her eyes.

Then Lucas was unhooking her bra and sliding his hands over her breasts, cupping them with sweet sensations, letting the suds soften his touch. Jessica moaned, stretching her lacerated nerves, almost unable to keep her fragile composure. They were meant to be together. She was being swept into a torrent of wanting.

Jessica lifted up her arms towards him, not saying anything, sending an unspoken message racing out to him.

Lucas slipped out of his clothes, and with infinite care, stepped into the bath. The water almost overlapped the side. He lowered himself down onto her and without a word, his body told her everything she had ever wanted to know. He held his mouth on hers, reluctant to break the spell, wrapping her body closely, hungry for her, their storm of desire gathering.

It was long after dawn when they awoke, in her bed, still wrapped around each other. Jessica could not believe that she was seeing Lucas's dark head on the pillow beside her. He was still asleep, long eyelashes fluttering, breathing soft and even. She studied his ruggedly handsome features and stretched her weakened body. She was spent and sated.

'Lily always charges in here, early morning,' she whispered in his ear.

'She knows me,' Lucas said, half asleep. 'I'm her daddy. She's seen me before.'

'But not in my bed.'

'She'll have to get used to it.'

'Will she?'

He turned and gazed at her, turning her face to kiss her tenderly. How easily and snugly their bodies fitted together,

'But I think we'll need a larger bed. How about a king-sized? When shall we go shopping?' Lucas asked with a wicked grin. 'Though there is a certain delightful togetherness about a small bed,' he added, pulling her close.

They had to savour these last few moments of privacy. Jessica could hear Lily padding along the landing, telling Floppy Ears to hop, hop, hop. Lily climbed onto the bed beside Jessica, then she saw Lucas on the other side.

She looked puzzled.

'Daddy? Did Jessica promise to read you a story and then

you fell asleep?' she asked.

'Something like that,' he agreed sleepily. 'It was a lovely story.'

'Are you going to tell me the story now?'

'It's got very long words in it,' said Lucas. 'You might not understand them. Floppy Ears would certainly be lost.'

Lily was instantly diverted. 'Floppy Ears has been extremely naughty this morning already. He wouldn't clean his teeth and he wouldn't wash his ears. He's not going to get any breakfast.'

'That rabbit has a hard life,' said Lucas. 'Shall I take him to the hospital with me as a punishment?'

Lily looked aghast. 'Oh no, he has to stay here. He has to keep Grandmother company while I go to school. That's his job.'

'Does your grandmother know this?'

'Yes, I 'plained it to her.'

'And what did she say?'

'She said she would put him in a cupboard and shut the door when he was naughty.'

Jessica took the opportunity to slip out of bed and put on her bathrobe. Lucas caught a tantalizing glimpse of her bare back, the curve of her spine, her hair falling over her shoulders.

'I'll go downstairs and make some tea. Everyone will be awake by now, all this racket going on.'

'Early morning tea in bed,' teased Lucas. 'I am being spoilt. Shall I get this service every morning?'

'No,' said Jessica. 'You'll be in the cupboard with Floppy Ears.'

They started laughing, their eyes warm with love. They could not take their eyes off each other. Lily joined in the laughter though she was not sure what she was laughing at.

Lucas had to go to the hospital. He had a list that morning and Maggie was still a concern. Laughter united them. He could not stop touching Jessica, loving every moment that she smiled at him. It was going to be all right. One day they would talk about it all, but now was not the time.

Jessica's arm encircled his waist as he ate some toast and marmalade standing up. Lucas was going, after the briefest of breakfasts in the kitchen.

'Tomorrow,' he said, 'I am going to take you out, firstly with a call to see young Maggie. When did you last have a day off?'

'I've never had a day off,' said Jessica, enjoying the consternation on his face. 'My employer forgot about days off. He's mean with days off. I've had a few hours off, but you could hardly call them a day.'

'Then I shall have to do something about that before you sue me or report me to some union. Do you belong to a union?'

'Of course, I do,' said Jessica.

'Tomorrow I want you to come with me,' said Lucas. 'It's very important. Can you arrange for Mrs Harris to stay the whole day? Lady Grace is so much better. She can cope, can't she?'

'She's got the trusty Fred.'

He was gone before Jessica could even say another word. His kiss was brief but permanent. It would last until he came home in the evening. Jessica knew she would love him for the rest of her life.

The morning rolled into its usual routine. Daniel seemed none the worse for his adventure. He did not share his feelings. He did not mention taking the seaweed back to the sea. But everyone knew that something had changed in the household.

'Nice to see you smiling,' said Lady Grace, over her breakfast tray.

'Has his lordship come to his senses?' said Mrs Harris. 'And about time too, if you ask me. We don't want to lose you, none of us does.'

'It was difficult for him,' said Jessica, not wanting to give away what had happened. 'But I think it's going to be all right now. I hope so. I can't go through any more.'

'We women always manage somehow,' said Mrs Harris, reminding Jessica of how she had managed for years, through love, to keep going.

'I couldn't do it.'

'You would, if you had to. Believe me, you would. Lots of women do.'

Mrs Harris nodded firmly but she could not conceal her delight.

'I wonder if it would it be possible for you to stay all day tomorrow?' Jessica asked. 'Lucas wants to take me somewhere. I don't know where, but he says it's rather important.'

'Of course,' said Mrs Harris. 'About time too. Lady Grace will be all right. She has that friend of hers coming to play bridge. Nice gentleman. Nice manners. I'll do them a bit of supper.'

'Thank you so much,' said Jessica, giving her a quick hug. 'You're a star.'

'More a burnt-out planet at my age,' said Mrs Harris.

Lucas was home early for once. The children ran to him, urging him to play cricket, What's the Time, Mr Wolf? and hopscotch. Tea was in the kitchen. It had turned too cold to eat outside. The table was laden with a healthy tea.

Lucas sauntered over to Jessica, his eyes sharp and bright. 'I was expecting to find you all wet,' he said, picking at the hem of her T-shirt. He bent and kissed her gently.

'Not a hope,' said Jessica.

'Later?'

'Don't count on your chances.'

It was an evening of enchantment. Daniel still drawing pictures of trees and rain, getting the nightmare storm out of his mind. He didn't seem to mind that the seaweed was living in a bucket. Jessica promised that they would take it back at the weekend. Lily was reading a story to Floppy Ears, which made a change. She knew the words by heart.

Lucas and Jessica went for a walk, leaving the rose garden and taking a path towards the Downs. He held her hand easily as if they belonged together.

Jessica saw the South Downs as he loved them, sweeping fields dotted with sheep. Hills with sturdy knolls of trees, those left from Henry VIII's deforestation, when trees were cut down to build his ships of war.

Lucas showed her corn circles from the top of the Downs. Where they came from, no one knew, but they were there for all the world to see far below. Great overlapping circles, patterned in the cornfield.

'Aren't they amazing? Even if they are made here, overnight, by some fun group of people after a few bottles of cider, they are still a work of art.'

Jessica had never seen corn circles before, apart from photographs in newspapers, and they were indeed strangely mesmerizing. She clung to Lucas's arm. 'It's lovely to see them, wherever they come from.'

'Is tomorrow still on?' she asked, as they began the walk back to Upton Hall. Mrs Harris had agreed to stay for the day. There was no reason why Jessica could not have the time off.

Lucas nodded. 'We'll go to see Maggie first. She's looking forward to meeting you. I've told her all about you and she's quite excited about having a visitor. Her grandmother has never been able to make the journey. The nurses make a fuss of her, but they don't have a lot of spare time.'

'Poor girl. How sad. I've some of Lily's toys and both children have made cards for her. Daniel wants to give her one of his drawings.'

'Then I'm taking you somewhere else, but I won't tell you about that until we get there. It's somewhere quite special.'

They reached the gate into the grounds of Upton Hall. They wandered through the rose garden, the night air still heady with the scent of rose.

'Come into my garden,' said Lucas. 'I want my roses to see you.'

EIGHTEEN

It was a cloudy morning and although Lucas said they were going somewhere special, Jessica did not think her smart suit was right for the occasion. Instead she put on her indigo jeans and a long-sleeved white sweater. There was a nip in the air.

'No need to dress up when you are going out with me,' said Lucas with a straight face.

'They are my best jeans,' said Jessica.

'I suppose that's something.'

She held out her left hand. The sapphire twinkled on her finger. 'And this is my best ring,' she added.

'Now that's really something,' he said, his eyes raking over her gently. 'I'm so glad you are going to share my life. I need you and I love you.'

'All this love talk before breakfast?' Jessica teased. 'I could get used to it.'

'Let's skip breakfast and do something more interesting,' he suggested.

'Not a good example to the children,' said Jessica.

Lucas almost said *damn the children* but held back. The children were arriving in the kitchen for their breakfast. Lily had her school shirt on inside-out and Daniel's jersey was on back to front.

'So much for letting them dress themselves,' said Jessica, sorting them out.

They all sat down together round the big kitchen table. A real family. Muesli and fruit, scrambled eggs, toast and honey. Mrs Harris was beaming. It felt as if they were her own family. They were her family.

'We're going to see Maggie in hospital this morning,' Jessica told the children. 'I've got your cards and Lily's toys and the lovely drawing from Daniel. Then this evening I will tell you all about it. I'm sure Maggie will be pleased. You see, she hasn't had any visitors.'

'You could take Floppy Ears,' volunteered Lily, making another ultimate sacrifice. 'He could be a visitor for Maggie.'

'How about another time?' said Lucas. 'Floppy Ears might be a bit tongue-tied going to a hospital.'

Lily looked relieved. 'He wouldn't like having his tongue-tied.'

Once the children were on the school bus, Jessica and Lucas could leave. She made sure that Lady Grace was up, doing her exercises, and promising to come downstairs.

'For goodness sake, stop fussing, girl. I can get myself downstairs by now. Go and enjoy your day off. I shall be glad to have a day's peace from your nagging.' Lady Grace was back on form. But there was little edge to her voice.

Jessica could not believe it when they were driving away from Upton Hall in the Porsche. It was too chilly to have the hood down. It reminded her of when Lucas had picked her up from the station, all those weeks ago. When she had felt drawn to him, despite wanting to turn round and catch a train back to London.

'So Maggie first?' said Jessica.

'And I have a few patients to look at before we can have a spot of lunch.'

'So not exactly a whole day off for you?'

'It's the whole afternoon off for me. You'll understand when we get there. Trust me, Jessica. Soon it will all become clear. I'm trusting you, my sweetheart. You will understand everything soon.'

Jessica felt the intensity behind his words. This was no day off for fun and laughter and a boozy pub lunch. It was some-thing more serious.

He drove more moderately. It was not one of his twenty-minute manic speed journeys to the hospital. The random buildings loomed ahead. They were serious hospital buildings, where Lucas worked and put faces back together. He had his own parking space.

Jessica was at home in the hospital environment. It didn't throw her. She recognized the smells, the hygiene, the silence in some areas. Her feet echoed along the corridors even though she was in her flat pumps.

'I'll introduce you to Maggie and then leave you,' said Lucas. 'These are my wards.'

Maggie had a side room. She was in a single bed with tubes attached to nose and mouth, feeding her both nourishment and liquid. Her face was heavily bandaged. The dogs had torn her mouth and arm. But her brown eyes shone brightly at the sight of a visitor.

'Hi, Maggie,' said Lucas. 'Jessica has come to visit you. She's the lovely young woman who looks after my two children. She's come to read you some stories.'

Lucas waved and left them together. Jessica sat beside Maggie. There was not much of Maggie showing, but Jessica found a hand. It was small and soft.

'Hello, Maggie. I'm Jessica. Lucas has told me all about how brave you are and I am so sorry about what happened.. But you will get better because Lucas is a wonderful doctor and he will do everything possible for you.'

Maggie had difficulty in talking. Her mouth was stitched up where the dogs had torn it. She would need plastic surgery to give her a normal, pretty mouth again.

''Lo,' she said, her eyes smiling. 'Story?'

She squeezed Jessica's hand. It was a touching moment.

'Lots of stories,' said Jessica. 'I've brought lots of books. I'll choose one, then you choose one. Is that all right?'

Maggie nodded, delighted. She snuggled down in bed, her

eyes on Jessica and the open book.

The morning fled. At some point, coffee arrived for Jessica and juice with a straw for Maggie. By then, they were firm friends. Maggie loved the cards from the children and she insisted that Daniel's shell drawing should be pinned on the wall. She was not so sure about Lily's toys. She liked the soft, rag doll with braided yellow hair, a pinafore dress and white socks and shoes.

'Baby,' she said, pushing the other toys away.

Jessica understood. Maggie was quite a grown-up five-year-old. It came from living with a much older person, her grandmother. She didn't have the same five-year-old bounce of Lily or the same tastes. She was much nearer in age to Daniel, especially as she now had difficulty in speaking.

Leaving Maggie was a wrench. Jessica was sorry when Lucas came to take her away. She knew she must not become attached to his patients but it was so difficult when it was a vulnerable child.

'I'll come again,' she promised, as they clung to each other.

'Please, please . . .' said Maggie.

'I promise,' said Jessica, near to tears herself.

Out in the corridor, Jessica needed a few minutes to compose herself. She had not realized that she would become emotionally involved.

'Not easy, is it?' said Lucas, taking her arm and walking her away. 'How do you think I feel?'

'I don't know how you do it. Maggie is a lovely little girl. I feel so sorry for her. I'll come again, of course, if I can.'

'Maggie will need a few weeks convalescing after the next operation to sort out her mouth so that she can talk and eat unassisted. Her grandmother would not be able to cope with her diet. How do you feel about having Maggie come to stay at Upton Hall, have fun with Daniel and Lily, be a normal child for a few weeks?'

Lucas was looking at her, full of respect, his words a trap. His kiss was only a breath away.

'Of course,' said Jessica. 'Maggie must come to Upton Hall. I will look after her. She will have a lovely time, perhaps regain what it's like being a child.'

Daniel might find it interesting to meet someone else who had trouble talking, and Lily would bounce Maggie back into childhood fun, show her the joy of running about, doing silly things.

Lucas folded Jessica into his arms, the outside world vanishing for the two of them.

'How about that boozy pub lunch?' asked Lucas, at last.

The boozy pub lunch was all that Jessica could have asked for. Two glasses of excellent Merlot went down well and rather fast. A jacket potato with grated cheese and a side salad was the perfect lunch. It was all that Jessica wanted. Lucas had a beer and a ploughman's. Sitting opposite Jessica was all he wanted.

The pub was a cosy, Sussex/Surrey pub. Oak beams and rafters, old hunting prints on the walls, a real log fire already burning in the hearth. Jessica was not sure which county they were in but it did not matter. Surely Lucas had no more surprises which could destroy their happiness?

He leaned over the table and clasped her hands in his. 'We have one more thing to do today,' he said. 'It may be very hard for both of us, but it has to be done. Our future happiness depends on this, and, oh my darling, I do so want us to be happy together.'

'Good heavens,' said Jessica, shaken. 'Where are you taking me? Newgate Prison or Tyburn? People were hanged at both places.'

Lucas let go her hands and sat back in his chair, staring at the ceiling. 'It was easier in those days to get rid of unwanted people.'

She did not understand what he meant. She did not want to know.

They both had black coffees. Lucas because he was driving, Jessica because she wanted to be alert for whatever was ahead.

What could be worse than seeing a five-year-old girl with tubes going in everywhere and hardly able to speak?

They drove through the rolling Surrey countryside. It was different to Sussex, more controlled, more sculptured, trees in staged groups as if being used for a television drama set. They turned in at a driveway, heavy iron gates opened for them after Lucas spoke to the man on duty. He was in a green uniform, belted. Surely it wasn't a prison?

Lucas seemed to know the way without any directions. He parked in an area marked for visitors. Ahead of them was a rambling two-storey white building with what looked like a chapel at the far end. Jessica caught the glint of a stained-glass window. There were gardens and flower beds and people strolling about in pairs.

'You have to tell me,' she said. 'It's not fair. Where are we?'

'This is a sanatorium for the permanently disabled,' he said. 'It used to be a convent called Saint Agatha's, I think. There are still nuns. Follow me.'

He did not take her hand this time but seemed wrapped in his own thoughts.

Jessica kept close to him in case he abandoned her, here in the wilds of Surrey, with no idea how to get back to Upton Hall.

The reception area was cool and empty, except for a vase of flowers and a strong smell of polish. No comfortable furniture, no paintings on the walls. Lucas went straight to the desk and signed in. He seemed to know what he was doing.

'This way,' he said, pointing towards the stairs. The oak treads had also been polished. They went along a wide corridor, doors either side with numbers. Again no decoration of any kind, only the occasional vase of flowers on a wall bracket.

He stopped outside room 24. He did not knock but went straight in.

Jessica followed him. It was a simply furnished room, plain white walls with flowered curtains framing a large window that looked out onto the garden. The bed was surrounded by pulleys and hoists which Jessica knew were only used for the severely disabled. A wash-basin was fitted in a corner. There was no television, no armchair, no table or bookcase.

Facing the window and the garden was a wheelchair. Jessica could only see the back of it. It was not a normal wheelchair, but a fully functional hospital chair with every device known to the medical profession.

Lucas went over to the chair. 'Hello, sweetie,' he said, bending low to speak. 'It's Lucas. I've come to see you. And I've brought a visitor, a very special person. This is Jessica.'

Jessica went over to the window, her heart thudding. The woman in the chair had her head held in a padded clamp. Her pale face was a mass of contradictions. Her greying hair had been combed back without any thought to style or appearance. She was wearing a cotton skirt and blouse, her thin legs bare, her feet in slippers. Her hands were immobile in her lap.

'Hello,' said Jessica, hesitating. 'I'm Jessica. How are you?'

It was a stupid thing to say. The woman could not move. Her back was obviously broken, if not more. She could not hold her head up by herself. Her face had been repaired but was probably only a caricature of her former feminine looks. She smiled at Jessica but gave no sign that she had understood.

Lucas came over, moving in his usual economical and lanky way. He stood close to Jessica, barely daring to touch her in case she flinched. He barely knew what to say. It could only be the truth.

'This is Liz, my wife,' said Lucas. 'She didn't die in the car crash on the M25. But she is here, in a living death.'

'You told me she had died,' said Jessica, barely able to find a voice. 'You said they had both died.'

'It was easier to say that she had died. She has in a way. This is not Liz, my wife, the mother of Lily and Daniel, this is just a shell, a body with no mind. She knows nothing. She remembers nothing. She says nothing.'

'How long?' Jessica choked.

'Since the accident. Liz went through the windscreen, severe spine and head injuries. He was killed outright, steering wheel trauma. No seat belts.'

'Who was he?'

'He was the man she was leaving me for, leaving her two children, leaving her home and her husband. Lily was only a baby, a few months old. He promised her a life without nappies and bottles and disturbed nights. He promised her Monte Carlo, racing at Goodwood and sailing regattas in the South of France. She wanted the high life and money to spend. She wanted fun.'

'How awful,' said Jessica. 'You must have been shattered.'

'I don't know how I felt now,' said Lucas. 'It was if a great fog descended on me. A bit like London smog. I barely knew what I was doing. Except when I was at the hospital. It was the only time I could think clearly.'

'This isn't much fun for her,' said Jessica, wondering if her plans were collapsing round their feet. She was unable to think how this would affect their plans. Oh dear God, she breathed, her eyes closed, don't let this be the end.

'No fun at all,' he said. He went over to Liz.

'Hello, Liz,' he said. 'This is Lucas. My friend Jessica has come to see you. Isn't it a lovely day? Look at all the flowers in the garden, they are so beautiful.'

Liz smiled as if she understood but it was obvious that she didn't. Her fingers had some movement. They curled and uncurled in her lap.

Jessica realized she was still carrying the bag of Lily's soft toys, the ones that Maggie had not wanted. Sometimes the feel of something different could stimulate an unresponsive mind. She went over to Liz.

'I've brought you some presents,' said Jessica. She prayed that there was something suitable in the bag. Her hand closed round a fluffy yellow duck. He was rather cute. 'Here's a little duck for you. Can you feel his soft feathers?'

She put the duck into the curled fingers and Liz smiled. Then she seemed to smile quite a lot, as if enjoying the sensation. Jessica found a furry kitten and put the toy into the other hand.

'And this is a furry kitten. His name is Sooty. Can you feel his soft fur?'

Liz smiled again, her fingers curling and uncurling round the toys.

'Are you expecting a miracle?' Lucas asked. 'It won't happen, you know. The brain damage is permanent. There is nothing that can be done.'

'I don't know what I'm doing,' said Jessica. 'I feel so helpless.'

'I think we should go,' said Lucas. 'She likes the duck and the kitten so that's good. Let's leave her now. The nuns will be round soon with tea.'

Lucas said goodbye to Liz but she gave no sign of hearing. He moved her chair, making sure that she had a good view of the garden. If she could see.

They went out into the corridor, Jessica almost slipping on the polished floor. Lucas caught her arm but Jessica shook it off.

'So is this my treat on my day off? Being shown the reason why we can never marry?' She tried to keep the disappointment out of her voice.

Lucas shook his head. 'No,' he said. 'We shall be married, I promise you. But first I have to divorce Liz. I've never made it legal before. It didn't seem necessary. I've always paid for her care and I come to see her when I can. She never gives any sign that she knows me. There's nothing there anymore, only a shell. But she could live for years more.'

'But can you divorce someone with a major head injury, who cannot say yes or no, who cannot agree to anything, who cannot sign papers?'

Lucas looked wearied by it all, the lines on his face etched more deeply. 'I have spoken to my solicitors. I am her legal guardian. I have power of attorney, but she has no assets. Divorcing a permanently disabled person is a relatively stream-lined legal procedure, apparently. I have to ask you to wait and be patient, just a little longer. Please, Jessica, I love you so much. We could be so happy together. I want you to be my wife. I want us to be together for always.'

Jessica's feelings were in a turmoil. Time was standing still. She was only now realizing what an enormous burden Lucas had carried for years. His demanding job, an autistic son, a difficult mother, and now she knew there had been Liz as well. She could imagine that her own arrival at Upton Hall had been like a ray of sunshine, Lucas suddenly seeing some light in all the gloom.

And Lucas had fallen in love with her.

As they walked towards his car, Jessica threaded her arm through his. She could share this burden. She was strong enough. Besides, she loved him. And she would stay with him, even if they could not be legally married.

'Would your roses like to see me again this evening?' she asked.

NINETEEN

There were busy weeks ahead that turned into months. Jessica sent a regretful letter to the hospital in Sheffield saying that she now had other plans and could no longer take up the contract.

Lady Grace saw her consultant and was reassured that both her legs were the same length. Though she was still not sure that she believed him. These consultants could say anything.

The consultant congratulated her on her speedy and successful recovery from the hip replacement operation.

'I keep strictly to everything that you told me to do,' she said, without blinking an eyelid.

'I wish all my patients were like you, Lady Grace, ' he said. 'Perhaps you'd like to come and give a talk to some of my pre-op patients sometime. It would give them such encouragement to see how well you have done.'

'Fred and me,' said Lady Grace, hiding a smile. She also had more secret plans for Mark Adams. She had not told a soul, waiting for the right moment. She had bicycles on the brain. That four mile promenade at Worthing was perfect for cycling, especially in the winter when Mark wasn't doing deckchairs.

And she had noticed empty premises on Marine Parade, on the front. Ideal for a bicycle hire business. She fancied being a silent partner in a business venture.

Swimming was now a regular part of the routine and either Jessica or Lady Grace drove over to Roxy's pool. They even met Roxy on one occasion and Lily was fascinated by her wildly bouffant hair, all different streaks of colour. Roxy rarely swam because of her hair. But she was great on paddling about on a lilo.

'She's got rainbow hair,' said Lily. 'Can I have rainbow hair when I'm grown up and singing in a roxy band?'

'Are you going to be a singer?'

'Oh yes,' said Lily with confidence. 'I'm going to be a rocky roxy star and have my own pool. Floppy Ears is going to learn to sing, too. Rabbit songs, of course.'

Daniel was starting to swim quite fast and with surprising stamina. Lucas wondered when it might be possible to take him to a full-sized pool. But not yet, not for a long time. They would take it one step at a time, or rather, one length at a time.

Maggie came to Upton Hall for two weeks convalescence and stayed for a month. She had scars on her face and arms but they were healing. She would need more surgery on her mouth as she grew older. She knew that Lucas would make her mouth smile again.

Daniel was fascinated that she preferred one word conversations and they became unexpected friends. They spent a lot of time together. He taught her to draw and she helped him with his alphabet. They made up funny names for the letters that he had invented.

Lily thought it was wonderful to have a non-stop playmate and Maggie soon lost her unhealthy pallor, racing round the garden and teaching Floppy Ears to do acrobatics. His new ambition in life was apparently to be a circus rabbit.

She brought the rag doll with her. The doll now had a name, Raggety Girl. Raggety Girl was soon participating in events, had her own chair at the kitchen table.

Arthur and Lady Grace expanded their games of bridge into a thriving bridge club. A group of friends met regularly at Upton Hall and Mrs Harris was in her element providing delicious nibbles for the group. She was asked if she would do the refreshments for a couple of village parties.

'Your canapés are absolutely delicious. And these dips. We

should be delighted if you could help us. We'd pay, of course, your usual rate.'

'Certainly,' Mrs Harris said. 'When I come back from my holiday. My friend and I are going on a coach trip to Scotland. We've always wanted to see the Highlands. Beautiful scenery, we're told.'

Jessica continued her research on the history of Upton Hall but she did not have much time or get very far. She did discover that the original farmhouse was built on the foundation of a long-lost Roman villa.

'Plenty of time,' she told herself. 'History won't go away.'

Jessica and Lucas planned their wedding. It would be a simple affair, they decided, with only a few friends. But they found time every day for a few moments together, walking round the garden, now in the autumn decline, the bronze colours replacing the fresh green of summer. The roses were almost over. Sometimes they found a hardy rose bud, determined to bloom at Christmas.

Jessica revelled in his touch and his closeness. Lucas had been a revelation these last weeks. She could not believe the warmth and passion of his love for her. Their time together was as if there was no one else in the world.

'Not long now, my darling,' said Lucas, pulling her close to him. 'We have our whole life ahead together.' He brushed his lips across her mouth. 'Is it time to chose that king-sized?'

'There are companies in the USA selling a super-king-sized. I found them on the Internet.'

'And I thought you were doing research on Upton Hall.'

"Different kind of research.'

The simple wedding in the village church with only a few friends grew and grew like Topsy. There were friends from several different hospitals with a group of grateful patients. Friends from the bridge club, friends from swimming. Friends from the village itself and the school.

Lucas grinned at Jessica in church. 'Be brave. We are

outnumbered,' he said as the service began.

The family Brussels lace was out, but Jessica wore it as a shawl round her shoulders. It went perfectly with her long cream velvet dress and it kept her warm.

Lady Grace was in her element, the perfect hostess at the reception back at Upton Hall. Mrs Harris was an honoured guest, in a new hat. Friends threw rose petals instead of confetti. The sun was clouded over, but warm enough for a late stroll in the garden.

Daniel was not sure what was happening but he looked content for once. Lily was a bridesmaid in a rose pink velvet dress with flowers in her hair. Floppy Ears was also a brides-maid with flowers in his ears.

'I'm going to have trouble with that rabbit,' said Jessica.